Agnes Hopper Bets on Murder

An Agnes Hopper Adventure, Book Two

By Carol Guthrie Heilman

AGNES HOPPER BETS ON MURDER BY CAROL GUTHRIE HEILMAN
Published by Lamplighter Mysteries
an imprint of Lighthouse Publishing of the Carolinas
2333 Barton Oaks Dr., Raleigh, NC, 27614

ISBN: 978-1-946016-43-0
Copyright © 2018 by Carol Heilman
Cover design by Elaina Lee
Interior design by Karthick Srinivasan

Available in print from your local bookstore, online, or from the publisher at:
LPCBooks.com

For more information on this book and the author visit www.carolheilman.com.

This is a work of fiction. Names, characters, and incidents are all products of the author's imagination or are used for fictional purposes. Any mentioned brand names, places, and trademarks remain the property of their respective owners, bear no association with the author or the publisher, and are used for fictional purposes only.

Brought to you by the creative team at LPC Books: Eddie Jones, Shonda Savage, Darla Crass, Andrea Merrell, and Brian Cross.

Library of Congress Cataloging-in-Publication Data
Heilman, Carol Guthrie
Agnes Hopper Bets on Murder / Carol Guthrie Heilman 1st ed.

Printed in the United States of America

Praise for *Agnes Hopper Bets on Murder* . . .

Agnes Hopper is back! The feisty redhead we've come to know and love has once again stuck her nose where it doesn't belong, and this time she finds a dead body. Will she be next?

~ Leanna Sain, award-winning author of *"Gate"* Trilogy, *Wish, Red Curtains*, and *Half-Moon Lake*

Dear old Agnes Hopper ... trouble follows her wherever she goes. But this feisty woman never gives up trying to find the truth and help her friends, even when her own life is at stake.

~ Karin Wooten, Author, Paper Crafter, and creator of Wicked Stitchery

The indomitable Agnes Hopper becomes a determined sleuth who bets on murder when she discovers a dead body—above ground—at the Beulah Cemetery in the charming village of Sweetbriar. Using her intuition and clever reckoning, Agnes tackles the mysteries that ensue, as she grows even closer to Smiley, the one who melts her heart.

~Ann Wirtz, author of *Hand of Mercy, Sorrow Answered, The Henderson County Curb Market*, stories in *Loving Moments, More Christmas Moments*, and *A Chicken Soup for the Soul Christmas*

Carol Heilman has done it again! I loved this story from start to finish. And her memorable character, Agnes Hopper, is at it once again. Naturally feisty and funny, Agnes turns gumshoe to solve the murder of her deceased husband's best friend while things at home are unsettled at best, uncertain at least.

~ Betsy Thorne, South Carolina Artist and Poet Member of the Community of Writers, Squaw Valley, CA

Dedication

For Mother and Daddy . . .
who dance in my dreams

Always do right. It will gratify some people and astonish the rest.
~ Mark Twain

ACKNOWLEDGEMENTS

I am thankful to the good Lord for this writing journey that has given me the opportunity to meet other writers and readers along the way. I am honored and humbled to know them. Each one continues to enrich my life.

Thank you, dear family, friends, and fans for loving Agnes and encouraging me to keep writing her story.

Thank you, writing sisters who endured those first drafts around our kitchen tables and in coffee shops. Many times, you have lifted me up and nudged me forward.

My outstanding editors, Andrea Merrell and Darla Crass, have shown me ways to improve my work through their examples and insightful suggestions. I have learned much from them and am deeply grateful.

And thank you, Eddie Jones, for believing in Agnes from the beginning of my first book, *Agnes Hopper Shakes Up Sweetbriar*. You knew her story would evolve into a series before I did. I appreciate your vision, your encouragement, and your tireless promotion of all LPC authors.

Chapter One

Resolved to calm my jitters, I plunked myself onto Sweetbriar Manor's porch swing to untangle my thoughts. It didn't help one iota. Something was amiss. In all my seventy-something years, my intuition had never steered me wrong, like the way my big toe warned me when bad weather was coming.

No matter what was brewing, my life could stand a little excitement. After I witnessed our former administrator, Miss Johnson, get carted off to the clink—thanks to me—things had been as bland around this retirement home as tapioca pudding.

Mama always said there's no use fretting about trials or tragedies lurking around the corner. I took her advice, closed my eyes, and lifted my face to the October sun. A shimmering vision appeared—my dear friend, Smiley, and me waltzing across a shiny wood floor. My red hair, freshly permed and dyed, bounced as we swirled in a cloud of Old Spice. My matching blouse and skirt glimmered like an indigo bunting—a real garage sale find. A flash of red flats completed my outfit as we danced the night away, despite my gimpy knee.

The red shoes, modeled on a QVC channel, had not only caught my eye on the sitting room's television, they had the power to melt my resolve to curtail all my frivolous spending. *But what if they've been marked down? Surely then I could—*

My daydream vanished like steam from a teapot when the front door slammed. Its beveled glass rattled in protest, and the now-familiar tune of "Dixie" filled the air.

Mr. Lively, the new administrator of the Manor, planted himself in front of me, casting a dark shadow with his ample form. As always, he smelled like he had emerged from an old, musty basement. "Learn to carry your cell, Agnes. And turn it on. I don't have time for these interruptions."

I peered up at his pinched face. "But no one ever—"

"It's Southeast Bank," he said, holding out his cordless office phone. "Bankers never call with good news." He scowled, thumbed his frayed leather suspenders, and rocked on his rundown loafers.

"Yes, I'm Agnes Hopper," I spoke softly into the phone, suddenly out of breath. The caller was brief and to the point. "Insufficient funds? Merciful heavens. Yes, I can come right away." I thumped the phone back into Mr. Lively's open hand and stood, ignoring a touch of vertigo.

"Humph," he said. "We can no longer manage our affairs, can we? More than a little forgetful too, I've noticed. Signs of … well, no matter. It's all documented. Perhaps it's time your daughter—"

My hackles went up. "Not a word to Betty Jo. I'll handle this myself."

He nodded, but there was no assurance he would comply.

❋ ❋ ❋

On his first day at the Manor, Mr. Lively had bent down to my face. It was the first time his too-close presence wrinkled my nose and caused me to hold my breath.

"So, you're the troublemaker Miss Johnson told me about," he said. "Mark my words. If one of us leaves Sweetbriar, it won't be me." He straightened up and turned his attention to a UPS man waiting for a signature as if nothing had happened.

How could he believe anything Miss Johnson said, the woman who had over-medicated and robbed some of my dearest friends? Could he actually claim I was incompetent? Could he boot me out? Call Betty Jo and tell her to come pick up her crazy mother?

❋ ❋ ❋

My thoughts were askew. *Signs of what? And just what does he have documented?*

"If one of us leaves Sweetbriar, it won't be me," I grumbled, trying to imitate his irritating voice. Grabbing my red purse—soft as a baby's behind and always kept within reach—I headed to town at as fast a clip as I could manage, thankful my dizzy head had cleared. Dressed in my nicest satiny purple jogging suit and like-new chartreuse tennis shoes, I was suitably dressed for visiting my banker, except for my confounded

2

cane. It was black with a silver handle. My daughter insisted it added a touch of class, but it slowed me down far too much. I considered it a temporary addition, even though my doctor said otherwise.

It was time to transfer some of my savings into my checking account. Pronto. *Forevermore, how did I get in such a fix?* Shame burned inside my chest, worse than when I once popped a whole jalapeno into my mouth. The humiliation was right up there with failing my driver's test after having a few fender benders and being told I would not ever be issued another license. Ever is a long time. At least my dearly departed husband Charlie was not around when I had to sell our truck, Big Blue.

No sir, it was time to face the cold, hard facts about my present predicament. Numbers did not lie. Instead, they fairly shouted: *In less than six months, you will be penniless and declared homeless in one fell swoop.* No one at the bank would have one ounce of compassion, but like it or not, they would hear my side.

My financial dilemma played over in my mind like a stuck record. At this moment in my life, red shoes—or any shoes for that matter—would be impossible. Even a purchase of Ginger Spice, my favorite hair dye. I had been longing for some excitement, but this was definitely not what I had in mind. My nose for spotting trouble—and then immediately setting out to make things right—did not include financial matters. Especially my own.

I stumbled on a rise in the old sidewalk, hidden by a pile of leaves, but righted myself in the nick of time. After that near disaster, I slowed down and put my cane to good use.

❋ ❋ ❋

The assistant bank manager, Rebecca Wills, ushered me into her office and shut the door. I sank into the nearest chair and studied her—a frumpy, middle-aged woman with a kind face. She would surely understand.

"You realize," she said as she rolled her chair up to her desk, "incidents like this will ruin your credit rating." Her voice dripped with sarcasm.

I gritted my teeth. *Certainly misjudged that one.* "I need to explain how I've come to this state of affairs."

She raised her eyebrows and crossed her arms like an elementary school teacher with an unruly student, but I plowed ahead. "When my husband was alive, I didn't have the time or inclination toward foolish

3

spending. Our expenses were necessary items like fertilizer, tobacco plants, chicken feed, and—"

"All well and good, but—"

I crossed my own arms and stared her down. "You need to hear the whole story."

"Mrs. Hopper, we don't have time to—"

"Can't you offer a senior citizen a little grace? Over three years ago, my Charlie crossed over Jordan, then my house burned down. I ended up in a retirement home because my daughter and I couldn't tolerate living with each other. Without Miss Margaret—Sweetbriar Manor bans all pets, even my precious pig—there's not much to do except knit and watch TV. Little wonder I got hooked on a shopping channel."

"You don't say." Miss Wills rapped a pen on her desktop and glared at me.

"I do say. And there's plenty more."

She pushed back, bumping her chair into the wall, and bounced up like a jack-in-the-box. "I'm certain Mr. Wilson can help you." She jerked the door open and marched to the nearest teller with me trailing behind her.

"Have a nice day," I said to her swiftly retreating form.

A blond, smooth-faced young man peered at me over his horn-rimmed glasses.

I took a deep breath, squared my shoulders, and tried to look taller than my five-foot-one-inch frame. "Need to transfer some money from my savings into checking."

"Name and account numbers?"

I looked at his name tag. "Willy, is that you?"

He straightened his tie and swallowed. "I go by Willard now, Miss Agnes."

I smiled, but he didn't smile back. "How's your grandmother these days?"

"Fine, I reckon."

I dug my checkbook out of my purse and passed it to him. "When you stop to visit, as I'm certain you will soon, say hello to Thelma for me, will you?"

"Savings account?" he asked without answering my question. This boy was all business. Must have been trained by Miss Wills.

"You'll have to look it up," I snapped, sounding like a grouchy old woman, which was exactly how I felt. I cleared a stubborn bullfrog from my throat and tried to do better. "I'll have you know, young man, I've never written a bad check in my whole life. Worse than unmentionables flapping on the clothesline for all the world to see."

"No worries, ma'am. Your private information is safe with us." He continued to type on his computer without looking up.

I stood on my tiptoes and raised my voice. "I'll also have you know I've resolved to give up my shopping channels. Might even cut up one of my credit cards." I loosened the scarf around my neck, picked up a brochure lying on the counter, and fanned myself. "Air's a mite stifling in here, don't you think?"

"How much do you want to transfer, Miss Agnes?"

"Two thousand ought to carry me for a while if I'm careful. Social security doesn't amount to a hill of beans these days."

"Yes, ma'am. Two it is."

A tall, skinny man with a handlebar mustache stood in front of the next teller's station. He turned toward me, saluted, and grinned as his bow tie quivered. "Money problems? Stop by to see me. If we purchase an item, we offer instant cash. Open nine to nine, six days a week." He turned back around, unzipped a fat, leather pouch, and pushed it across the counter. "Yep," he said. "A big deposit this time around. Business has been good. Mighty good."

Talk about hanging my unmentionables out to dry. How much had Boss Brown heard about my personal affairs? Never in a million years would I be desperate enough to enter his Last Chance Pawn Shop. Even though he had been part of Charlie's checker-playing group, my dear, late husband didn't like or trust him. And although I couldn't remember exactly why, he must've had a good reason.

By the time my transfer was finished, Boss was gone. I hooked my cane over my arm and picked up a sugar cookie from a tray in the lobby. I paused on the front sidewalk to savor my morning treat as Boss and a short, stocky woman with spiked hair linked arms and crossed the street in front of the bank. I couldn't see her face, but I didn't remember ever seeing her before.

No matter, there were more important matters on my mind. I headed home, ready to be away from this place that treated senior citizens so disrespectfully.

Sweetbriar Manor came into view—a lavender Victorian house with two identical attached wings painted to match. My room was the fourth of five rooms down the left wing coming from the main house. The right wing had the same number of rooms, all carpeted in sea-foam green with matching floral bedspreads and drapes. My room had a lumpy bed and a crooked rocker, but it was home because of the friends I'd made there—a prediction made by my sweet Charlie who still offered advice whenever I needed it, even though I'd been warned to give up this game of conversing with my dead husband. Maybe someday I would. For now, it gave me comfort.

I picked up my pace, but soon any thoughts of comfort turned into worrisome ones. Maybe my wide-brimmed, black-feathered hat pushed my bank account over the edge. It was an extravagant purchase, I had to admit, but at the time, I had become purely worn out with being frugal. Not to mention being bored to death. Surely, I didn't have to give up my charge cards—the ones tucked inside my billfold looking as innocent as a flower bouquet.

✳ ✳ ✳

I was in no mood to chat with anyone, but perhaps it would be okay to rock on the porch with Sam Abenda, or Smiley as we all called him. I not only envisioned him as my dancing partner but maybe someday as something much more. Since my first day at the Manor, this kindhearted man had smitten me with his big brown eyes. I had become accustomed to his red suspenders, knobby knees peeking out from his walking shorts, and the black dress socks he wore with sandals.

Smiley reminded me of a little bird whenever he pumped his elbows and scurried down the hallway toward the dining room. No one would believe it by looking, but that man loved to eat. His Old Spice aroma added to his charm. Our late afternoon rocking routine would soothe my nerves without needless chatter.

My heart sank as I maneuvered my way up the steps. Not only was no one sitting outside, the empty rockers were all clumped together, moved by a stiff breeze sweeping across the porch. Ralph, our weatherman on my favorite bluegrass radio station, had predicted arctic air would not only reach as far south as Sweetbriar, it would set a record for October.

A shiver coursed through my body as I moved beyond the foyer and retired to my room. The tall, drafty windows in the old house hummed. My knee throbbed, and my joints ached, worse than when I had chopped weeds all day with my garden hoe.

I turned on my radio, sank into my rocker, and tried not to think about my problems. It didn't work. Not even with Johnny Cash belting out his "Orange Blossom Special," one of my favorites.

The usual suppertime chatter around our table was missing—as if someone had pushed the mute button—and I was in no mood to get any ball rolling. Smiley leaned close to my good ear. "I said, could you please pass the mashed potatoes?"

"No need to shout," I said, thumping the bowl beside his plate.

Soon afterward, I excused myself, feigning a headache, and returned to my room, even though Smiley questioned me with his eyes—those eyes that never failed to melt my heart. I turned in early, filled with anxiety, and tossed and turned while trying to pray until well after midnight.

✸ ✸ ✸

The next morning, long before breakfast, my eyes popped open. The light outside my window shade turned from gray to soft pink as my mind whirled with possibilities. I threw back the covers and set about cleaning my room. My best solutions always emerged alongside busy hands.

Knitting would normally be my next choice, but I had finished a multicolored cap complete with earflaps and hadn't yet found a pattern suitable for Miss Margaret's sweater. My precious little pet pig would be toasty warm during the day with Henry, my son-in-law, content inside his cozy hardware store. But at night and over the weekends, she stayed at Ben's Llama Farm. Whenever she roamed his fields in the approaching winter or was confined in his drafty old barn, she needed a nice wrap to keep her warm.

Armed with energy, as well as lemon-scented Pledge, I moved into the quiet hall, cradled Alice's framed poem against my chest, and dusted the shelf beside my door. My deceased friend, an accomplished author, would always say, "The antidote for frustration is action. Take action, Agnes!" Oh, how I missed that gentle soul and the words of wisdom she always offered at the right moment.

What would my dearly departed husband say if he could speak to me now?

"Charles Eugene Hopper," I said to the empty hallway, "I'm coming to visit. I've made a big decision, and you need to be part of it."

I dug out my cell phone from underneath my tabloids, called my daughter, and then dressed in jeans and a warm sweater, Cardinal red, for my trip to Beulah Cemetery. Spread over rolling hillsides overlooking Sweetbriar, some headstones were dated as far back as the days of Daniel Boone. I loved to read the names, dates, and inscriptions, but today my focus would be on visiting with my Charlie.

✳ ✳ ✳

I stopped by the dining room, poured myself a cup of coffee from a side table, and took a sip, burning my tongue in the process. Smiley turned completely around in his seat, stared with raised eyebrows, then pushed up from the table. Before he could steady himself and get going good, I hurried over and patted his arm. "I'll be back in no time. Save me a biscuit." Waving to my tablemates, I made my exit and kept going before anyone could ask questions.

On the porch, I slipped into a fuzzy jacket, threw my favorite purple scarf around my neck, pulled my knit cap onto my head, and descended the steps. My knee twitched, but a glance at my watch proved there was no time to go back for my cane. Betty Jo was always punctual and didn't like to be kept waiting. Maybe on this trip we could begin our time together without a spat rising between us.

My daughter tucked her shiny, brown hair behind her ears, where it never stayed. "You're late," she said as I closed the door of her Buick. She pulled away from the curb.

I tapped my wrist. "Early by my watch."

She pointed to the dashboard clock and glanced my way.

"Want a peppermint?" I rummaged in my purse and held one out.

She shook her head. "Bad for my enamel." She turned on the radio, tapped her ocean-blue fingernails on the steering wheel, and hummed along with James Taylor. I had other things on my mind and tuned out both of them. There was no way around it. Our farm, mine and Charlie's, had to be sold. My savings might see me through the next six months, but only by becoming a miser.

Any rental income on my little yellow house—which I'd bought on a whim—had shrunk close to non-existent. But I refused to turn Juanita and her toddler, Frankie, out on the street. She was a single mother with few resources and no family. Besides, she was no freeloader and was doing the best she could.

I needed help but would never share my financial problems with my daughter. If so, it would be an admission that I'd made a bad decision about buying a rental in the first place. And I certainly would never confess to ordering everything from steaks to sweat suits from my television set.

I could hear Betty Jo's accusing voice. *What were you thinking, Mother?*

If I could no longer afford to live at Sweetbriar Manor, my friends and I couldn't gather in the dining room for a home-cooked meal. No longer would we play bingo or some silly card game, or share the latest gossip. Our days of rocking on the front porch whenever we took a notion would come to an end. I couldn't walk to Blind George's Poolroom for one of his famous chili dogs, to Begley's Drugstore for a strawberry milkshake, or slip into another world altogether at the movie theatre. My retirement home was only a few short blocks from all that our small town had to offer. My dear Sweetbriar Manor friends would probably be the last ones I'd have on this side of heaven, and I planned to do everything in my power to keep them.

"Are you sure you don't mind carrying me out to the cemetery?" I shouted over "Carolina Girls."

Betty Jo turned down the volume. "Not easy to rearrange my schedule, but I managed."

"Don't forget to stop by Fran's Florist. To pick up some mums. Purple, your daddy's favorite."

My daughter rolled her eyes. "You asked me not more than five minutes ago."

"Just making sure."

She turned the volume back up. "I was listening."

As we entered an older section of Beulah Cemetery, Betty Jo slowly navigated around mud puddles scattered along the grassy lane. She was a fanatic about keeping her black Buick spotless. We parked near a life-sized statue of Jesus holding a lamb. A place of comfort and peace.

Beyond the statue, a pathway led to Charlie's gravesite and then continued a short distance to a war memorial in honor of those from our county who had served in WWI and II. The curved black marble had been inscribed with the names of those once held dear. It was comforting to imagine my husband, a Vietnam veteran, trading stories with those who understand the heartache and horrors of war as only soldiers can.

I leaned down between my feet for the plant we had stopped to pick up. Discounted and probably headed for the landfill, but the other choices were expensive, and I was determined to tighten my belt.

"No, you stay in the car," I said as Betty Jo reached for her door handle. "Did you bring a book to read?"

If looks could kill, they would soon be planting me in the ground next to Charlie. "Doggone it, Mother, You promised this would be a quick trip," she said.

I bit my tongue and got out of the car, balancing the droopy plant.

A worn path led to a small hill, a shortcut to Charlie's grave. After days of rain, the earth felt spongy. Tree limbs swayed above my head, and raindrops splattered around my feet. When I sidestepped yet another puddle, something shiny caught my eye.

My fingers plucked a small pocketknife from the wetness. It looked similar to one Smiley always carried. I rubbed my thumb over a raised design, then dropped it into my jacket pocket to examine later.

As I approached my husband's grave, my eyes moved across the familiar words on his headstone. Charles Eugene Hopper, Beloved Husband, Father, and Friend. "Charlie, I don't have much time to visit this morning so I'll—"

What in tarnation was that noise? Wind moving through the trees? A moan?

The dried leaves of a pin oak rattled. I pulled my hat down over my ears and retied my scarf tighter around my neck. Then there was a clunk, sounding like a heavy glass object falling onto a hard surface. The noise seemed to come from the direction of the war memorial, a wall surrounded by a brick walkway. I squinted but saw nothing out of the ordinary. Maybe it was from the other side of the wall. A chill raced up my spine, and the hairs on the back of my neck bristled. I was not alone. As sure as my big toe throbbed, someone was close by. I placed the potted mum on a nearby bench, crept closer, and left Charlie's grave behind me.

"Who's there?"

A startled crow flapped to a nearby limb. The bird cocked its head and peered at me with one glassy eye.

I approached the memorial in a crouch, even though my knee protested. When I reached one end of the marble wall and leaned against it, a terrible odor assaulted my sensitive nose, causing me to hold my breath. It was like stepping inside a nursing home where old carpet reeked of urine. I gagged, and the sound of my heartbeat thumped in my ears. Never, in all my visits to Beulah Cemetery, had I been the least bit afraid. Today, fear threatened to suffocate me. I fought the urge to turn back. Instead, I peered around the names of dead soldiers.

"Oh, my. Merciful heavens."

A man lay on a stone bench with his back to me. His bulky form barely fit onto the small concrete slab. A frumpy hat lay over one side of his face, and an overcoat covered him like a blanket, except for his bare feet. They hung off the edge of the bench in the damp, chilly air.

The breeze stopped, and the stench grew stronger. I fished a handkerchief out of my pocket, held it over my nose, and inched closer. An empty whiskey bottle lay underneath the bench. Maybe the man had passed out in a drunken stupor, and the bottle had slipped from his grasp.

The morning sun disappeared, but I told myself I could do this as I took a deep breath, held it, and approached the bench. I leaned forward and poked the man's arm with one finger, then stumbled backward. He was as hard as a bundle of tobacco sticks.

"Lord a mercy!"

This man was dead.

Chapter Two

The coat slipped from the stone-like body and bunched around my feet. I was vaguely aware of something floating upward but turned my attention to the dead man lying on the hard bench. He wore a tattered brown sweater and grungy, torn jeans. The tip of a red paisley scarf peeked from underneath his bare feet. It was impossible to stop trembling, inside and out.

Once again, I held my breath and bent over his head. Who was this man? He seemed familiar somehow, but I didn't know any bums or homeless men. Those people weren't a part of my world. Surely, our mayor kept them from loitering in Sweetbriar, not to mention Beulah Cemetery. Natural curiosity got the better of me, so I lifted his filthy hat. Sunlight bathed his face, and I gasped.

Josiah Goforth.

His mouth hung open, and his blue eyes stared into space. I swallowed a mouthful of bile and refused to throw up. He had been Charlie's friend. I had once known him well, though I had not seen him since … since Charlie's funeral when he had played "Fallen Soldier" on his bagpipes.

I calmed myself and gathered my wits enough to say a silent prayer over him, even though my heart threatened to jump out of my chest. My hands clutched at my jacket as I tried to think, immediately suspecting two things. Number one, Josiah did not die near Charlie's grave on a stone slab in Beulah Cemetery. Number two, his death involved foul play. I would bet my life on it.

I backed away until the rancid smell lessened, then slumped against a giant live oak dripping with Spanish moss. I closed my eyes and remembered Josiah at another time, more than three years earlier.

Months before Charlie's heart attack, the two men had talked at the end of a workday, a habit of theirs. They had become as close as brothers over the years. Both were veterans, the younger of Iraq and Charlie of Vietnam. They stood outside underneath an open window while I peeled potatoes for supper.

"Told him I was done. Wanted out," Josiah said.

With my paring knife suspended, I leaned closer and strained to hear.

"Did you talk to the sheriff?" Charlie asked.

Josiah laughed. "Not itching for jail time."

"What are you going to do?"

Josiah laughed again. "Turn over a new leaf, like I told him, like I promised you. It's over. If I turn up dead, you'll know where to start looking."

Charlie struck a match, and the aroma of his pipe tobacco drifted through the window screen. "You'd best watch your back. Guys like him play for keeps."

Later, in our bed, I turned toward Charlie and reached for his hand. "Josiah's in trouble, isn't he?"

"Made some bad choices, but he's trying to do what's right," he said as he patted my hand. "I'm figuring out how to help him, even though he told me not to get involved."

Charlie never shared Josiah's secret. Then my dear husband died of heart failure one evening as the sunset burned streaks of red and orange across the sky. And now, Josiah had turned up dead. Charlie would have known where to start looking, but since he couldn't, it was up to me.

A horn beeped twice, then twice again. Betty Jo's code for chomping at the bit.

As I turned to go, my cell phone slid forward in my jacket pocket. I had forgotten I had picked it up before leaving the Manor with my daughter. Another example of my short-term memory loss? Mr. Lively would never know that tidbit of information, nor that I had followed his advice to carry my phone.

After calling 911, I walked close to Josiah's body once again, managed to turn on the camera, and took two photos. I didn't check, but they were probably blurred because my hands shook as if I'd been struck with palsy.

I picked up his coat and spread it over him as best I could, out of respect. A large feather rose into the air, lingered suspended for a moment, and then dropped back down. I picked it up. Was this what I had seen earlier, or perhaps one like it? It was shiny, black, and edged with iridescent blues and greens. A gamecock feather? Walter Jones, who owned the farm next to ours, raised them. I added it to my other pocket, thinking it was worth keeping, like a shark's tooth on the beach. But how did it end up in Beulah Cemetery?

There was no choice but to turn away and leave Josiah as Betty Jo laid on her horn, making me jump like a scared rabbit. Normally, I would have dallied a bit on purpose to let her stew a little, but today was no time for us to be at odds with each other.

Nearing Charlie's grave, I huffed my way past an ancient magnolia. Without any warning, a flock of crows flapped out and then upward, cawing like rusty saw blades biting into a wet log. Startled, I picked up the pitiful, discounted flowers and plunked them beside Charlie's headstone. At least they were his favorite color. I hadn't talked to my dear husband as planned, but I knew he would understand.

As I headed down the small hillside, my feet slipped on soggy leaves. I slid the rest of the way on my rear. A car door slammed, and my daughter helped me stand.

"Mother, are you hurt? Where on earth is your cane? Didn't the doctor—"

"Forget the blasted cane. I had to call 911, which I've never done in my life."

"You called 911? Whatever for? What happened?"

"Josiah Goforth's up there on a bench. Stiff as a poker."

In spite of her heavy makeup, the color left Betty Jo's face. "No. Not Josiah. An ambulance is coming, right? Show me where he is. Maybe we can stay with—"

My hand rested on her shoulder. "He's already flown to heaven. The coroner and the sheriff are on their way."

My daughter's face had now turned paler than death. "I need to see him."

She offered her arm, for which I was grateful, and we slowly climbed back up the hill. We stayed with Josiah only a moment, even though handkerchiefs covered our noses. I patted his cold feet before we walked back to the bench beside Charlie's grave to wait for the sheriff.

"I didn't realize you thought so highly of him," I said. "Even though he and your daddy had a lot in common, both being veterans—"

"He saved my life once," she said, barely above a whisper.

"What? When? How come I didn't know?"

My daughter bowed her head as tears slid freely down her cheeks. I handed her a clean hanky, put my arm around her shoulder, and pulled her toward me. She didn't resist like I expected her to do but sank into me. A rare moment of closeness we hadn't had since Charlie's funeral. My mind was in a whirl. *What memory had triggered such emotions?*

"Can you tell me what happened?"

Betty Jo took a ragged breath, sat upright, and blew her nose. "I had dressed for prom night and paced back and forth on the front porch waiting for Henry to pick me up. He was late like always." A little nervous laugh spurted out. "My sweet man hasn't changed a bit, has he?"

"Not at all, but—"

"Remember my white dress with the red sash?"

I nodded.

"Josiah was practicing his bagpipes behind the barn. I decided to show him my new dress. He had always seen me in jeans and tee shirts and loved to tease me about being a tomboy."

She shuddered, and I took her hand in mine. "Go on."

"Albert was still in the barn, milking."

Guessing where this was headed, my mouth turned as dry as a tobacco field in August. "Where was I? Where was your daddy?"

"Trying to get our old camera to work. Searching for batteries or something."

"Mercy me. What did Albert do?"

Betty Jo shivered. "Pulled me into the barn. Penned me against a stall. His breath smelled like whiskey and his hands like … like sour milk. He tried to kiss me, jerked up my dress, grabbed my panties, and yanked them down. I screamed, and the next thing I knew, Josiah was there. He threw Albert to the ground. Told him to get out and never come back."

My heart was breaking, thinking about what my daughter had gone through. "I'm so sorry. I never knew. Why didn't you tell us? Why didn't Josiah?"

"Because I was ashamed. Even though I've come to understand it wasn't my fault, I thought at the time it was. I asked Josiah to never tell you or Daddy. And he didn't. What do you think happened to him? Why was he here in Beulah Cemetery?"

"I don't have any answers … yet. But I can tell you one thing for certain."

"What?" she whispered.

"He met up with foul play."

* * *

Sheriff Caywood's generous paunch pressed against the steering wheel as we talked for nearly an hour in his patrol car, parked behind Betty Jo's Buick. Then he turned silent. He held a buckeye in his right hand, rubbed it with his thumb, and stared out the front window. A deep frown scrunched his bushy eyebrows together.

"You're going to make a hole in that thing," I said.

"My granddaddy always carried this very one in his pocket. Said it was good luck. Could use some of that right about now."

The coroner had taken Josiah's body away. My daughter paced back and forth on the driveway. She and I were both anxious to leave, especially since I had answered the same questions three times.

"Let's go take another look," the sheriff said.

We both got out of the car. He dropped the buckeye into his pocket and gave it a pat. We trudged back up the hill as a car door slammed. I hoped my daughter didn't leave without me. It would not do my reputation any good to be transported back to the Manor in the sheriff's patrol car.

Larry, the sheriff's lanky deputy, had strung yellow tape around the bench where Josiah had laid, the memorial wall, the oak tree, clear around Charlie's grave, and back to the bench. It was now a crime scene. I squinted to read the words on the tape. *Caution. Wet Paint.*

"Wet paint?" I asked.

"Only tape we had on hand," Larry said. "It'll do."

I pointed toward Charlie's grave. "Did you have to include my husband in this?"

He scowled at me, removed a handkerchief from a back pocket, and wiped his sweaty face. *Really? On a chilly morning like today?* Maybe he was not well. He was as nervous as a cornered barn cat. I had never liked the man since the time he accosted my friend, Jack, in Blind George's parking lot and accused him of kidnapping me. That was the night I left Sweetbriar Manor without permission and walked downtown to a movie.

"I'll be coming back to visit Charlie. Soon," I said. "I'll remove this tape if it's still here."

"Interfere with the law, and you'll be in a heap of trouble," he muttered. His Adam's apple danced as he lifted his lip like a cranky mule.

My eyes moved from his lip to his waist. "Is that a stun gun? You always carry one of those?" It was in a small holster hooked to his belt.

"Never know when it might come in handy." A twitch pulsed across his left eye in waves, making him appear even more nervous than before.

Had Josiah been subdued with such a weapon? An Atlanta newscaster last week told of an officer using a stun gun too aggressively, causing the captured man to die of heart failure.

The sheriff cleared his throat. He had apparently been saying something to me.

"Would you mind repeating that?" I said.

"You've got to let us do our job, Miss Agnes."

"Your deputy not only ought to have more respect for the dead, he ought to be more courteous to the living."

Sheriff Caywood pinched the bridge of his nose and blew out a slow breath. "Tell me again how you knew Josiah."

"I hope you realize I'll soon need to visit a ladies' room."

He nodded. "Yes ma'am."

"As I told you, he used to work for us, especially when we were housing tobacco. Charlie called him Slim when he was actually about as broad as he was tall. Dependable as the sun rising. Polite too."

The sheriff remained silent, so I went on.

"Josiah loved to play his bagpipes, which he would do for special occasions. Weddings or funerals, dressed in his Scottish finery. He didn't hail from Scotland, but his love of bagpipes drew him into anything Celtic. He had quite a collection. Old coins, metals, even swords. He participated in the Highland Games near Grandfather Mountain every year without fail. Practiced his bagpipes along about dusky dark. He would stand on a hillside behind our barn and—"

"I get the picture."

"It's important to know what matters to a person. Speaks to his character."

He rolled his eyes, a bad habit of his—just like my daughter. "Go on."

"Josiah said maybe he wouldn't offend anybody except a few cows and chickens, so he played out there before he headed home. Who would want to harm such a gentle soul? Miss Margaret loved him. And his music. Whenever he was around, she was his shadow."

"Saw him loitering near Sweetbriar Manor a few days ago," the sheriff said. "Told me he was waiting for someone, but I asked him to move along. Not too steady on his feet either."

"In all the years he worked for us, I never knew him to touch a drop." *Merciful heavens. Near the Manor? Who did he hope to see? If he was in some sort of trouble, why didn't he come to me? If he had, could I have done anything to ...*

"Maybe you didn't know him as well as you think you did," the sheriff said. "People change. He could've taken up drinking after his life ended up in shambles. He hung around the old train depot a lot over the past year or so, playing cards and gambling and such. Evicted from his house on Big Willow, he sometimes slept in a shack down along the river. Looks to me like he was a ne'er-do-well."

My thoughts were jumping ahead. "Who's going to play music for his funeral?"

The sheriff shrugged. "I doubt there'll be one."

"Breaks my heart," I said. "When will the coroner have his report?"

"Could be soon. Or not. Some deaths are complicated, although I predict the liquor caused him to pass out, and he died from exposure like I said. Drunks'll die that way sometimes."

"You're wrong, Sheriff."

"About what?"

"Footprints don't change. Circumstances change, and people have to adapt, but since Josiah was an honorable man when he worked for us, he was the same when he died."

The sheriff adjusted his hat and squinted at me as if studying what I'd said. "Anything else you want to tell me, Miss Agnes?"

When I slid my hands into my pockets to warm them, my fingers touched the small knife and the feather, but I said nothing. I wanted to ask about Josiah's bagpipes. Why weren't they sitting beside him? He had always kept them close by in a frayed leather bag. And why was he barefoot on a chilly, wet day? And besides, why would an expensive-looking scarf lay on the same bench with a homeless man? Too many things did not add up.

"Well?" he asked. He hitched his pants over his belly—where they did not stay.

"If I think of anything, I'll give you a call."

The sheriff took my arm as we left the crime scene. Sometimes he could be a real gentleman.

I reasoned that Josiah must have gotten himself into a mess of trouble with some unsavory characters. If I told the sheriff the words I had overheard, spoken underneath my kitchen window years ago, would he listen? No. He didn't care about the death of a bum. Josiah had flirted with something he should have stayed clear of. Now he was dead. He had tried to correct his mistakes. Over the years, Charlie had confided in him, and today I learned so had Betty Jo. She probably owed him her virginity if not her life. My whole family had been blessed by him. And besides, Miss Margaret loved him dearly, and I've always trusted her judgment.

Betty Jo and I rode back toward the Manor in silence. I suddenly missed Charlie's sweet presence. A heavy weight would press upon my chest when I least expected it, like after finding Josiah. My Charlie would've been distraught over his friend's death. I spoke to him from my heart and made him a pledge—a silent one so my daughter wouldn't question my sanity, which she tended to do even on ordinary days.

Charlie, I will find out what happened to Josiah Goforth. If you were here, you would do the same. I'll not rest until I've uncovered the truth about his death. I promise.

When we reached the Manor, I offered to get out at the curb so my daughter could make her garden club meeting on time, but before I spoke, she cut off the engine.

"I can be late for once, or even absent," she said as she gathered her purse and a package from Tim's Toy Shop. "You need to check your blood pressure. Use the blood pressure cuff like I showed you. We're both upset and will be for a long time to come. Finding Josiah on a bench in Beulah Cemetery, of all places."

"He didn't deserve to lay out in the cold like he didn't matter to anyone."

"No, but he could have gone to the homeless shelter," my daughter said sadly.

"I plan to find out what happened to him." *Whoops. Didn't mean to say that out loud.*

Betty Jo's brows rose above her sunglasses. "Nonsense. Our sheriff has this whole situation under control."

I held back what I thought about the sheriff and his control. "Exactly."

"If your blood pressure's high, let me know. I'll make you an appointment with Doc Evans."

"You worry too much. Next time we're in Walmart, I'll use their machine." I didn't like the contraption Betty Jo bought me, and I had put it underneath my tabloids in the bottom drawer of my chest, where it would stay.

She got out and shut the door, mumbling to herself … another bad habit of hers. "I've decided Juanita could use a break," she announced.

Before Miss Johnson had spent one night behind bars, she had hired Juanita—the young, single mother who lived in my rental—as a daytime caregiver for her mother, Ida Mae. She hired another young woman as a nighttime nurse. Juanita also had to keep an eye on her toddler, Frankie, but the one-year-old and the ninety-two-year-old doted on each other, making the task a breeze. In many ways, our last administrator was evil to the core, yet she loved her mother. I had to give her credit for that.

Betty Jo and I paused for a moment beside a *No Parking* sign. "The meter maid will be making her rounds soon," I said. "You're sure to get a ticket."

"Never have. Park here all the time."

"Suit yourself," I said. We continued up the walkway. The brief, tender moment at the cemetery with my daughter had vanished. We were back to normal.

I wouldn't discuss any of my suspicions about Josiah's death with Betty Jo. In fact, she needed to think I had dropped any speculating like she urged me to do. I knew my daughter well. She had been deeply shaken this morning, but like she had denied a traumatic event in her life years ago, she was ready to dismiss the fact that a kind, decent man—as well as her daddy's best friend—had been murdered.

"You would be amazed what Juanita can do with Frankie strapped to her back, but I'm sure she would appreciate some help," Betty Jo said. She was determined to deny what we had witnessed, and I would play along. For now. With no children of her own, she was enjoying playing grandmother to little Frankie.

I glanced at her package. "You would think Frankie was our own kin. What did you buy him this time?"

Her eyes lit up when she smiled. "A John Deere tractor. He'll love it."

We climbed the stone steps and followed the walkway bordered with yellow mums and purple cabbages planted by Betty Jo's garden club. Today, the flowers melted into a blur of colors. Sweetbriar's incompetent sheriff, his irritating deputy, and Josiah's untimely death dominated my thoughts—until I spotted a red, white, and blue sign: *FOR SALE by Southern Realty.* We both stopped short and stared. The sign was surely a mistake. Or even a practical joke stuck into the ground next to our large, purple Sweetbriar Manor logo.

A gust of wind swirled around the signs, making the smaller one rattle. My knees shook, in danger of collapsing altogether, but since I hadn't brought my cane, I reached for Betty Jo's arm and leaned on her. "What's going on?" I finally managed to ask. "That ridiculous sign was not there when we left this morning. Do you think it's a Halloween prank?"

We didn't come up with any answers as we continued toward the porch. I considered climbing the steps but chose the handicap ramp instead. Too much trauma in a short span of time had taken the starch out of me. The handrail was warm from the sun, and the sky had turned a Carolina blue. The morning chill had given way to a beautiful fall day—even though my world had tilted completely out of kilter.

Betty Jo waited for me on the porch with her arms folded, a take-charge mother's stance. "Looks like you may have to consider Shady Acres after all," she said. "On the whole, it's geared to care for Alzheimer or dementia patients, but they do have one building for independent living. Then, if you developed those kinds of problems, there you would be, first priority to have a room with a trained staff twenty-four-seven."

My insides twisted into a knot. "You don't say." *Did Mr. Lively put a bug in her ear and recommend such a place?*

She kept talking like it had already been decided. "I've heard it's expensive, but you don't have to worry. Daddy left you financially independent. Certainly a relief, isn't it? I'll give them a call as soon as I get home."

"Not on your life!" I shouted. Heat rose clear to the tips of my red curls. "I'd rather live in the apartment over Blind George's Pool Hall, even with the tattoo parlor across the street flashing *Open* in red neon—probably twenty-four-seven." *It was the only place I would soon be able to afford anyway.*

She folded her arms tighter and glared at me. "You've never seen what Shady Acres looks like."

"Don't plan to either," I said. "If I ever do have to move, that's the last place I'm going. And you might want to stop in the ladies' room to fix your hair. The wind at the cemetery has turned you into a wild woman. And while you're at it, put on some lipstick. You'll scare little Frankie to death."

I pushed open the Manor's front door, setting off the sounds of "Dixie"—Miss Johnson's idea. It had always alerted her to anyone coming or going, and apparently Mr. Lively intended to keep it. It was quite annoying, just like the two of them.

This morning had turned out worse than the time I got lost in an endless corn maze. In the middle of July, no less, with those pesky no-see-ums biting my scalp. Questions nagged me like a yippy dog nipping at a vagrant's heels.

Was my retirement home truly for sale? Was I desperate enough to sell my farm? But even more than changes in my life jumping over the horizon and charging toward me, I had to discover who had killed a good man. And why.

Chapter Three

The Manor's grandfather clock struck eleven, but instead of dozing or watching television, even with the newly installed cable, the residents were gathered in the foyer outside the dining room. They sounded like a swarm of hornets shaken from their hive.

My daughter whispered in my good ear, "When you find out what's going on, fill me in later. And I would advise you not to share anything about the *situation* out at the cemetery with your friends. No need to stir up gossip. Are you listening?"

"I hear you," I said, trying to remain calm in spite of my rising anger, and most likely my blood pressure. She left me in search of a toddler who would keep her from thinking about seeing a friend's dead body. We had to come to terms with what we had witnessed, each in our own way.

William, my barrel-chested friend, stood a foot taller than the other residents gathered around him. He scowled and chewed on his ever-present cigar stump, but when he held up his hands, the grumbling ceased. "We've got to stand together, folks. Come up with a plan." This kind, bear of a man ran his fingers through his thinning white hair. Normally, he greeted me with, "Hi ya, Red. Whatcha know?" Then he would often add, "How about a stogie?" He delighted in teasing me, not only about my hair color—which reminded him of his mother's—but my years-ago resolve to never smoke again.

Today he didn't glance my way.

I needed to talk with someone about Josiah's death, but not William who apparently had taken charge of Sweetbriar Manor's crisis. Besides, his friend, Francesca, was parked by his side in her wheelchair. She reminded me of a pampered, rich lady with her soft, pink skin, long pearls around her neck, and sparkling rings on every finger. I called her Diamond Lil—to myself. She was also a busybody and would be thrilled to hear of a murder in our small, quiet town. She smiled up at William, her face flushed and full of pride. She was a friend, but she could be as irritating as all get out.

Smiley was always a good listener. Where was he anyway? I didn't see him or Pearl. I hoped Pearl was glued to her soap operas because when she learned our home was for sale, she would be thrown into a tailspin. She would tug on my sleeve and ask, "What's happening? Is there something I need to know?" At this point, I couldn't reassure her. Pearl and I had been inseparable at Southern High until she left for Atlanta to study art, and I fell head-over-heels in love with my Charlie. She and I were finally together again, only sometimes my tall, slender friend seemed standoffish. Her memory came and went like the tides, but how could she possibly forget our high school friendship? Most days she was sharp as a tack, while other days she didn't know me from the mailman. It was amazing that Mr. Lively hadn't shipped her off to that Shady Acres place.

Another worrisome thought crept into my mind. *Were Pearl and Smiley sitting on her sofa watching some sappy love story? Together?* My suspicious nature said they were. I'd noticed sweet-as-sugar looks pass between them when they thought no one noticed. My years-ago best friend and my first friend at Sweetbriar Manor ... together? If only he were available to talk. *Shoot a monkey. I need him this instant.*

With no one else to talk to, I had no choice but to jump into the middle of the ongoing exchange in the foyer. "I'm gone for a couple of hours and look what's happened. Someone fill me in."

Francesca, beaming like sunshine, flounced about in her wheelchair and waved her arms. "Oh. Oh. You'll never guess what's happened. Simply dreadful. Mr. Lively called a meeting after breakfast and introduced a lady Realtor, Lee Ann Spivey. She informed us Sweetbriar Manor will be sold, and she has someone interested and ..."

She stopped to take a breath, and William leaned over and patted her back. "Now, now, sweetie. Calm yourself down."

Lord-a-mercy, if we were all scattered to the four winds, I would even miss Francesca, as bossy and annoying as she could be. She was *confined* to her wheelchair, at least in public. But one day, when I knocked and then opened her bedroom door, she was walking about in her room without holding onto anything. I suspected she enjoyed the attention she gained from her handicapped status, and for certain she delighted in another person's misfortunes.

"What happened to your talk about buying this place?" I asked her.

Her face flushed beet red, and she twisted her pearls into a knot. "You know I can't. Not with my dear son facing an investigation of his bank. Of course, he's innocent, but lawyers are expensive." She lifted a tray from its slot, clicked it into place, and whipped out her well-worn tarot cards. I didn't need them to tell me her crook of a son would keep on until he swindled his mother out of her last penny.

"Wait a minute," Smiley chimed in as he appeared among us in a poof of Old Spice. "Maybe someone who wants to run a retirement home will make an offer. Let's think positive."

"So glad you could join us," I said, looking behind him for signs of Pearl.

"Even Dale Carnegie couldn't find a positive card in this deck," Francesca said. "Looks like the future of Sweetbriar Manor is doomed." She gathered her cards and dropped them into one of her many pouches, then leaned forward and shook her finger. "These potential owners want to operate a halfway house for recently released crooks from some women's prison before they let them out in society. Can you imagine? Right here in Sweetbriar? We'll be evicted. Set out on the front lawn with our possessions like we're the criminals. There ought to be a law. We've got our rights." She banged her fist on her tray, causing everyone around her to jump.

"You tell 'em, sweetie," William said.

"William's right," I said. "We need a plan. Has anyone seen Mr. Lively?"

Everyone had an idea as to his whereabouts and shared it out loud. I held up my hand. "One at a time."

Lollipop—whose real name was Elmer McKinsey—offered up garbled words around his ever-present sucker. I learned my first day at the Manor that he had been given the nickname because his shirt pocket always bulged with cherry, orange, and lemon suckers, which he never shared. His brother kept the supply coming. Miss Johnson had doled them out a few at a time and had charged him for them to boot— one of her many schemes to line her pockets and keep the residents under her control. This gentle soul also repeated himself and talked so fast no one could understand him. Until recently, he had always been underfoot with his forever question, "Wanna be my girlfriend?"

"What in tarnation did he say?" I asked.

Somehow Smiley always understood. "Mr. Lively left with the Realtor."

Francesca paused in her primping, compact and cherry red lipstick at the ready. "We had better start looking for places to live. Nobody takes up for seniors these days. We're out of sight and out of mind."

Everyone either nodded or voiced their agreement.

Francesca wasn't finished. "I hear there's a new retirement home opening in Saluda. I'm going to get my name on their waiting list. How about you, Willy?"

William grinned all over himself. "Why of course, sweetie. We'll only need one room though." He looked up, wiggled his eyebrows, and fingered his cigar like Groucho Marks.

Smiley turned to me. "Maybe we'd best get our names on the same list. For two rooms."

Was he informing me he and I would never need one room? *Humph. How could an intelligent man be so dense about my feelings for him?* If I weren't around, who would comfort him after his recurring nightmares? Or share in his reminisces of his days as a Fuller Brush salesman. Nor could we have our hot tea late at night when neither of us could sleep. Sometimes I shared private thoughts with him I'd never told anyone before—except Charlie, of course, or Miss Margaret.

I rummaged in my purse, found my funeral home fan, and cooled my face as I scanned the gathering. "Are you really ready to pack up and move this minute?" Not one person would look me in the eye.

"We don't have a choice, Sis." *Sis.* Smiley's name for me since my first day. "Sure as shooting, flood waters are coming, and we've got to move to higher ground," he added.

I laid my hand on his arm. "What's happened? A minute ago, you were hopeful, then you flipped to doom and gloom."

"Francesca's right," he said. "No one's gonna listen to us. We're outranked and without any financial resources. If the Lord don't show up, we're done for, don'tcha know."

Yes, Sweetbriar Manor could be done for, and without the Lord's help, Josiah's honor could also be done for. Smiley had spoken the gospel truth. A chill ran over me. I could not get the image of Josiah's bare feet out of my mind or the way he might have died. The sheriff said no one cared about his passing, but Charlie would have. I did. And Betty Jo too.

A hush fell over our gathering until gradually, the bubbling of our large fish tank—a welcomed addition from Sweetbriar's Women's Club—brought me back to our immediate crisis. "The Lord gave us brains, didn't He?" I said. "Let's think."

Even as conversations began again, some in low tones and others swelling in volume, I envisioned a killer hiding in Beulah Cemetery when I came to talk to Charlie. Maybe I had startled him and caused him to drop the whiskey bottle. No, the horrible smell indicated Josiah had been there awhile. Someone must have placed him there. But he had been a heavy-set man, and even heavier when dead. It would've taken at least two men to carry him up the hill and then arrange his body on the small concrete bench.

The sheriff was wrong about the cause of death. What had Josiah gotten himself into? What was he trying to leave behind? I hadn't insisted Charlie tell me the details of our friend's troubles, but I sure wished I had.

I edged back over to Smiley and leaned close to his ear. "I need to talk to you. It's urgent."

He took my hand. "Urgent? What's wrong, Sis? Other than Mr. Lively knocking the wind out of our sailboat. You look as pale as talcum powder."

"Let's slip into the dining room," I said.

We eased around the corner and out of sight. I collapsed into the nearest chair while Smiley scooted another one over to face mine.

He sat down, reached for my hands, and held them in his. "If we lose our home, it will be like watching a grand old ship sink to the bottom of the ocean, don'tcha know. But we'll survive, Sis. Somehow."

I nodded, for I could not find my voice. He said *we* would survive. He and I.

"My stars. This must be something worse," he said as he stood and placed a hand on my shoulder. He bent over and looked into my eyes. "Is that why you didn't say two words last night at dinner and why you left in such a hurry this morning? And you said you'd tell me what you've been up to when you returned. And then … heavens to Betsy … I totally forgot. Been preoccupied lately, but that's no excuse. What's wrong? Are you ill? Why have you been avoiding me? Why didn't you eat breakfast this—"

"I'm fine. Well, not so fine either. I need your help, and it's important."

"You've got my attention. Shoot."

"Josiah Goforth's been murdered."

He frowned, lifted his Reds baseball cap, and scratched his head. "Who? Murdered?"

"A man who worked for us. He and Charlie were close, like brothers. They met years ago at a veteran's benefit where Josiah played his bagpipes. Turned out both men suffered from survivor's guilt from two different wars, Iraq and Vietnam. Over the years, they helped each other work through some of their issues. I found Josiah's body on a bench at the cemetery."

"You did? But why would you think—"

"I'm as sure as my name's Agnes Hopper. But I can't prove it. Not yet. Will you help me?"

"Help you? I don't see how, but—"

"Agnes!" Francesca called from the foyer. "Where did you go?"

"Why do you feel a need to investigate his death?" Smiley asked as we made our way back to our friends.

"You weren't listening. I promised to find out who killed him."

"Oh, indeed. Who did you promise?"

"Charlie and Betty Jo, although she isn't aware I did."

"Well," Francesca said. "Look who has graced us with their presence. As I was saying, let's get a petition started."

I tried to concentrate on her words, but a dead body, bare feet, and an empty whiskey bottle kept swirling around in my mind.

"Agnes can ask those people who hang out at Blind George's Pool Hall. I'm sure she knows them all. Her son-in-law, Henry, comes in contact with the merchants in town, and Betty Jo rubs shoulders with scads of people through her social committees, and—"

"We get the idea," I said. "You and William will be in charge. When you've collected all the signatures you can think of, bring the list to me."

"You can count on us, Red," William said with a broad grin as he whipped out a small, black comb and ran it through his hair.

"Good." I turned toward my burly friend. "Here's what else you can do. If you can find out when the property inspectors are coming, maybe they'll find a little sand in their gas tank."

Francesca snapped her compact mirror shut and dropped it into a pouch. "Aha! Just like Agnes to be devious, cunning, and plain underhanded. If you think it will—"

"Let's get started," I said. I had more pressing issues on my agenda, and this detour was frustrating, to say the least. "What do inspectors look for?"

William rubbed his chin. "Plumbing problems, electrical issues, termites."

"What can we do to make the potential buyer think this place is in shambles?" I asked.

Francesca said, "I'll point out the crumbling stonework around the fountain."

William warmed to the challenge. "Do any of you see lights flicker in your room? Maybe the two wings added to this house weren't built to code. And maybe this old house was never brought up to modern standards."

"Wait a minute," Smiley said. "New construction might not stand the test of time, but this house has been here since ... since forever. Maybe it's a little run down, but it has a certain charm like it is, don'tcha know. And if they had modernized it when they added on our ten rooms ... why, they would've ruined it."

Groans rose in the air.

"Remind me to lock this man in his room if we spot any potential owners on the premises," I said.

Lollipop grunted and unwrapped a new sucker.

"I've got an idea," William said. "Lights flickering. Footsteps in the middle of the night. Doors creaking open. The swish of a skirt and the scent of perfume. What if we infer Sweetbriar Manor is haunted?"

"Maybe even hint Sherman himself is rattling around here, looking for his lady friend," I added. "She's the reason our home, and probably the town, was never torched."

"Have you lost your minds?" Francesca said.

"I wonder if he smoked a cigar?" William said as he stared into space. "Give me an excuse to light this puppy."

Francesca wagged her finger at him. "Over my dead body," she said. "You could burn the place down."

"I'll plant the seed on social media," William said, ignoring her. "My grandson will help me. Facebook, Twitter, and Pinterest to start."

"You've lost me," Smiley said. Agreements rose all around.

"You'll be arrested. Mark my word. And the rest of us will be charged with aiding and abetting your crime," Francesca said.

I turned toward William, intending to ask him if he would actually carry out his plans, but when our eyes met, he winked, and a grin spread across his face. He would proceed and could hardly wait. Could he be charged with spreading false rumors? Francesca always delighted in imagining the worst.Our group turned mute as a fence post. If we lost our home, we could be scattered between here and yon, our friendships disrupted forever

As chatter began once again, Pearl appeared at my side. She was dressed as usual in a long skirt and peasant blouse, but her stringy white hair hung loose from her normal ponytail, and her face had twisted into a deep frown. She edged closer to me, clutching a vase of sunflowers. The flowers trembled, and her bangle bracelets jingled like little bells. After I finally convinced her to ease up on her grip, I placed the vase on a nearby table. She reached for my hand, which she rarely did unless she was deeply troubled.

"Pearl," I said, "look at me." I craned my neck back, for Pearl is tall, and I'm considered short. When our eyes met, I said, "If we should have to move, I will not go anywhere without you. Do you understand? You and I will stick together. You will not be alone. Ever. And that's a promise."

She nodded, but her eyes looked as wild as a horse aware he was headed for the slaughterhouse. Pearl definitely had some mental issues, possibly the beginning of dementia, and her condition had worsened by Miss Johnson's cruel treatment of her. In the last month or so, however, she had greatly improved. Would our predicament set her back? What if Mr. Lively deemed the two of us incompetent? Would he wait for the sale of our home to declare all of us homeless at once?

Smiley edged over and took Pearl's other hand. I tried not to notice, but my whole body stiffened in spite of myself. She needed our help, our friendship. Even Smiley's. But I didn't like being a witness to his compassion. Was my jealousy unfounded and totally out of control? I asked the Lord's forgiveness and ended up feeling like a scoundrel.

The residents of Sweetbriar Manor moved as solemn as a funeral procession into the dining room. They had a right to be upset. But for me it was so much more—more than the uncertainty of Smiley's feelings toward me, my dwindling savings account, Mr. Lively's unfounded scrutiny of me, Pearl's fears, and even more than the anxiety surrounding the sale of our home or claiming it was haunted.

The murder of Josiah Goforth weighed heavy on my heart.

Chapter Four

Francesca and William fell into a heated discussion. *Haunted. Sherman. Cyber Space.* Would William stand his ground or cave-in to his sweetie?

Lollipop gave his full attention to slurping his soup, humming as he ate. It was hard to believe I was leery of him when first coming to the Manor. He was a simple man who had suffered a brain injury from a car accident and meant no harm. My protective instincts took over, and one day I asked our cook if she could use his help in the kitchen. The routine calmed him, and she was delighted to have the assistance.

I leaned over to Smiley. "I've got a few clues," I whispered.

He questioned me silently with wide eyes.

"Meet me on the porch after lunch," I said. "It's warm enough."

He reached over and patted my hand. "I'll be right there."

I pushed my empty soup bowl aside and stood. "No, you go ahead and finish."

Shirley stepped out of the kitchen with a heaping plate of cookies, probably straight from the oven. Shirley Monroe had been our cook since our former administrator fired the old one. A decision I applauded. Besides manicuring our nails—one of her former duties at the Kut 'N Loose Beauty Salon—Shirley never failed to whip up three delicious and hearty meals a day. Earlier, her blonde poof, caught securely in a hairnet, had bounced against her satiny red blouse as she served us cheesy potato soup and chicken salad sandwiches on toasted wheat. Now she moved from table to table offering the residents dessert.

Since the night Shirl and her boyfriend, Jack, had come to my rescue in front of the Royal Cinema, we had become fast friends. She was one person I could always count on. Why, I'd bet my bonnet that Shirl wasn't afraid of anything or anybody.

The aroma of warm peanut butter caused my stomach to lurch, a sure sign my worries were getting the best of me. I hurried to the powder room and splashed cold water on my face.

✾ ✾ ✾

The old boards creaked underneath my feet as I paced back and forth across the front porch. The wind had died down, and the rockers were still. *Would Smiley help me?* He didn't like conflicts. In fact, he steered around them whenever possible. He would probably agree with Betty Jo and say to leave the investigating up to the authorities.

"Sis," he would most likely say, "if there's anything amiss, the sheriff will find it. Rest assured."

Well, I was not assured one bit.

I headed inside to see what might be keeping Smiley, when he appeared in the foyer. We returned to the porch where I chose a rocker on the other end, away from the door. He pulled his over to face mine— our knees almost touching—then leaned forward, engulfing me with the aroma of his aftershave. I ignored my unsettled stomach, found a peppermint in the bottom of my purse, and popped it into my mouth. Maybe there would be some peanut butter cookies left for later. Then I reached inside my jacket pocket, pulled out the silver knife, and laid it on my outstretched palm.

"What've you got there?" Smiley asked. He took the knife, opened it, and whistled. "It's a Case and a beaut." He snapped it shut. "Has some initials on it." He pulled reading glasses from a shirt pocket, slipped them on, and turned the knife to catch the light. "Fancy ones." He handed it back to me.

I held it in the right spot for my bifocals. "They're a little worn, but the initials could be MB or VB or even WB. I found it near Charlie's grave. It could be evidence."

"Don't you think you ought to—"

"Turn it over to the sheriff?"

He nodded.

I pushed myself up with my cane. "Are you with me on this or not?"

He stood and folded his arms across his thin chest. "Now, Sis, you know I am. Even if it's against my better judgment. What can I do?"

"For starters, you can listen. Maybe you can spot a clue I've missed.

We can talk more on our way to Henry's store. If we take our time, my knee will hold out. You will go with me, won't you? Or have you committed your afternoon to Pearl?"

He gazed at his penny loafers as if studying them. "Uh, she's busy, I think. Yep. Busy." When he looked up, his eyes shone with pure delight. "She's a woman who's blessed with talent. Overly blessed," he added.

"Well," I said, looking away from his flushed face. "It certainly is a blessing to be blessed."

"Yep," he said, getting his baseball cap settled on his head.

I bit my snippy tongue. "I'll meet you back here in ten minutes."

When I returned to the porch, Smiley met me with a question. "Why are we going to Henry's store?"

"So you can convince Betty Jo to help us keep our home," I said as I buttoned my jacket.

"Me? Why me?"

"She likes you. She would come closer to listening to you than to her mother."

Smiley looked confused. "What can she do about Sweetbriar?"

"For starters, she has more political connections than Carter's got little liver pills. Betty Jo could enlist enough big-name protestors against this halfway house business to stop them in their tracks. She's an active member of the town council and has known the mayor practically forever."

"How do you know she'll be there?"

"Shirley told me she bundled up little Frankie, strapped him in his stroller, and off they went to visit Henry. My son-in-law is as crazy about Frankie as Betty Jo. That little boy is like the grandchild they never had, and they've discovered a joy they never knew they missed."

Smiley still didn't look convinced. "So … while I talk to Betty Jo, what will you be doing?"

"Asking Henry some questions. He might have seen Josiah wandering around town since he was part of the homeless community. Maybe he can offer some insights into his habits or … oh, I'm not sure what else, but Henry is observant."

"One thing is a puzzlement to me," Smiley said, scratching his head.

We stepped onto the Manor's walkway. "Well, are you going to share it?"

"The sheriff. Is he as blind as you say or is he doing his own investigation on the sly because he realizes you're itching to get involved, and he doesn't think that would be wise?"

"Either way, our detective work is moving forward. Our situation reminds me of the year Charlie and I fought hail, drought, and floods on the farm, all in a few months' time."

"Sounds exhausting. What did you do?"

"Got mad. Worked hard. Prayed a lot. Charlie admired Winston Churchill. *Never, never, never give up* was a favorite quote. No matter what happens, we can't give up."

"Not until every rabbit's been run out of the cabbage patch." He grinned at me.

I stared at Smiley. "I won't ask you to explain."

He chuckled. "Ah, Sis, I want to learn everything about this Josiah fella. Plus, we've got to figure out the *why* of it. Murder's got to have a motive, don'tcha know."

"My thoughts exactly," I said as I pulled on my knit cap and tied it underneath my chin.

We continued on our way as Mr. Lively walked toward us with a swagger in his step. He was flanked by two big-boned women, one tall and the other short and stocky. They wore navy skirts, white shirts, and matching navy blazers, and looked like they might be from the women's prison and wouldn't put up with any nonsense. A chill snaked its way clear up to the top of my curls and stayed there, despite my new hat. The three of them laughed as if they had reason to celebrate. Had they already struck a deal and hung us out to dry?

Smiley tipped his baseball cap, scooted around the threesome, and kept going. I stopped, leaned on my cane, and tried to smile like I meant it, but I only managed to make my cheeks hurt with the effort.

"Good afternoon," I said. "Do we have visitors, Mr. Lively?"

The trio came to a stop in front of me. "We certainly do." He threw his arms around the women's shoulders as if to draw them closer. Instead, his hands slipped to their backs, which he ended up thumping.

They both rolled their eyes.

My sentiments exactly.

Smiley reappeared as Mr. Lively gathered his clumsy hands, stuffed them in his coat pockets, and rocked on his heels—which he seemed to find great pleasure in doing. He didn't look me in the eye, another irritating habit of his. Instead, he stared into the trees high above my head. "We—our Tennessee firm and myself—are tickled pink the Correctional Institute for Women has chosen a Chicago firm to represent them. They have chosen Sweetbriar Manor as their center for matriculating the rehabilitated back into society. A mighty fine and worthy goal, and we are honored to be a part of it."

"Our SRCW will be one of the finest halfway houses in the southeast," the taller woman said. She brushed her black bangs out of her eyes and glared at me.

"Exactly," said the chunky one with spiked hair and a rose tattoo on her neck.

Is this the same woman I saw cross the street with Boss yesterday? I was almost certain, even though her clothes were not the same.

"SRCW?" I asked.

"Sweetbriar's Rehab Center for Women," answered the two of them together as Mr. Lively's head bobbed in agreement, his eyes focused on the sidewalk. A bad feeling settled in my bones.

"What if your deal doesn't go through?" I asked. "Will you choose some other town or search for a place out in the country?"

"Why would we?" the tallest woman asked. "We've done our research. Sweetbriar Manor is an excellent choice. Most of our women don't have a driver's license, so they'll need to walk to most anywhere they need to go. The mayor has assured us the town will be supportive, and the merchants will hire them when jobs are available."

"That's all well and good, but what about the seniors who call Sweetbriar Manor home? We have some rights in this situation."

Mr. Lively scowled at me. "You'll stay out of this or—"

I took a step forward and matched his scowl. "Ever hear of the first amendment?"

The women looked at each other and then back to me. The stockier one said, "This place is destined to be sold to someone. It's on the market, after all. I'm sure we will give ample time for each person to find a place to live. We're not heartless, you know. Right, Milton?"

Milton? I never knew his first name. They had certainly gotten chummy.

"Uh … right. Absolutely," he said, dragging the toe of his shoe across a crack in the sidewalk.

"Those ladies from your prison deserve a second chance," I said. "But none of us are happy about this predicament. As a matter of fact, we're pretty steamed up. We love our home here. Today, you folks have turned our peach cart upside down."

"Now, Sis," Smiley said as he gave my sleeve a slight tug. "No need to talk ugly to these ladies. It's not their fault those Tennessee folks want to sell our home. Besides, the prison system has made a legitimate offer."

"I know," I said, jerking my arm away. "But who's to say those women won't bring a criminal element into our town? Doesn't anyone see the danger?"

The women glowered at me like I had sprouted horns.

"Humph," Mr. Lively said. "Typical. Causing trouble. Again. Let's go, ladies."

The discussion apparently over, I motioned to Smiley, and we moved past the troubling threesome. We had walked more than halfway to Henry's hardware store when I spotted two red rockers tucked underneath an awning outside Begley's Drugstore. One called my name. A place to catch our breath. A glance at my dear friend told me he must've had similar thoughts.

"Would you look at those?" I said. "Let's give 'em a try."

We settled ourselves. He leaned back and shut his eyes, a smile on his face.

I couldn't help but chuckle. "I never knew a man who enjoyed rocking as much as you do."

His smile widened. "Hmmm. One of the pleasures of getting older."

While we rested, we discussed some details I had noticed in Beulah Cemetery such as the gamecock feather, the fancy scarf, Josiah being barefooted, and the empty whiskey bottle lying on the brick walkway.

"I'm considering my former neighbor, Walter Jones," I said, "as a person of interest because of a possible gambling connection. Josiah was addicted as long as I knew him."

Smiley stopped rocking. "But you don't have a scrap of evidence."

"Even so, let's think this through. If Josiah'd been trying to leave the sordid business behind, maybe he got in too deep to walk away. He could have been betting on cockfights and lost more than he could repay. Walter raises gamecocks and probably takes bets on his birds coming out as winners. But his name doesn't match the initials on the knife." I took it from my pocket and studied it.

"Its owner might not even be from around here. Or a man might've used a girlfriend's initials, don'tcha know," Smiley said as if reading my thoughts.

I returned the knife to my pocket and stood. Then, on an impulse, I leaned over and gave Smiley a bear hug. "I never would have thought of those possibilities."

"Well, uh, I … I …" he sputtered as he straightened his cap and tried to recover. "We need to consider every angle."

"Exactly," I said, helping him stand. We steadied ourselves and continued on our way at a much slower pace. I was thankful we didn't have much further to walk. "Don't mention any of our discussions to Betty Jo," I added. "Or to anyone, though I'm considering asking Shirley to join us in our detective work. What do you think?"

"Mum's the word. Shirley? Perfect. She's up to her eyeballs with wisdom and street smarts."

"Yes indeed." I linked my arm through his.

After Mr. Lively recognized Shirley's cooking talents, she was given Alice's old room. Rent-free. She had first come to Sweetbriar Manor as our manicurist from the Kut 'N Loose, and she made no bones about being our chief advocate. Her hair was always teased into a mass of blonde poof, her nails painted a bright red, her floral perfume powerful, and all the residents loved her dearly.

But could the three of us go against any suspect we uncovered, including Larry, the sheriff's deputy? In my mind, he and Walter Jones had both become persons of interest.

❋ ❋ ❋

Inside the hardware store, I rested on an antique chair while Henry helped a customer decide which type of bird feed to buy. I caught a glimpse of my precious pig, Miss Margaret, bolting away from Frankie's outstretched arms. The child seemed determined to tweak her snout. Betty Jo was not far behind as Smiley struggled to catch up.

"What do you think? Do we have a leg to stand on?" he yelled.

My daughter barely rescued Frankie—who had stopped chasing Miss Margaret—from swallowing a handful of something, probably nails or screws. Straightaway, she fastened him into his stroller, though he wailed to the top of his lungs like she had taken a switch to him. As soon as she plugged his pacifier into his mouth and handed him his toy tractor, he hushed. She dressed him in his jacket and cap, and they were on the move.

"Nap time," she said as she jogged past me.

"I'll see you back at the Manor," I said to Smiley as he shuffled past, trying to keep up with Betty Jo.

As soon as they were gone, I heard Miss Margaret's hoofs clatter across the wooden floor and caught a glimpse of her pink, fuzzy body.

Even at forty-four pounds, she quickly ducked behind an Almanac display, headed for her bed. By the time I managed to squeeze into the small space, reached down and rubbed her behind her ears, she was sound asleep. As always, she had tucked her favorite stuffed monkey underneath her chin. She let out a little sigh and promptly began snoring. I grieved for the lost warmth of her presence and her sweet companionship but carried such special memories of our time together—especially the time Miss Margaret visited me at the retirement home and got so excited she relieved herself all over Miss Johnson's feet. I can still see those black high heels doing a backward tap dance. Too bad animals were not permitted at Sweetbriar Manor. They would bring such comfort to the residents.

"Mother Hopper," my son-in-law called. "I can take a break now."

Henry and I moved outside to a Charleston-style bench in front of his store.

"Betty Jo told me about you finding Josiah in Beulah Cemetery," he said. "Went all to pieces and upset Frankie so much he started whimpering. Took me awhile to calm them both. Didn't realize she thought so much of the man, though I suppose she had known him for years. A tragic situation."

"Yes, indeed. I'll fill you in later when you're not so busy."

He studied me. "What's on your mind?"

"I understand the homeless often wander downtown, rest on the benches, use the public restrooms, visit the library when it's raining or cold, but I've never seen any such people myself. Do any of them actually live around Sweetbriar?"

Henry stuck his glasses on top of his bald head and rubbed his eyes. "I call them the invisible people. They're around. Some even live in tents back in the woods outside town, but most folks choose not to see them."

"Oh." I was one of those *most folks*. "Did you ever see Josiah, maybe going through your dumpster out back? It's a puzzle to me why I never caught a glimpse of him in the past year or so. Since I moved to the Manor, I've frequently walked down Main Street. Never saw him one time."

"Maybe he didn't want to be seen. Maybe he was too proud to ask you for help."

"Oh, my. You could be right. Makes me feel terrible. I hardly gave him a thought after Charlie died, and then I had to leave the farm and—"

"Don't be so hard on yourself, Mother Hopper. To answer your question, I never saw Josiah anywhere near my store." He stood and straightened a nearby arrangement of corn stalks and pumpkins.

"I guess my intuition's on the blink," I said, rubbing the soreness out of my knee.

Always one to tease, Henry turned toward me and grinned. "But I did see him across the street. Every Wednesday morning for the last three months. I always sit on this bench at exactly nine forty-five Monday through Saturday with a big cup of coffee and gaze up and down Main Street. Unless the weather's nasty. Then I stand inside at the windows. Love this town. Been my routine for twenty years."

I looked around and wondered what Henry had seen. "Did Josiah sit on the bench across the street? Did he have his bagpipes with him? He always carried them in an old leather bag."

Henry returned to the bench. "Had his bagpipes, but he didn't sit."

My curiosity was growing. "What did he do?"

"Climbed the steps of First Presbyterian and went inside."

"My word, Henry. Anything else?"

"Jack Lovingood stopped him one morning, halfway up the steps. About two weeks ago. They argued, but I couldn't hear what was said. Jack left in a huff, and Josiah continued on inside. Don't know if any of this means anything. Come by after work one day. I'd like to hear all about your investigation."

"Better yet," I said, "you and Miss Margaret stop by the Manor. Call me first. Come around to the back, and I'll let you into the beauty shop. It's in the enclosed porch. The only other door leads to the kitchen. Nobody would know we were there except Shirley, and as soon as she sees Miss Margaret … why, she'll be more tickled than finding a rhinestone bracelet."

"Now, Mother Hopper, you understand I'm not much for breaking rules."

"No pets in the Manor is absurd. That rule deserves to be broken."

Henry squinted at his watch. "Speaking of Miss Margaret, it's nearly time for our constitutional."

"First, a few more questions. Are you sure you saw Jack? What connection could Shirley's boyfriend have with Josiah? Why would they even be acquainted? Makes no sense whatsoever."

He shook his head. "It was him all right. He's the only man in Sweetbriar who drives a red scooter. He came to a screeching stop in front of the church, jumped off, and flew up those steps even with his stiff right leg. Not to mention his long, thick hair most women would die for, swinging as he went."

"Betty Jo tell you I'm going to find out who murdered Josiah?"

He nodded and frowned. "She doesn't like it, but she also knows her advice won't stop you. She's worried about you. Be careful."

"My daddy always said, 'If you can't be good, be careful.'"

"If I think of anything else, I'll give you a call," Henry said. "I hear you're using your cell phone these days."

I shrugged. "Trying to. Well now, looks like I need to visit the church."

"Hmmm. Not sure what good it will do, but the sheriff's not going to answer any of your questions either."

I brushed a stray piece of cornstalk off Henry's shoulder. "Any other suggestions?"

"Nope," he said as he helped me to my feet.

Before Henry went back inside, I made sure he had my phone number and asked him to please reconsider coming to the Manor to bring my precious for a visit. The old back porch would be the perfect place. I crossed the street and eased down on the bench.

Henry, along with Miss Margaret on her leash, appeared in the hardware's doorway. Her little catnap must have done her a world of good, for she stepped along as if she were a much younger pig. They turned in the opposite direction, away from downtown, and trotted down the sidewalk. Probably going for a quick walk in the park. I considered joining them but pushed myself up with my cane and pressed on toward the Manor, tomorrow's detective work percolating in my mind like fresh-brewed coffee.

After walking two more blocks, I spotted Smiley sitting on a bench in front of Feather Your Nest.

"Are you alright?" I asked as I flopped down beside him.

"My feet are killing me. Going to rest 'em a spell."

"It would help if you'd spring for some good walking shoes." I studied my pale-faced friend. "You look a little tuckered out. Do you want me to wait with you?"

"No indeed, Sis. I'm perfectly fine. I'm also stopping at Begley's. Need new corn pads don'tcha know."

"No, I didn't know."

"Did you talk to Henry?" he asked.

I nodded. "Glad I followed a hunch. Seems Josiah visited First

Presbyterian on a regular basis. Have no idea why. If he needed to go to confession, Saint John's is nearby. After all, he was Catholic."

Smiley stretched his feet out in front of him and wiggled them back and forth. "Maybe he went there to play his bagpipes."

"He could have practiced anywhere down along the riverbank where he might have slept in an old shack like many of the homeless. He liked to play out in the wide-open spaces, like on the hillside behind our barn, not in a closed sanctuary."

"A pure puzzlement, Sis. Like a jigsaw with a missing piece."

"Exactly. What did Betty Jo say? Did you have a chance to talk?"

"Yep. Little Frankie snoozed away before we had gone half a block." He pulled his feet back in and took off his shoes.

I held my breath waiting for his answer. "Is she going to help?"

"Sort of. But on her own terms."

"I'm not surprised. What exactly did she say?" I could picture the look on my daughter's face when Smiley asked.

"She said, 'I will talk to the mayor, but not the town council. I could be accused of meddling in Sweetbriar's affairs or even profiling these women as hardened criminals, which I understand they're not.'"

My shoulders sagged. "I guess some assistance is better than none."

"A stewpot half full looks mighty good to a starving fellow."

"Guess I understand." I stood to go. "Soak your feet tonight. I'll bring you some Epsom salts, good for all sorts of aches. Tomorrow morning, try out your new corn pads. We're going to pay a visit to the church. My doctor's been telling me to get more exercise, but we'd better not overdo it. I'll see you back at the Manor."

I left him there with his shoes off. When I looked back, he had taken off his socks as well and was swinging his bare feet like a schoolboy. Hopefully, he wouldn't get a chill and take a cold, which could turn into pneumonia before you spun around twice. Then my mind reflected on Josiah's bare feet hanging off the edge of that cold bench. He would never have gone anywhere without wearing his cowboy boots. His shoes—and especially his bagpipes—were his pride and joy. *Where were they?*

My body shuddered at the thought. *Maybe I should go back and tell Smiley to take better care of himself.* But I didn't. Surely, he could think for himself. This fella could be as stubborn as all get out—and for sure too much of a ladies' man—but he was also my closest friend. I didn't know what I'd do if anything should happen to him.

Thankfully, my knee was behaving for the moment. I passed Blind

George's Pool Hall, the Kut 'N Loose Beauty Salon, and Rodeo Rags before arriving back home. *Home.* Sweetbriar Manor—rumored to be a house of ill repute during Sherman's day—had also been run as a bordello by a woman named Dakota during my daddy's day. It had become my home, a Victorian-style house with wraparound porches filled with white rockers. Who would've thought such a thing could be possible?

Was my home destined to become a halfway house for criminals?

Chapter Five

I made a mental note to call Fruitland Bible College. Some of the strongest prayer warriors, professors, and students worked and lived there, and I could use their help. Once again, my cell phone would be put to good use. Drastic times called for drastic measures. This old dog was determined to learn as many new tricks as possible.

It would be easy to ask them to pray for us to somehow keep our home, but how could I ask people to pray for the Lord's help to find a killer without getting specific? This detective business was no easy matter. Nothing seemed simple and clear-cut like those reruns of *Matlock* and *Murder She Wrote*.

I headed to my room to shed my jacket, gloves, and hat before asking Shirley to join forces with Smiley and me. When I reached for the doorknob, my hand froze in midair as it turned from inside my room. When the door opened, there stood Nellie Watson, the Manor's newest resident. We stared at each other without speaking. Nellie was a tiny person who wore her gray hair pulled into a tight bun on top of her head and no makeup whatsoever on her wrinkled face. She reminded me of Mother Goose's old woman living in a shoe, of all places. She often claimed to be Minnie Pearl's cousin, twice removed.

"What are you doing? You don't even live on this wing," I said when I finally found my voice.

One of her hands fluttered to her throat. "Oh …"

Her breath sent the aroma of chocolate into my face. No need to tell me. She was stealing my candy—again. Whenever she was around, nothing loose was safe. She had slipped packets of sugar and crackers from the dining room—as well as someone's forgotten coin purse and a personal letter left on a coffee table—into her pockets. More than once, I told her to return what she had taken, which she would do with a surprised look on her face but without one ounce of guilt.

"Don't you dare come back unless invited, which won't happen," I snapped. "From this moment on, my door will stay locked."

She left in a huff as her tiny feet scurried down the hall.

After opening my nightstand drawer, best I could tell there was a missing Snickers and a Hershey with almonds. She could have stolen some of my valuables, but there was no time to look. I dropped my jacket onto the end of my bed and made a much-needed stop in my bathroom. After rummaging in my purse, I found my room key which had not been used since Miss Johnson had roamed the halls checking on our whereabouts.

After all attempts to lock my door failed, I said, "Drat, drat, drat, Charlie." I thumped the end of my cane on the floor three times for good measure. Then I caught a whiff of a distinctive odor.

"Who's Charlie?" Mr. Lively asked as he appeared behind me. "Is there a man in your room?"

"Don't I wish. Hey, my key doesn't work."

"Give it to me. You're probably not turning it the right way." After many attempts, he said, "I'll have another one made. Looks like you've bent this one. Frustrated and angry, are we?"

"You're too busy," I said. "My son-in-law can make one for me."

"Suit yourself," he said, plopping the key into my open palm.

I tried calling Henry on my way to the kitchen, but his store's phone was busy.

Shirley stood at the restaurant-size stovetop mashing a kettleful of sweet potatoes. At the sink, Lollipop waved a soapy hand and turned back to scrubbing another large pot. *Gee whiskers. How can we talk with him around?* He often gave the impression he wasn't listening, but sometimes he would repeat what he'd heard, even if he didn't always understand it.

I sat on a stool at the kitchen island, formerly an antique workbench, and tried to think of a way to get rid of him. Shirley removed cornbread muffins from the oven and slid in three large casserole dishes of sweet potatoes with brown sugar and pecans on top. My stomach growled.

She must have sensed I needed to talk to her in private. "When you finish settin' the tables, dear sir," she said as she led Lollipop to the dining room door and handed him a basketful of silverware and napkins, "go to the front yard and fill this basket with some pretty leaves."

"Lady talk?" he said as he shifted the basket to his other arm.

"Exactly." She shooed him on his way.

I glanced at the swinging door. "I think that dear sir has a crush on you. He used to follow me around everywhere I went. Has he asked you to be his girlfriend yet?"

"Law, at least once a day—even though I tell him yes every time." She removed her apron, smoothed her tight black pants, and pulled up another stool. "I can tell you're dyin' to talk to me. And if it's between us, my lips are sealed. We've got about thirty minutes before the gravy needs to be thickened."

I jumped right in. "Did you know Josiah Goforth?"

"Slim? Sure do. Played for my mother's funeral and wouldn't charge me a penny. One of the kindest men in Sweetbriar, or probably the entire South. After his wife left him, he used to wait for me outside the Kut 'N Loose and walk me home after work. And here lately, right before dark, I've spotted him down on the street corner near the Manor, but he's never come up to the house. I think he needs a friend to talk to, but, honey, between you and me, he wants more—if you understand my drift. I've never encouraged him, you understand, but if Jack found out … well, you know how jealous he is."

"No, I haven't noticed," I lied. So, Josiah had been hanging around the Manor to see Shirley. *Maybe she was the reason the two men argued on the church steps.* "When did you last see him? And where?"

"Funny you should ask. It was last Saturday mornin' as I was leavin' the library. I always go there as soon as they open to check out some movies for the weekend. They've got some good ones. He asked if he could carry my bag. I tried to be polite and all but told him the movies didn't weigh hardly nothin'. Besides, I had to hurry back to the Manor. I left him standin' on the sidewalk with his old ragged bag sittin' beside him. He looked like a lost teddy bear, but I certainly didn't want Jack to happen by and see us together."

My thoughts bounced around like a hayride down a bumpy road. *What if Jack had found out about Josiah trying to court his Shirl? Could he have flown off the handle and killed him in a rage? Was such a thing possible? Jack might be rough around the edges, but I always thought he had a tender heart. Could his jealousy have pushed him over the edge?*

Shirley hopped off her stool, hurried to the drying rack, and grabbed a pot and a towel. "Reckon I can work while we talk. I heard Josiah fell on some hard times lately. There's talk of him hangin' around with the wrong crowd. Gossip that's gotten out of hand, I'd say."

Normally, I would have jumped down to help her, but I stayed on my perch to rest a bit. "I don't think you understood me. Josiah's troubles are over. He—"

"Wait a minute, Miss Agnes." Shirley slung the towel over her shoulder and turned toward me. "You said *did* I know Josiah, not *do* I know him."

"I suspect he's having a grand time praising the Lord on heavenly bagpipes right about now."

The pot in Shirley's hand clattered to the floor. "Josiah's dead? Lord-a-mercy! Tell me it ain't true."

"That's not all. I'm certain he was murdered."

Shirley's face blanched white as flour. "Josiah? Murdered?" She returned to her stool, and I reached for her trembling hands. I told her about finding him in Beulah Cemetery near Charlie's grave. Then I shared the two photos I'd taken, even though they were disturbing to look at.

Her pale blue eyes filled with tears. I fished around in my purse, found a clean handkerchief, and handed it to her. "The sheriff says he probably had too much to drink, passed out, and died from exposure. I don't believe it for one minute."

She blew her nose. "Thanks, honey." She sniffed and blew again. "I'll do this hanky up nice before I return it. Any evidence to prove the sheriff wrong? Wait a minute. Josiah didn't drink."

"Absolutely. And did you notice the bottle in the pictures? He would have never had the money to spend on Maker's Mark liquor, even if he did drink. Whoever put his body there planted it so the sheriff would think exactly what he did. He fell for a set-up as obvious as … as the wart on Nellie's chin."

I remembered my unlocked room and called Henry again while Shirley composed herself. His clerk answered. Henry was out making deliveries, and he didn't own a cell phone. *Merciful heavens. We needed to talk about that.*

Shirley peeked in the oven. "Ten minutes more ought to be about right. What else has our officer of the law missed?"

"Josiah had no shoes on his feet." I slid my cell phone back in my pocket.

Shirley's head tilted to the side as she considered what I'd said. "Why do you think that's important?"

"Because he loved his cowboy boots. When he worked for us, he always kept them shined and polished."

Shirley's frown showed her confusion. "I don't understand."

"He would never have walked around with bare feet, but if he had, his feet would have been muddy after all the rain we had last week. I looked. He didn't have a speck of dirt or one blade of grass on them. One of the pictures shows clear evidence he didn't walk to the bench."

"Oh, my. What else did you notice?"

"His bagpipes were nowhere around, and he always carried them with him, everywhere he went." I picked up a dishcloth and folded it into a little square.

Shirley nodded and looked as if she were deep in thought. "Come to think of it, you're right. Never saw him unless he was totin' his worn leather bag."

I leaned in and lowered my voice. "Another thing. There was a fancy silk scarf hanging out from underneath him."

"Maybe someone threw away a perfectly good scarf, and he happened to find it."

I leaned in even closer and looked around to make sure no one was listening. "I also noticed some marks on his neck like somebody had to subdue him—maybe with a stun gun—before they killed him. He was a big man, you know."

"This is awful … simply awful. A murder. Here in Sweetbriar." Shirley paced back and forth in the small space between the counter and the stove.

"That's not all," I said. "I think someone could've pushed him up there in a wheelbarrow."

Shirley's hand went to her mouth. Her brain was probably spinning as fast as mine. "You do?"

"Yep. I had plenty of time to look around after the sheriff escorted me back up the hill to the crime scene and then spent twenty minutes talking to his deputy. I couldn't take more pictures, but there were some tracks. Looked to me like one wheel had cut into the soft ground. And it was wobbly."

Her bright red nails tapped the counter. "Did you tell the sheriff all this?"

"Nope. He's either wearing blinders or planning a cover-up. Election year's around the corner, you know."

"Law have mercy. There's thunderation in Beulah Cemetery for sure. A murderer among us and our law's doin' nothin' about it." Shirley fanned her face with her hand.

"My thoughts exactly." I pulled a pile of laundered napkins closer and began folding them. I barely noticed their fabric-softener scent.

"What are you gonna do, honey? Do you have any other suspects?"

"I've got an idea or two, and Smiley mentioned someone I hadn't thought of. I'll share everything with you later, but we've got to keep it under our hats until we can gather enough evidence—before we make any accusations."

"Sweetbriar ain't had a murder since I can't remember when. Maybe ten or twelve years ago. And it proved to be self-defense, so it don't count." She walked toward the oven, stopped, and turned to face me. "Did you say *we*? Under *our* hats?"

"Will you help us, me and Smiley, investigate? Undercover?"

Shirley flew back to my stool and hugged me tight. "Honey, I would be as pleased as pineapple sherbet. Whoever killed Josiah has got to get what's comin' to him. Besides, being a detective is bound to be more excitin' than … than my Baby teachin' me how to fly fish. Well, almost."

"Can you keep our discussion to yourself? At least until we get the proof we need?" *And what if our evidence led us to Jack, the jealous lover? Shirley's Baby.* A sour taste rose into my mouth. Thankfully, I found a peppermint from Captain Tom's in my pocket.

Shirley stood straight and tall and placed her right hand over her heart. "I pledge my allegiance to do my best as your assistant. I will treat every scrap of evidence like top secret." Then she sniffed the air and rescued the sweet potato dishes. "In the nick of time," she said.

I walked to the door leading to the dining room and turned to face Shirl. I had to find a way to ask Jack some questions. "Say, when will you be seeing your fella again?"

"Tonight, after supper. Said he'd wait for me in the sittin' room and try to be invisible. Mr. Lively don't much like him hangin' around."

"Mr. Lively's afraid you'll get married, and he'll lose a cook," I said, trying to make light of the matter and keep my thoughts under control. Did our administrator also have a crush on her or had he discovered a shady side to Shirley's Baby? Did Jack have a criminal record? Had he come to Sweetbriar in an attempt to leave it behind? Francesca had always been suspicious of his motives from the day he delivered fresh strawberries to our porch. Maybe she had been right all along.

Regardless, Shirley could never find out I planned to watch Jack Lovingood.

I left the kitchen with its wonderful aromas of Thanksgiving, including chicken and dressing—in October no less—to freshen up before suppertime. My earlier queasiness had flown the coop, and I was starving.

The who, why, and how of Josiah's death elbowed their way to the front of the line. They all demanded answers. They were out there somewhere. But where? In the meantime, a murderer was free.

Betty Jo bumped into me as she headed to the front door.

"Oh," I said. "Hoping you would still be here. Have you thought about—"

She looked at me with squinted eyes and pursed lips. "Mother—"

I held up my hand. "Let me finish. We're going to stop this women's prison business in its tracks, with or without your help."

She stepped back, stood stiff as a board, and clenched her jaw.

But there was more to say, and I wasn't about to stop. "And whether you like it or not, I'm going to investigate a murder. I don't want to have to answer to your daddy or the good Lord for not keeping my promise."

"What promise? You're talking nonsense. I'm glad Daddy's not here to witness your decline," Betty Jo said, wagging her finger at me.

"If your daddy were alive, we would work this case together. He thought the world of Josiah, and I'm sorry I didn't keep in touch with him like I should have."

"I don't know about that. I'll think about what I can do to help save Sweetbriar if we can move forward legally. But you can't do anything about the tragedy we witnessed this morning. Absolutely nothing." My daughter's face was almost as red as my hair.

"You're wrong. And I'll prove it to you."

Betty Jo waved her hand as if dismissing me. "You're confusing me so much I can't think straight. We both need a good night's sleep."

"Don't think I can't see through your smoke screen," I said. "You're upset over Josiah's death, but you're refusing to look at the facts." I shook my finger at her this time, but I might as well have been talking to a flock of chickens.

Excuses spilled out of my daughter. "I've got to stop at the Winn-Dixie, and fix supper, and my bridge club's coming …" She paused when the Manor's grandfather clock struck once for the half hour. "My goodness, it's five-thirty already. I need to get a move on. Maybe I'll see you tomorrow."

I waved a halfhearted good-bye as she hurried away. We needed to talk. She knew like I knew, Josiah's death had not been accidental. Why could she not face the truth?

When I entered my room, my bottom dresser drawer was hanging open a good four inches. Had I forgotten to close it? I opened it further and looked inside. My tabloids seemed to be undisturbed, as well as Betty Jo's blood pressure contraption underneath them. As soon as the drawer slammed shut, I made a decision. I would go to Blind George's on Saturday night where many Sweetbriar residents gathered to celebrate the end of a workweek. If I got lucky, some of the murder suspects might be there.

Or maybe I should send Shirley instead. She would blend in where I would stick out like Miss Margaret wearing a pink sunbonnet.

Chapter Six

After supper, I stopped by the sitting room, wondering if Jack would be there. Standing in the arched doorway, I leaned on my cane and scanned the room. Maybe he had decided not to come. It took a moment to spot the silver tips of his cowboy boots. He had chosen a chair beyond a tall palm and the piano. Almost invisible.

As I thumped over to him, he jumped up and stuffed his newspaper underneath his arm. "Miss Hops. You needing a ride somewhere?" In the past, he had given me a lift if his produce truck was headed my way, but this time I would not let his kindness muddy the water.

As usual, I jumped in with both feet. "Did you know Josiah Goforth?"

A startled look swept over his face. "Why are you asking?" He patted his shirt pockets. "Could use a smoke. Don't suppose you … Nah, you said you quit." He took a deep breath and blew it out. "Sure, I knew him. A pure shame how he died."

"Bad news travels fast. What did you know about him?"

"Addicted to gambling, owed some people money, and hung around some shady characters. Not good. Why all these questions?" He threw his newspaper into the chair and retrieved his cowboy hat.

"Some things about his death don't set right," I said, shifting my weight to my good knee and leaning on my cane.

Jack said nothing but questioned me with his eyes.

"I knew him for many years," I added. "He was a friend. Used to work for me and Charlie."

"He certainly had his share of problems," Jack said as he edged toward the door.

I nodded. *Were my questions making him nervous?* "You ever gamble?"

Jack retrieved a bandana from his jeans and wiped his neck. "Maybe, but it ain't none of your—"

"Where were you last night?" *How many more questions would he tolerate?*

"What's it to ya?" He jammed his bandana into a pocket and plopped his hat onto his head. "Seems to me you're sticking your nose where it don't belong."

I decided to push a little harder. "Weren't you supposed to take Shirley to a movie?"

"Could be." In the next instant, he stood within inches of me.

I held my breath against a strong odor. *Was it from the sweat of a hard-working man or fear?*

"Now you've gone to meddling," he said. "Where I am and what I'm doing is my business."

"One more question," I said as I stepped back and bumped into the piano. *Trapped.* "Did you have an argument recently with Josiah? On the church steps? Maybe about Shirley?"

A flush crept over a bulging vein in his neck. "What if I did? I thought you were my friend. Looks like I was mistaken."

"I am your friend, but I'm looking for some answers."

"You're barking up the wrong tree." He grabbed his jacket and brushed past me, but then whirled around. In two steps, even with dragging his stiff leg along, he leaned down to my face. His breath smelled like stale cigarettes and a bucketful of beer. "You think someone killed Josiah? Well, it wasn't me. Carl Swain is the one you ought to be checking out. The two of them got into a shoving match."

I reached behind me and pressed my hands into the piano, wondering how much closer he could get. "Where was this? And when?"

"Cockfight. Last Friday. But if anyone asks, I'll deny being there. Not exactly a legal place, you know. As far as my whereabouts last night, I was working on my scooter and lost track of time. All of a sudden, I remembered my date with Shirl, stopped what I was doing, and ran into Three Points Grocery on my way to the Manor. Bought her a big bunch of flowers. Anything else, Miss Hops?"

"That about covers it," I said. I had not seen any flowers. If his story were true, Shirley would have shown them off to everyone. Had he come here with a peace offering like he claimed? "Unless you overheard what Carl and Josiah argued about," I added, hoping he would share it if he did.

"Didn't listen. But could have had something to do with what I seen in the alley behind Begley's Drugstore. Reckon you could use that information too." He walked around to the piano bench and slid himself onto it. He took his hat off and heaved a sigh. He seemed calmer, so I joined him, thankful for a chance to sit.

"Happened late one night. A couple of weeks ago. Since you seem determined to be a regular snoop, this might interest you." He glanced at me with a crooked smile.

I ignored his insult. "What were you doing back there?"

"Don't have to answer to you, but I was walking. Scooter was out of gas, and the alley is a short cut to my apartment." Jack fiddled with the piano keys.

I rubbed my knee, wishing for an ice pack. "Go on."

"Josiah was going through the dumpster. We spoke. I moved on. Next thing I knew, Carl come out of Begley's and handed a package to some heavy-set guy. Something didn't set right and, since I found myself in the dumpster's shadow, I stood there and watched. Soon as the big man left, Carl spotted Josiah. They stared at each other, and then Carl said, 'Forget what you saw, or you'll be sorry.'"

The detective in me was turning somersaults. "Oh, my. You could be an important witness. Would you testify … if need be?"

He turned toward me and held up both hands. "Nope. Don't exactly get along with the law, as you well know."

I thanked him for sharing what he knew about Carl.

He stood, reached for my hands, and pulled me up from the bench. "Tell Shirl I'll be back in about an hour. Need to walk. Clear my head."

Jack left the sitting room pulling his stiff leg along. His jerking gait caused his long hair to swing back and forth across the back of his leather jacket. He had given me some damaging information about Carl—if it were true. But Jack's whereabouts when Josiah was killed? Even though Jack was a kind man who loved my dear friend Shirley, his alibi did not hold water.

❊ ❊ ❊

Retrieving a nice, fresh notebook out of the bottom drawer of my chest, I found a pen to my liking. Blue with white script on the side advertised the Dixie Diner. Its purple ink would flow easily across the page.

Propped up in bed, I began my investigation by making notes about Josiah Goforth. What did I truly know about him? What had he shared with my Charlie underneath my kitchen window? Had I remembered their exact words or forgotten an important detail? The photos on my phone provided some clues, plus evidence found at the cemetery but not shared with the sheriff. What else could be important?

Then I remembered. Pen and notebook laid aside, I went to my jacket hanging on the back of my rocker. The knife was recovered from one pocket, but the gamecock feather was not in the other. I searched the floor and underneath my bed. No feather. How could I have lost it? It could be an important piece of evidence.

Pacing the floor and fussing at myself for being so careless got me nowhere. Charlie would have said, "Work with what you've got instead of fretting about what you don't have." A smile traveled clear to my toes, and I managed a small jig step. My dear husband could always get me back on track.

Back in bed, I studied the knife more closely underneath my bedside lamp. The initials looked more like a WB than anything else. Like Smiley suggested, maybe those two letters stood for someone's girlfriend. Did the silver knife belong to Josiah's killer or an innocent visitor to Beulah Cemetery?

Sheriff Caywood immediately came to mind. Didn't Shirley tell me he was dating someone from Newberry? A Wanda something? What was her last name? Bradley? Hadley? Even if his grandfather used to bring me bushels of the best tomatoes in the whole county, I didn't trust our sheriff. He had shut his eyes to a murder. Had he become blind on purpose, or was he protecting someone?

After much deliberation, four men became people of interest in my notebook, each one occupying a separate page.

Deputy Larry. Not a suspect yet, but a person to watch. A man too anxious to use his stun gun and more nervous than he should have been when we were at the cemetery. Did Larry come upon Josiah loitering somewhere, possibly Beulah Cemetery? Did the deputy become more aggressive against him than he should have, which resulted in heart failure?

Walter Jones. An apple farmer and my former neighbor, who also raised gamecocks—which was a shady sideline, at best. But his connection? Did Josiah owe Walter money? Josiah had gambling troubles back when Charlie was alive. Maybe he was trying to give it up but owed someone too much money and fell into the trap of *one more time and my luck is bound to turn around.* Perhaps the feather was a link. If some feathers had been underneath Josiah in the wheelbarrow, one could have clung to his coat when they lifted him to the bench. That same wheelbarrow might have transported dead birds.

Did Walter kill Josiah to keep him quiet? Surely the sheriff realized Walter held cockfights. Was he blind due to ignorance or on purpose? Or maybe my imagination was running away like a loose steer.

Carl Swain. The new assistant manager of Begley's Drugstore. If I could believe Jack, Carl had threatened Josiah in the alley behind the store. Had Josiah witnessed a drug deal? Why had Carl shoved Josiah at the cockfight? I needed to know what had gone on between the two men. Jack's testimony could be reliable, or he could be trying to distract me from the truth of his own involvement.

How many Sweetbriar men were in this circle of crime? Working on the farm with Charlie all those years, I had no idea our small town was not postcard perfect.

Francesca's son, Edward, was also a possible suspect because he had ties to the Mafia, but I didn't have enough to go on. Gambling. Possible debts. Strong-arm tactics if a man couldn't pay. All motives to harm Josiah if he was about to be a whistle-blower. Was he or was he simply in over his head and wanted out?

Jack Lovingood. I added his name because he had the strongest motive of the other men—the universal love triangle. Did Jack and Josiah argue about Shirley on the church steps? Jack admitted he and Josiah had attended the same cockfight a week before the murder. Maybe he was the one who got into a shoving match instead of Carl. Maybe they argued about Shirley then too—the real reason he left early.

Another thought nagged me. What about the bagpipes? What happened to them? Had Josiah become desperate enough to sell them? Surely, they were not worth stealing.

The killer had to be a man. A woman could never subdue a big fellow like Josiah unless she drugged him first. *Hmmm ... Carl would have access to all sorts of drugs at Begley's.*

Working until nearly eleven, I was frustrated with a lack of real progress. Close to midnight, I padded to Smiley's door and tapped lightly, but his room remained dark and quiet. Further down the hall, a strip of light under Shirley's door and the sound of Elvis' "Crying in the Chapel" indicated she was very much awake.

After two firm knocks, she threw open her door. "Law, honey, looks like we've got the same problem."

We shuffled into the kitchen in our nightclothes and slippers, me in pink flowered pajamas and Shirley in a flimsy, short gown—bright red. She handed me a package of frozen peas for my knee before pouring us hot tea in purple mugs, with Kut 'N Loose Salon emblazoned in a fancy, gold script. In her former place of employment, she had shampooed heads and manicured nails. She had tacked up a note, *Part-time beautician wanted at Sweetbriar Manor*, on the beauty shop's bulletin board, but no one had applied for the job.

We talked about our men and how sometimes their actions made no sense to us. Then I opened my notebook, and we discussed each suspect on my list—except I never turned to Jack's page, of course.

She agreed with me. Any one of the men could have killed Josiah. And the same motives applied to nearly every suspect. Perhaps Josiah had borrowed some money in order to satisfy a gambling debt. Maybe he sold his bagpipes for the same reason. Then Josiah could have lost more money gambling, as he was prone to do, and couldn't repay his loans.

Shirley opened the refrigerator and set a large Tupperware bowl on the counter. "Stewed chickens," she said. "Might as well get these pies ready to bake. Can't sleep anyhow."

"Better than tossing and turning," I said.

She handed me a pair of rubber gloves. I stayed on my stool at the island and tore chicken from the bones and chopped it into pieces while she peeled and diced potatoes, carrots, and onions and cooked them in broth.

"Something's bothering me about those bagpipes," I said. "I don't believe Josiah sold them."

Shirley's knife stopped chopping. "What makes you think he didn't?"

"He would never get rid of them, no matter how desperate he was." I leaned toward the garbage can and threw in a handful of chicken bones.

"Law, honey, what does this mean?" She went back to her chopping.

"Maybe someone stole them, though I can't imagine they would be worth fooling with."

"What are you gonna do, honey?" Shirley's expression was serious.

"Pay a visit to Boss' Last Chance Pawn Shop. It's possible they ended up there. Want to join me?"

Shirley broke out in a grin. "Do you think I'd let you go there by yourself?"

I grinned back. Before long, we had four large potpies ready for tomorrow's oven.

✳ ✳ ✳

The next day, soon after breakfast, Betty Jo came like she said she might—but not to see me, for she was soon gone again.

Shirley informed me my daughter had taken Frankie and headed to Begley's Drugstore for more diapers. Not for the toddler, but for Ida Mae, our former administrator's mother, a frail old woman with dementia who most certainly belonged at Shady Acres. Betty Jo seemed determined to avoid me. No matter. Sooner or later, we would air our differences, and, settle them or not, we would move on.

I searched for Francesca and found her parked beside the fountain in the garden. The residents of Sweetbriar Manor needed her help. I needed her help. But would she agree?

William saluted as he hurried past me. "Blanket," he said with a grin as he returned inside. Always happy to serve his sweetie.

I pulled a patio chair close to her wheelchair as a squirrel scampered away, a treasure in his mouth. "You've got everyone buzzing about the shortcomings of this place. Once you inform any potential owner, we won't be able to give Sweetbriar Manor away on a silver platter."

"I doubt it," Francesca said as she shuffled tarot cards on her tray. She pointed to the fountain's wall. "Going to collapse. Mark my words."

"You have a good, critical eye for such things," I said, making an appeal to her already inflated ego.

She smiled and sat up straighter. "We've nearly got the petition ready. You can soon carry it to Blind George's."

"Excellent. Are you ready for another assignment?"

She dropped her cards into a wheelchair pocket and shook her finger at me. "Why are you delegating so much these days? What have you got up your sleeve?"

A sudden breeze sprayed us with water from the fountain. We both squealed as I pushed Francesca to a sunny spot near the back steps. I leaned close to her ear. "Can I count on you?"

She twisted around and glared at me. "Who do you think you're talking to?"

"Good." I moved to the steps and plopped down in front of her. "Organize the residents to form a protest march down Main Street. Keep it under the radar, away from Mr. Lively's ears as long as possible. He always suspects I'm up to something, and this time, he's right. Contact Betty Jo and tell her we need a permit. Decide on the date and make some posters."

"You realize I'll use some tough, in-your-face language," she said. "Nothing wishy-washy. We have to make a stand."

Something nagged me to clarify what I expected, but surely she had some judgment and would use it. "I'll leave the wording up to you. Use your creative, inventive side." *Oh, my. Had I unleashed a tiger?*

She studied me with brows knitted together. "Whatever is keeping you from taking charge of our protest march yourself must be important."

"Exactly." I pushed myself up with my cane, anxious to leave before she began demanding answers.

"I'll need poster board and markers, bold colors. And balloons. And Betty Jo's phone number," Francesca said.

"No problem. Uh, would you like to contribute to the cost?" I certainly hoped she would.

She pulled a leather billfold from a wheelchair pouch and handed me a fifty-dollar bill. "That enough?"

Francesca would organize the march, but would she push the envelope too far with rude signs and turn the community against us? Could I actually concentrate on the murder investigation or not?

William nearly knocked me over in his rush to get back outside with a pink throw draped over his arm. "Sorry it took so long," he said to Francesca as he kissed her cheek. "Got the last two signatures and made duplicate copies of our list." He handed me some papers stapled together.

As I left them, Francesca asked for William's phone. My daughter would be no match for my bullheaded friend. And I imagined the town of Sweetbriar would never again see the likes of her protest march.

❋ ❋ ❋

Soon on my way into town, I stabbed the sidewalk with my cane. Had I made a mistake enlisting Francesca's help? Only time would tell. I had to concentrate on other matters at hand.

The morning was still young, with plenty of time to visit the pawnshop, the church, and Begley's Drugstore before noon. I was going alone. Shirley had forgotten today was nail day, and she had five customers to squeeze in before starting lunch preparations. Smiley absolutely could not go, even though after breakfast he had offered. His corns and bunions were talking trash. He also admitted he had a scratchy throat.

"But, Sis, you shouldn't go to the pawnshop by yourself. You could meet up with all sorts of unsavory characters."

"Hogwash. I'll be back in two, maybe three shakes of a donkey's tail. You get some rest. Ask Shirley for some orange juice."

He nodded. "I don't like this. If a hound dog catches a skunk, he's in a world of trouble."

After giving him a quick hug, I was on my way. "Or hot tea with honey wouldn't hurt," I added from the doorway.

Pausing on the sidewalk, I pulled on my hat and gloves. "Boss Brown, Carl Swain, and First Presbyterian, here I come." Some of my questions could soon have answers. A lighthearted feeling lifted my spirits, and I yearned to skip along like a schoolgirl, even though it was impossible with my old bones. Determined to behave, I watched where my feet would land on the uneven sidewalk and plodded along.

Chapter Seven

I paused outside Begley's Drugstore, where Carl Swain was a murder suspect with a question mark beside his name. I was not sure what his connection had been to Josiah, if anything, but right now, my main concern was the bagpipes. They could have been left in a pawnshop. If so, there was no guarantee how long they would stay. I decided to stop at the drugstore on my way back home, hopefully to talk with Carl as well as purchase poster board.

Past Henry's Hardware, I turned right onto Short Street and then immediately left on Pine—not a familiar part of town. The storefronts, dirty and dull, needed a fresh coat of paint and a window washer. My feet navigated over and around some trash. The town also needed to send a street sweeper.

Yet across the street in the next block, the Last Chance Pawn Shop shone as bright as a movie theatre's marquee. A total surprise. The large brick house, painted white, looked like it had once served as a funeral home. I could imagine a black hearse parked in the circular driveway as I followed it around to the front door. A prosperous-looking establishment, the pawnshop stood between a used bookstore, called Hooked on Books, converted from an old carriage house, and an art gallery that perhaps had once been a caretaker's residence.

An old wicker chair on the porch offered me a chance to sit. I sank down and rubbed my knee. Maybe all my walking lately had been too much. What if I had trouble getting back home? Certainly had no money for a taxi. I'd have to figure things out as they came. I slowly pushed up and got my bones moving.

A bell on the door jingled as it opened. Two men stood behind long counters stretched along either side of a wide foyer. Beyond them, seated at a roll-top desk, a chunky woman with spiked hair stopped whatever she was doing and closed a large black book. She was the same woman I'd seen with Boss, as well as with Mr. Lively. All three people stared at me as if I had interrupted a private—and important—conversation.

Finally, the tall skinny man wearing a shiny black suit rushed over to me.

"Hello, Boss. I assume you're open for business." *Was that a smirk hiding behind his mustache?*

He rubbed his hands together. "I've been expecting you," he said as he adjusted his plaid bow tie. "Always told your Charlie, a friend in need is a friend indeed. Are we selling or pawning today? In no time, you could walk out the front door with a pocketful of cash if you play your cards right."

Boss was never my husband's friend. Or mine. He reminded me of an overly anxious salesman. "I'd like to look around first," I said as I backed away from his too-close presence. His three-piece suit smelled like it had recently been unpacked from an old trunk filled with mothballs, which gave me a sneezing fit.

"Help yourself," he said with the sweep of his arm. "Had a feeling you might need my services one day soon." He inched a little closer. "If by any chance you're coming to make a purchase, every room is filled to the brim with treasures. We have a special collection upstairs if you're interested in musical instruments or any item related to the Celtic culture—from kilts to a framed Irish Blessing. And special for you, we have an easy-payment plan to accompany anything you'd like to purchase. Or we can draft your bank account each month—a brand new convenience we offer. You let me know what strikes your fancy."

My ears perked up. *Celtic items?* I was not anxious to climb the long staircase, nor did I want to appear too eager in my search for a set of bagpipes. I had no idea Boss specialized in anything. Maybe I had hit the jackpot.

I browsed through vinyl records stacked in a wooden crate, examined an antique tea set, and gazed through a glass case of estate jewelry.

"Any piece in there remind you of something you'd like to sell?" Boss asked from behind the counter. "A ring or a watch perhaps? Widows always have forgotten treasures tucked away. Perhaps in a safety deposit box? Instant cash."

"Maybe. I could use some cash—for certain. Let me think about it."

I glanced around the shop. When the thickset woman with horn-rimmed glasses and spiked hair rose from her desk chair, a rose tattoo on her neck became visible. She wore loose, flowered pants and a long, flowing purple top. She gathered her book and a stack of papers and exited through a side door. How did Boss know one of the women who represented the women's prison system? What was she doing here? Was she an accountant on the side? In Sweetbriar? Something smelled worse than rotten cabbage.

I needed to stall, not only to pretend an interest in something besides bagpipes but to ask this woman some questions if she should reappear. However, a subtle approach would be best, and since that was not one of my strong tendencies, I had to give it some thought.

On the wall behind one of the long counters hung an array of rifles and shotguns. I walked closer. In front of the display, inside glass encasements, were shelves of handguns, a few sets of handcuffs, two stun guns, and boxes of ammunition. I turned toward Boss who stood close by. "I've been thinking about buying a small firearm for protection, something I could slip inside my purse. What would you recommend?"

He hurried over, zipped behind the counter, unlocked the glass doors, and slid them open. "We just happen to have a couple of beauties," he said. "You're in luck." He unfolded a piece of black velvet and laid two pistols on it.

I picked one up and examined it, then looked closely at the other one—taking my time as if studying them. "These are not what I had in mind. Neither would stop even a small person standing as close as you are to me. Don't you agree? I'll ask Sheriff Caywood to advise me and come back another time."

"Suit yourself," he said as a frown washed across his face. He returned the guns to their case and locked it.

"Say, didn't you mention kilts when I first came in?" I asked. "An out-of-town friend is looking for some in a particular tartan plaid, but I can't remember which clan. Maybe if I could see the name or the pattern, it would ring a bell."

"Certainly. Turn to your right at the top of the stairs. Take your time. I'll come up directly to see if you've found anything." A young man carrying an oil painting entered the store, and Boss was gone in a flash. I was thankful for the distraction.

The staircase looked like it stretched up to the sky, but I took one step at a time, favoring my bad knee. *Was surgery in my future? A knee replacement?* Absolutely no time for such nonsense.

In the upstairs hallway, guitars in all sizes and colors stood in rows in their individual stands. Made me wish I could lift one up and play it alongside my favorite radio program, *Going 'Round the Mountain*. I turned right and stepped into The Celtic Room. On either side of the arched opening stood a mannequin dressed in Scottish finery from head to toe. On a far wall hung a set of bagpipes. I didn't remember exactly what Josiah's looked like, but I suspected they were not a common item in Boss' store. I moved closer to read the tag.

"They're top-notch, a real prize," Boss said.

I jumped and spun around, not realizing he had walked up behind me.

Boss held onto his jacket lapels, and his face fairly beamed. "Contacted one of my special customers who I knew would appreciate such a prize. Sold them in no time. Picking them up this afternoon. Who would've thought a pawnshop in our small town of Sweetbriar could acquire such an item. Yes sir, made me right proud."

"Where did they come from?" A fair and easy question, I assumed.

Boss turned away, grabbed a feather duster, and tackled a sword display. "Transactions in this store are confidential."

"So ... you won't say who bought them either?"

"Absolutely not." He threw the duster onto a countertop and scowled at me. "Why are you so interested anyway?"

This encounter was not going in a good direction, but I refused to panic. Maybe I was overreacting. "A friend of mine needs to replace some. I think they were stolen."

Boss fingered the tips of his handlebar mustache. "We don't touch hot merchandise. My deals are legit. Apparently, you didn't come here to do any business, and I haven't seen any credentials authorizing you to ask questions. I suggest you leave or my nephew can escort you out."

Oh, my. My intuitions about Josiah's bagpipes had been right. A bald man appeared, out of nowhere it seemed. Dressed in black pants and a black tee shirt, he looked as hefty as a sumo wrestler. I tried to smile. What had I gotten myself into?

"Have a good day," I said, making as quick an exit as I could manage. The woman I had seen when I first came in—and whatever she was doing here—would have to remain a mystery. For the moment.

After hobbling down the stairs and out to the circular driveway, I put my cane into service and headed straight to the sheriff's office to inform him someone had brought Josiah's bagpipes to Boss' pawnshop. Had Josiah been desperate enough to pawn them, thinking he would rescue them when a gambling bet paid off? For sure, someone had bought them. Smiley was right. This hound dog had found a passel of skunks.

When I rounded the corner of Short Street onto Pine, I nearly ran into the burly nephew from the pawnshop. With feet firmly planted, he towered over me with his tattooed arms folded across his black tee shirt.

I pointed my cane at him but couldn't keep it from wobbling. If he grabbed me, could I scream? "I hope you realize the sheriff is expecting me. In less than five minutes." My voice quivered, and my stomach knotted into a lump.

He frowned and shifted his eyes toward the sidewalk. My cue to skedaddle. I only wished I could break into a run.

The sheriff was not in his office, but his deputy was there with feet propped awkwardly on his desk. He looked up but didn't offer to stand. Neither did he ask me to sit. I did anyway, sinking into a rickety folding chair.

"Please tell Sheriff Caywood to call me. It's important," I said placing both hands on my cane and leaning forward.

"I'll consider it," he said as he opened a pocketknife and began cleaning his fingernails. "Isn't it about time you dropped your ridiculous detective business before you get hurt?"

I felt like bopping him on the head with my cane. "I've been visiting the Last Chance Pawn Shop. Do you know Boss?"

He raised his eyes and glared at me. "Yeah, reckon I do. You shouldn't be messing around down there."

"What's his real name?"

"Beats me," he said as he inspected his nails. "Never needed to know. Why?"

"No reason." I held onto the desk's edge and pulled myself up. "Wondered if he had one. A real name."

"You are one weird old woman." He snapped the knife shut and stood.

I moved toward the door then turned back. "Seventy-something is not old. Tell the sheriff what I said."

"Good-bye, Miss Agnes," he said as he saluted.

I would show him. He was not about to dismiss me that easily.

✻ ✻ ✻

I managed to slowly navigate up the church's long handicapped ramp. Boss Brown had become a person of interest, and the deputy had moved up several notches on my list of irritating people.

The dimly lit sanctuary was whisper-quiet and stuffy. I collapsed onto the nearest pew to catch my breath and allow my eyes to adjust. A woman sat near the front with her head bowed. Saying a prayer myself, I asked for the Lord's guidance.

What on earth did I expect to find out by coming here?

My watch, as near as I could tell, indicated it was almost ten o'clock. If Josiah had met someone here each week, the same someone would have no reason to show up today. I couldn't even remember why it was so important to come here. I jumped when a side door squeaked open and then shut with a thud. A man sat down at the organ. Even though expecting some music, I gasped as he pounded his first notes. Maybe Josiah had come here to play his bagpipes after all, and he had met no one. The praying woman rose from her seat, removed some cloths from her apron, and began dusting the pews. A cleaning lady. Maybe she had seen or heard something.

"Ma'am," I said as I moved close behind her. She didn't respond, so I touched her arm.

She jerked around with a surprised look on her face. "Land's sake! Where did you come from?"

"The street. Can I ask you some questions?"

"Are you in trouble? Is someone after you?" She sat down and patted the cushion beside her.

"Do you remember seeing a man come in here with his bagpipes, every Wednesday morning around ten o'clock? I asked. "He probably looked like a bum. Only he wasn't."

She nervously rubbed her hands together. "Who's asking?"

"Josiah used to work for my husband. He was a kind man and a friend. Someone has killed him."

The woman pulled a tissue from her waistband and dabbed underneath her glasses. "Exactly what I thought might've happened to him. He was in trouble."

"What kind of trouble?"

"Not sure, but maybe the sheriff could tell you, or maybe he wouldn't."

I knew that man had something to hide. "Why him?"

"He and Josiah met here every week. Talked a good fifteen minutes every time."

I hugged her and thanked her for her help. "Would it be all right if I come back another time, maybe talk some more?"

She smiled and nodded.

What reason could the sheriff have to meet with Josiah? Obviously, they wanted privacy. Except for the cleaning lady—and probably the deputy—they had accomplished their goal.

My next stop was Henry's store. While his clerk made me two new keys, I shared what I had learned at the pawnshop and the church.

"You don't say. Mighty interesting," Henry said as he poured himself a cup of coffee that looked as black as tar and smelled worse. "What's next on your agenda?"

"Mike's Garage, Begley's Drugstore, and Blind George's. Drugstore first."

Chapter Eight

Henry refused any payment for my keys. As I headed back toward the Manor, with a stop along the way to talk to Carl, the courthouse clock struck eleven.

Inside Begley's, I caught my breath and gathered my thoughts at the soda fountain. With my purse down by my feet and my cane hooked on the counter, I sipped on a cherry coke. The aroma of hamburgers and French fries almost made me forget my resolve to watch my spending.

How to approach Carl was my main concern. Made no sense to walk up to him and accuse him of murder when he was not even a number-one suspect. No one had earned that position. Not yet. I needed a plan. Still not certain what to do, I slipped off my stool, found a cart, and strolled to the school supply aisle where I found ten pieces of white poster board on a shelf. Since I wanted at least fifteen, it was a good excuse to speak to the assistant manager. *Perfect.*

Mr. Watson announced Carl's name over the loud speaker. He soon appeared at the end of the aisle, flipping his dark, greasy hair away from his pockmarked face.

I pushed my cart closer to him. "Do you happen to have any more of these in the back?" Even another color? Yellow would work."

He shook his head. "Been a run on poster board lately."

As I looked down at the shoes he wore, something else caught my eye. I was flabbergasted and hoped my face didn't show it. Was that the end of a scarf peeking from a pocket on his pharmacy jacket? It looked similar to the one underneath Josiah's body. Or was my imagination running wild again?

"What in thunder you staring at?" Carl asked. He thrust his hands into his pockets, and the scarf disappeared.

"Uh … your shoes. You always work in those boots?"

He took a step back. "Maybe. Maybe not. What's it to you if I do?"

"I knew a man who always wore some like those. Exactly like them, matter of fact."

Carl's face turned as white as the cardboard in my cart. "I've got to get back to work." He turned, picked up an empty box, and collapsed it with his fist.

I was on to something. Felt it in my gut. "Did you attend a cockfight on the night of October twenty-fifth?"

"What if I did? It's none of your business." He collapsed another box by stomping on it.

"The possibility might interest the sheriff." My voice had risen to a thin squeak. But nerves could not get the best of me.

"You don't know what you're getting into," he said in a menacing tone.

Was he threatening me? Sweat ran down my neck and trickled between my breasts. "Where were you that night anyway?"

"Can't remember exactly." He loaded a stack of flattened boxes into a cart.

"Humor me and think about it," I said, hoping my voice sounded braver than I felt.

He looked up from his cart. "I was … uh … working late. Yep. Working late. Almost midnight by the time I left here."

"I suppose Mr. Watson could verify your hours."

"We're done here." He turned to leave, but I was not finished.

"Not quite. Heard you acquired a black belt recently. Could come in handy, self-defense and all. Ever have to use it?"

Carl jerked around and shot daggers at me with his eyes. "What if I did?"

"If I had another option, I would take my business elsewhere. By the way, your wheelbarrow of pumpkins outside … its front wheel is full of red clay." *Like the dirt out at the cemetery.* "And it's looser than a tooth fixing to fall out. Might collapse altogether with the weight of those pumpkins."

"You keep your hands off private property," he snarled.

I gripped the handle of the shopping cart to keep my hands from shaking. "So, the wheelbarrow belongs to you."

"I never said such, old woman."

Who was he calling *old*? "If you stole a dead man's boots—which I suspect you did—you're nothing but a scumbag."

In an instant, Carl stood within inches of me. He smelled like fear itself. His pockmarked cheeks puffed up like balloons, and he flexed his hands. *Would he actually hit me?* I stepped back into a pen display and sent it toppling over.

"Get out of here," he said between clenched teeth.

I did exactly that.

❋ ❋ ❋

Shirley had saved me some split pea soup and a fat slice of sourdough bread. The dining room was nearly empty, so she pulled a chair close to mine while I ate and shared my morning's detective work.

"What do you think?" I asked, scraping my bowl for the last bite.

"Law, honey, somebody's as guilty as sin, but I'm not sure which one. And what in thunder do you reckon the sheriff was up to?"

❋ ❋ ❋

Later that afternoon, as Pearl clicked on her soap opera reruns, I delivered five pieces of poster board and a box of colored markers to Francesca.

She frowned at the items, then at me. "Is this all you could get?"

"They said they'd call me when more comes in." I counted out the change onto her tray. If Francesca relied on her tarot cards for advice, she was liable to blame the women criminals for everything from bad weather to the crumbling fountain in our garden. Her signs for our protest march could be a catastrophe, and I regretted asking her to make them. But it was too late.

Smiley received the remaining five pieces. He was soon hard at work drawing and sketching, quickly and purposefully, to complete his special assignment. We talked back and forth, wording our signs so we would not offend anyone. After all, we didn't want to sound like a bunch of grouchy old people who were against women getting a second chance to turn their lives around. The residents of Sweetbriar Manor could alienate the whole town. And what good would that do?

Smiley snapped the top down on the last marker just as the buzzer sounded for supper. Where had the time gone? I had shared every detail about my encounter with Carl. Smiley only nodded or grunted.

"Tell me what you think," I said. "Surely the evidence against him is incriminating."

"Not so sure, Sis. I've reconsidered from when we talked earlier. It all seems circumstantial."

"Seriously? But you should have seen him—"

"Ever read Thoreau?"

Why was this man always talking in riddles? "What does he have to do with anything?"

"Some circumstantial evidence is very strong, as when you find a trout in the milk."

"Oh. So you think—"

"You could have a whole mess of trout in this bucket of milk, but it won't satisfy the law." Smiley shook his head as if the matter were closed.

We hurried to the dining room where ham, macaroni and cheese, pinto beans, collard greens, and cornbread awaited us. Charlie's favorite supper. It made me yearn to sit across our kitchen table from him one more time.

While we ate, Francesca expounded on her latest prediction—no doubt extracted from her favorite cards. According to her, Sweetbriar Manor was headed for an impending disaster.

I leaned over and whispered in Smiley's ear. "Can you come to my room in a little while?"

He nodded. "Does she actually believe in such garbage?"

"Afraid so," I said around a mouthful of cornbread.

If Smiley would come sit in my crooked rocker, we could share a Snickers, his favorite, and listen to *Going 'Round the Mountain* on my Philco before we got to the pressing detective business at hand. We had to plan our next step, which included confronting Carl. Again. Either with the sheriff present or on our own.

Smiley was the perfect listening friend if he had kept his daily routine. He didn't like to miss his morning newspaper reading time or his afternoon nap time. Sometimes it was hard to tell the difference between the two—but then lately he didn't have his normal routine because of ... because of Pearl. *Was she the reason he seemed so ... so beside himself with happiness?*

This man could be a comfort or a total frustration, and I never knew which one to expect. I seemed to be the one who could upset him most, and he was quick to fly off the handle when I did. Like the time he jumped all over me because he thought I had gone to visit our friend Alice at Mission Hospital without him. I hadn't, of course, but he never did say he was sorry for saying those hurtful words. Not like my sweet, even-tempered Charlie who had flown to heaven going on three years ago.

When I opened my door to see if Smiley might be on his way, voices and laughter floated from Pearl's room next door to mine. Curiosity got the better of me. Who could be there? She never had visitors. When I knocked on her door, it swung open. There stood Smiley with a silly grin on his face.

"Agnes. It's … it's you," he sputtered.

"Of course it's me," I said, suddenly feeling flushed from head to toe.

"I was looking for you," he said.

"Well, you must've discovered by now I wasn't in Pearl's room." Did he think I was totally clueless?

His face turned as red as a clown's nose. "Nope. Not here."

"We need to talk," I said. If he wanted to play dumb, so could I. Pearl hummed as she worked behind her easel. "We've got to plan our next step," I added. "Strike while the iron's hot. Don't you agree?"

"No. Yes. Talk would be good." He studied the green carpet between us for a moment, gave me a sideways glance, skirted around me, and headed down the hall, pumping his elbows in the air like a little bird trying to take flight.

I moved into the hallway and fought against the urge to go after him. "I thought you … I'll be waiting," I hollered to his back.

He waved but kept moving. *Shoot a monkey.* Obviously, he wasn't coming to my room to discuss anything.

I reentered Pearl's room and shut the door. She was totally absorbed in her work, and I hesitated to disturb her. I couldn't confront her about Smiley. If hanky-panky was going on between those two, I blamed him—not my high school friend who these days seemed more childlike and innocent than when we were decades younger.

Since Miss Johnson could no longer threaten Pearl, it was like she had discovered her talents for the first time. These days she practically painted nonstop. Her watercolors of the town of Sweetbriar graced the walls of Henry's store. And she had sold a half-dozen or more, giving a portion of her profits to the Juanita and Frankie Fund as we had named it, to help our single, young mother who struggled to make ends meet.

Yes, Pearl had improved, and I prayed she would continue. But what was Smiley doing in her room tonight? Didn't I have a right to know his intentions and where I stood?

An hour dragged by, and he never knocked on my door. Frustrated, I ate my Snickers and then tore into his. Still no Sam Abenda, my so-called friend. *Humph.* I went down to Shirley's room. It looked like we both had complicated men in our lives.

She answered the door with her face shining with cold cream. "Law, honey, there's nothin' worse than a two-timin' man. I can see he's made you madder than a wet hen."

"My thoughts exactly. We need a drink. Hot tea with lots of honey."

Over several cups, with gingersnaps on the side, I brought Shirley up to date on the investigation. We both agreed Carl Swain could be the killer, but we weren't sure if we were ready to make an official accusation.

Looked like we had reached a stalemate.

Chapter Nine

At breakfast the next day, I had planned to give Smiley my coldest shoulder, but that would have to wait until another time. The obituary in the *Timely News* sparsely announced Josiah Goforth's passing. *Forty-eight years old. Died in Beulah Cemetery on October 25, 2016. Born in Waco, Texas, Mr. Goforth was a drifter, a farm hand, and a bagpipe player. He will be buried on Saturday. No service is planned.*

"No," I said, quickly refolding the paper. "I cannot let this happen. I will not."

"Sis, what's happened?" Smiley said, leaning close with his hand on my arm. "Are you crying?" He patted my arm, then handed me his napkin. "We'll go to the porch and sit in the sun. You can tell me all about it. A good bit warmer today, but I'll bring my African just in case."

I dabbed at my eyes. "Afghan." He was such a dear, I almost forgot about being mad at him.

He stood and helped me out of my chair. "Exactly what I said. African. My Lucinda made it."

***

We settled ourselves underneath the crocheted lavender coverlet. "Want you to know," I said, "I haven't forgiven you for standing me up last night. You have some explaining to do, but we have more urgent things to discuss."

"Sis, I can—"

I held up my right hand to stop him and shared the death announcement I'd found in the newspaper. "Will you help me plan a service for Josiah?"

"No wonder you were upset this morning," he said, removing his Reds' baseball cap and turning toward me. "I would be sorely disappointed if I couldn't be a part of it."

I took his hand in mine and gave it a squeeze. I considered planting a kiss on his cheek, or even a big smooch on his lips. Maybe in due time. I certainly didn't want to frighten him away. If I did, what woman would he run to? *Hmmm ... exactly.*

We decided to take a look at the funeral arrangements our friend Alice had made before she died. Hers had been a beautiful service, and her program would be an ideal one to follow. We made plans to meet in the dining room after everyone turned in for the night.

"Perfect," I said as I folded the obituary page and slipped it into my purse.

With that settled, we discussed the dead ends I had acquired by visiting the pawnshop, the church, and the drugstore. I still thought Carl was a number one suspect, but we needed to be absolutely certain.

"I know where we should go next," I said.

"You do?"

"Mike's Garage. Saturday afternoon."

Smiley looked puzzled. "What on earth for?"

I leaned close to his ear. "Trust me," I whispered. "And come Saturday night, you and me are going out again."

Now, Smiley looked totally confused. "We are? Where?"

"Blind George's Pool Hall. Shirley's going too."

He grinned and shook his head. "Forever more. Good thing I take my vitamins every morning."

A sudden, cool breeze caused me to shiver.

"Scooch closer, Sis," he said as he placed his arm on the back of the swing. "Air's got a nip to it. Feels fresh, though, don'tcha know."

I scooched as close as possible. A warm tingle ran all over me as we touched. He reached for my hand.

Oh, my. Is he feeling guilty for something?

※ ※ ※

Shirley was busy loading the dishwasher as I pushed open the kitchen's swinging door. "Did you see Josiah's death notice in the paper?" I asked. "Smiley and I are planning a service here. Saturday morning."

She straightened herself and brushed off her apron. "I saw it. A poor excuse it was too. I figured you'd do somethin' to set things right. Did you say a service?"

I nodded and smiled. "I was hoping you might help us."

Her face lit up like a sunny day. "Count me in. I'll fix a light lunch for everyone, but I've got to get cracking, or Mr. Lively will ask me to explain why I haven't delivered his second breakfast. Besides that, our Swiss steak will be tough as shoe leather come supper."

Shirley filled a bowl with steaming oatmeal and set it on a tray. "I'll keep my ears open in case I hear more, but our new boss man is about as talkative as a lump of coal and as dense too if he thinks our town don't have any crime." She added small dishes of butter, brown sugar, and raisins, a plate of toasted English muffins, and a glass of orange juice. Then she picked up the tray, looked me in the eye, and winked. "These days I'm a regular snoop. Detectives have to be on the alert." She leaned to my good ear. "I'll talk to the sheriff. See what I can find out about his meetin's with Josiah. He's always liked me. And Saturday night, I'm headed to Blind George's. Wanna come?"

I reached up and patted her back. "Great minds think alike, but I don't want to cramp your style. No need for the two of us to show up together. Smiley said he'd go with me. Some of the suspects on our list could be there if we get lucky."

Back in my room, I called the sheriff. "What time is Josiah's burial on Saturday?"

"Early I expect, he said. "No money for a funeral, you understand."

That's what he thinks. "We're having a memorial service here at the Manor. Eleven o'clock."

"Kind and thoughtful of you, I'll have to admit," he said.

"You're welcome to come."

"Thank you, but I've got other duties to attend to," he said over the sound of papers being shuffled. "Good-bye, Miss Agnes."

I turned on my radio, a display item from Henry's store he had given me when I moved to the Manor. Mine had melted into a blob during the fire. Who would've thought forgetting a pot of beans on the stove could burn a house clear to the ground? Johnny Cash sang "Desperado." His words always spoke to the heart of the matter.

❋ ❋ ❋

By ten o'clock, a hush had settled over the Manor except for Pearl's television. She was probably working late on a painting or sound asleep in her recliner, where I often found her if I visited her before breakfast. I had to admit I hadn't stopped by her room in the early mornings lately. Had I been avoiding her because she and Smiley might have a thing going? What kind of a friend was I anyway?

Thumbing through my Bible revealed the program from Alice's service. I grabbed a notepad and a pen and headed to the dining room with the help of my cane. Seemed dependence on it had become a habit more and more lately. Smiley was already there. He jumped up when he spotted me, pulled out my chair, poured us some hot tea, and we tackled Josiah's service. Smiley was polite, but neither of us mentioned Pearl or what he might be doing in her room. Gave me a pounding headache.

The two of us put together some pretty snazzy arrangements on short notice, if I do say so myself. We followed some of Alice's ideas, but instead of using a student pastor from Fruitland Bible College, I contacted the Salvation Army. Turned out to be the perfect choice because the lady who answered the phone said they knew Josiah personally.

Come Saturday morning, two trumpets, a trombone, and a guitar made sweet music in our sitting room. Francesca refused to join us. She sat in the foyer all puffed up because we had not asked her to play the piano. Soon, however, she edged her wheelchair closer and closer to the arched doorway. During a prayer, I walked over and whispered in her ear, "Get over it. This is not about you."

She flashed her eyes at me and twisted her pearls into a knot. After a bit, she gave up her hissy fit, wheeled inside, and parked next to William. They held hands, and she joined in when we sang "Amazing Grace."

Captain Gilbert spoke of "our fellow soldier being promoted in glory."

Josiah might have been living like a bum in the eyes of society, but he was a man who not only cared about other people—he did something about it. He visited the tent camps where the homeless lived, where others could not or would not go. I had no idea such places even existed near Sweetbriar. The vision of Josiah receiving his rewards gave me a measure of peace, but it also fueled my determination to find the person who killed him.

The captain told stories of men and women Josiah brought to the shelter, not only for food or a shower but for medical attention—sometimes critical. We all shed many tears for Josiah's compassion and his determination to help others.

After the service, Shirley invited us into the dining room where she had set a table filled with an assortment of finger foods. China platters and silver trays were piled high with chicken salad, pimento cheese, cucumber, and Benedictine sandwiches. She had also prepared deviled eggs, crisp veggies for dips, and brownies and pumpkin bread for dessert.

I filled my plate and found a seat next to Captain Gilbert, who looked like a slightly smaller version of Burl Ives.

"Call me Bill," he said as he polished off a cucumber sandwich. "I understand Josiah used to work for you and your husband years ago."

"Charlie said he was one of the best. A hard worker. Polite too. How did he fall on hard times?"

Bill rubbed his chin. "It's complicated. Guess you heard his wife ran off with another man."

"Yes. A pure shame." I took a bite of my sandwich.

"Soon afterward, he took stock of his life. Came to the conclusion he hadn't done much he could be proud of. Knocked on our door with his glorious bagpipes and asked how he might help. He had his own demons to fight, you understand, but he was trying to rectify a sticky situation."

"He had a gambling addiction before my Charlie died. I didn't ask enough questions at the time, but now I'm trying to set things right."

Bill excused himself, filled his plate with second helpings all around, and returned. "Don't know when I've had such delicious food," he said as he popped an entire deviled egg into his mouth. He closed his eyes and chewed slowly. After he finally swallowed, he continued without losing a beat. "Not many people in Sweetbriar knew of Josiah's troubles, except a dozen or so people living on the edge of society. And they try to stay under the radar ... if you know what I mean."

I reached for a pitcher of Shirley's sweet iced tea and refilled our glasses. "I'm fairly certain I saw his bagpipes in the pawnshop. He must have been desperate."

Bill frowned. "He was a gambler. Couldn't seem to get a handle on it. But his bagpipes? He would never give those up."

"If he didn't, then maybe someone did it for him."

Bill turned toward me with a worried look. "You be careful, Miss Agnes. Some of those fellows he hung around with won't hesitate to protect themselves. Josiah could have discovered some of their crooked ways, and maybe they felt threatened. I'm not saying any one of those characters killed him, mind you, but I have a hunch you're right about one thing. Someone did."

As soon as the captain left, I told Smiley to meet me in the kitchen. This new information needed to be shared with him and Shirley. Bill Gilbert also thought a murder had been committed, even if our sheriff was incompetent—at the least. Or an accessory to murder—at the most. And the bagpipes I saw at the pawnshop? If they had belonged to Josiah, who brought them there? And who had purchased them?

These were things I had to find out.

✳ ✳ ✳

That afternoon, I headed for the swing on the front porch, my favorite spot to ponder and sort things out. Before long, Smiley appeared carrying Lucinda's afghan. He settled himself beside me and spread the covering over our laps.

Nellie, clutching her frumpy sweater close to her chest, climbed the front steps and glanced our way. She had obviously snatched something from no telling where and had hidden it inside her clothing. Thankfully, she crept to a rocker on the opposite side of the wraparound porch, away from us. Only her black schoolmarm shoes were visible.

The air was cool as clouds hid the sun. I decided to speak my thoughts out loud. "I wonder if Milk Toast watches his lava lamp all day while he thinks up ways he can make trouble." The lava lamp sat on top of a file cabinet in his tiny office and reminded me of my first day at the Manor and my first encounter with Miss Johnson—or Prissy as I soon nicknamed her. Mr. Lively had demanded Shirley and the residents reimburse him for the lunch after Josiah's service. That would not happen if I had my way.

"Who?" Smiley asked in a bit as if startled out of his own thoughts.

"That wimp of a man we ended up with. He's one grouchy man with no backbone whatsoever. Ill-suited for running a retirement home, and he smells worse than a stack of old library books. Beats me why he was ever hired in the first place. Miss Johnson was a pain in everyone's backside, but at least she had some gumption." The afghan slipped off my lap, and I pulled it back.

"Miss Johnson always looked crisp as a starched shirt," I added. "But she was rotten to the core. Mr. Lively looks as shabby as a tramp, plus he has a strong dislike for people, especially me. Aren't there any normal people in this world?"

Smiley clicked his tongue. "We all have our faults, don'tcha know."

"Exactly. Josiah's killer has serious shortcomings, and they'll help us snag him."

"They will?"

"Yep. For instance, think about Walter Jones. What faults does he have?"

"Hmmm …" Smiley scrubbed his chin with the palm of his hand.

"Fear and greed. What if Walter couldn't let Josiah walk away? Afraid he knew too much about his whole gambling operation. What if he talked? Walter didn't want to lose his lucrative gamecock business. Could have killed Josiah to keep him quiet."

"Sounds possible," Smiley said. "What about the other suspects?"

"Carl Swain. Pure fear. Blind George, like most bartenders, has accumulated a wealth of information about some of his customers, including Carl. Told me he confided in him one night. It seems Carl works for someone … on the side. He'd like to quit, but he can't see any way out. I'm not sure what this has to do with anything, but I'd bet my bottom dollar it does." *Or maybe I should be betting my bottom nickel.*

I shook off my thoughts and continued. "Did you realize Carl has a black belt in karate? Could have killed Josiah with one blow."

"Oh, my," Smiley said. "Surely not."

Nellie rose from her rocking chair and ambled our way. "Ignore her," I said. "Can't trust her any further than you could throw the moon."

Even so, he offered her a little wave—as she did him—as she slowly moved past us and entered the Manor.

Smiley opened a package of Juicy Fruit gum. The sweet aroma made my mouth water. We both unwrapped a piece and chewed in silence for a moment.

"Now, where was I?" I said as the memory of our conversation returned. "According to Jack—if he's a reliable witness—Carl spotted Josiah in the alley behind the drugstore and threatened him. It seems Jack and Josiah saw Carl pass a bundle to a big man, probably a thug. And probably drugs. So, whoever Carl is working for is a thug too. My theory is Carl killed Josiah to keep him from talking about a drug deal."

"Remember what I said about too many fish in the milk?"

"Yes, but—"

"What about our deputy?" Smiley asked.

"He's a puzzle and an irritating one. Definitely someone to keep an eye on. We also have to find out why the sheriff met Josiah every Wednesday morning at First Pres. I've added Jack as a person of interest, but you have to promise to keep it from Shirley."

"Certainly. Go ahead and tell me why you've got Jack on the list. I hope you're wrong. What motive would he have?"

"Jealousy. Josiah was sweet on Shirley. Maybe Jack found out. Henry witnessed Jack and Josiah arguing on the church steps, but he was too far away to hear what they said. Jack has a flimsy alibi for the night of the murder. Says he was working on his scooter. Of course, no one could verify he was."

Smiley fingered the afghan. "How are we going to get to the bottom of the barrel before the fish rot?"

I cut my eyes over to him. "Maybe one day I'll understand what you're talking about. Somehow you, Shirley, and I will solve this crime. We're SBI agents. Sweetbriar's Bureau of Investigators."

He chuckled. "Almost sounds official. What's your plan?"

I sat up straight and faced him, making sure we had eye contact. "Several suspects, including Walter Jones, come to Mike's Garage on Saturday afternoons to play checkers. Since his farm is next to ours, he always offered to pick up my Charlie, who would make excuses to drive himself. Not sure why. Charlie sometimes told me things about his checker-playing buddies, but at the time, I halfway listened. What if he mentioned something important about one of them? A bit of information to help solve the case. I've wracked my brain, but for the life of me, I can't pull anything up. Maybe it'll come to me when I'm not trying so hard."

Smiley tapped his forehead with one finger. "Like when a squirrel finds a nut he forgot he buried."

"Exactly."

"Surely an apple farmer would never kill anyone."

I hoped he was right, but there was no way to be sure. "Stranger things have happened. First of all, Walter raises gamecocks and sells them. Isn't such a business frowned upon by the law? He was also holding cockfights on the sly. If Josiah couldn't pay his gambling debts, maybe he figured he'd blow the whistle, close Walter down, and not have to pay up."

"One crime can lead to another, like a goat in a china shop," Smiley said as he opened his pocketknife and began cleaning his fingernails. He was being as uncouth as that irritating deputy.

I turned my head. "You mean a bull." I shuddered and tried not to listen to his scraping blade.

"Anything else?" he asked.

I threw the afghan aside, pushed myself up with my cane, and stepped away from the swing. One day I would have to address his manners. "We have to investigate each suspect and keep an open mind, or we're bound to miss an important clue. We're going to a checkers game this afternoon."

He peered up at me and shook his head. "What could we possibly gain by going to Mike's? No crime in playing checkers."

"It's right across the street and the perfect place to ask some questions, especially where Walter is concerned. Otherwise, we would have to convince someone to carry us out to his farm five miles outside of town. And what would be our excuse for showing up at his door? We don't need to buy a bushel of Pink Ladies or a gamecock."

"But we don't have any reason to show up at Mike's Garage either."

I blew my breath out. Would this man always remain clueless? "Don't you have a hankering for an orange soda and a Moon Pie?"

"Can't say as I do," he said as he snapped his knife shut and dropped it in his pocket.

"Well, you've got about thirty minutes to work up a craving. It's a lovely day for a walk." I lifted the afghan off his lap, folded it, and handed it back to him. "I'm going to the bathroom before we head out. Bring your billfold. This outing can be your treat. I'm a little short on cash this month." *And maybe for many months to come.* "On our way over there I'll tell you what I've got in mind."

I caught a whiff of Old Spice as he stood and brushed my shoulder. "I'm sure you will, Sis. I'm sure you will."

Whatever faults Smiley had, whatever he was doing in Pearl's room these days, I found myself forgiving him in spite of myself. But I turned away before he could look into my eyes and see my soft-as-a-marshmallow feelings for him.

Chapter Ten

We crossed the street to Mike's Garage, ignoring the *Closed* sign on the door. A jangling bell announced our entrance. The cavernous space smelled of grease, dirty concrete, and gasoline fumes. To our left were three darkened bays, two empty and one with a truck hoisted onto a lift. We passed shelves of auto parts and a potbellied stove and made our way toward two light bulbs suspended by cords from the tall ceiling. Underneath the dim lights, a checkerboard rested on an upturned wooden barrel. Three metal folding chairs and one ragged wingback sat in shadows, even though they had been scooted as close as possible to the board game.

Walter Jones sat in the only comfortable chair. He turned his tan, weathered face toward us as we got closer. He wore his usual bib overalls. His pale, red-headed friend, who wore a greasy jumpsuit with *Mike's Garage* stitched across his chest pocket, was engrossed in cutting himself a plug of tobacco. The men had been hunched over their checkerboard until we interrupted them. A man with a blotched, pockmarked face had been observing their game—Carl Swain. The three men stared hard at us, but I was not about to let them intimidate me.

"Good afternoon, gentlemen. My friend, Smil … uh, I mean Sam Abenda and I, we're … we're seeking information about Josiah Goforth being found dead in Beulah Cemetery. You probably read the small article in the *Timely News*, but we're not sure it told the whole story. You see, it's a puzzle to us exactly how he ended up there, and we're trying to piece together some of the details. Seems some of his family can't rest until the truth comes out."

Walter's chair scraped against the concrete floor as he stood and reached for a set of crutches. "And who would that be? Never spoke of any family. Paper stated the facts. Sounded cut and dried to me. Accidental. None of us knows anything more about it. Right fellas?"

The other two men grunted in agreement. Walter lumbered toward the door. "Got to have a smoke," he said. His face scrunched up as he tried to navigate the short distance.

"How long you been all crippled up?" I asked.

He stopped and looked back with a scowl, his face glistening with sweat. "Two months. Botched knee surgery. Thinking about suing the quack." He turned away, mumbling under his breath.

"Did Josiah ever gamble?" I said to his back.

"Didn't exactly hang out with the bum," Walter said. "I'm a law-abiding citizen." The others laughed. He slowly managed to get through the door and make it outside.

How could this man possibly kill anyone, especially someone as big and strong as Josiah? I moved closer to the men who were waiting on their friend to return. "When my Charlie used to join your group, he said all kinds of betting went on here. I never asked him if he was a part of it, and I don't need to know. What about Josiah? Was he a gambler?"

"Yeah, he was addicted for sure," Mike said around a jaw full of tobacco. He spat into a Pepsi can and wiped his mouth on his sleeve. "Last few years he got down on his luck. Gambling debts. Owed me money too. Finally told him I couldn't work on his rattletrap of a truck no more. Suppose he sold it, but he never came around here much after that. Heard he slept down along the river. Used to talk about people walking the straight and narrow when it turned out he couldn't do it his own self."

"Mike runs an honest business here," Carl said as he crossed his legs and swung one foot. I could hardly tear my eyes away. *How could he have the nerve to continue wearing Josiah's boots?* "We don't come here to do nothing illegal," he added. "A little betting among friends don't hurt nobody."

"I understand," I said, although my blood was starting to boil. Carl had to be guilty as sin. "I'm not here to stir up trouble, but I keep wondering about Josiah. Some circumstances about how he supposedly died don't set right."

"Why do you care, anyhow?" Carl said with a smirk. "He wasn't nothing but a tramp. Sneaky too. He lurked around everywhere, even Sweetbriar's alleyways. Don't suppose he was any kin of yours."

I swallowed my anger. "Josiah had his troubles, but he was as close as family—especially to my Charlie. He was trying to turn his life around. My husband would have helped him, but he passed away before he could. I promised to find out the truth about his death."

Carl laughed. "You promised your *dead* husband?"

"Him and the Lord."

"You must be one of them crazy fanatics."

I clasped my cane and resisted hitting him with it. "Trying to do what's right."

"What in tarnation is making you question how he died?" Carl asked.

"An empty bottle, for one thing. Found underneath the bench where Josiah's body was discovered. Expensive bourbon. You may have noticed it on the pool hall shelf, square-shaped, sealed with red wax. Blind George says he only serves it to customers with money to burn."

Carl jumped up. His metal chair clanged onto the floor. His face turned a fiery red as he coughed into a handkerchief.

But I wasn't finished. "And another thing. A gamecock feather was floating around in the cemetery. I'm wondering how it got there, of all places." No need to mention I no longer had it. "And I have other evidence, including a dead man's boots."

Overcome by a coughing fit, Carl made a beeline for the back of the garage.

"Told him to get some medicine for that cold," Walter said as he maneuvered his crutches to rejoin his friends. "I don't know nothing about feathers in a cemetery, but all the folks around these parts know I raise gamecocks. Good lookers too."

"Who do you sell them to?" I asked.

He lowered himself into the threadbare chair, fished a handkerchief out of a pocket, and wiped his sweaty face. "Ship 'em all over the southeast, but I don't have no control what folks do with them birds after they get 'em."

"I see," I said as if satisfied with his answer.

"Is there anything I can get for you, Miss Agnes, before you and your sidekick have to leave?" Mike asked after a long silence.

"As a matter of fact, yes. We'd like a couple of orange sodas and Moon Pies. Right, Smiley?"

Mike hurried to do my bidding.

Smiley—who hadn't said a word since we walked in—took the bag from Mike and handed him a five-dollar bill. When he got his change, he held the door open for us to leave. Before stepping outside, I caught a glimpse of Carl, hunched over his phone next to a tire display. He was talking low, but his words met my ears loud and clear. "Told you it wouldn't work," he said. "Didn't I tell you?"

Smiley and I sat on the bench underneath the Stagecoach Express sign. It creaked in the cool breeze. By the time we had eaten our pies and drained our drinks, our teeth chattered so loud even I could hear them. We carried our empties to the recycle barrel at the edge of the building as a vehicle rumbled up to Mike's. We managed to duck out of sight and peeked back around the corner. A Case Produce truck came to a screeching stop. Jack jumped out of the cab and rushed inside.

"He's in a mighty hurry," Smiley said.

"Hmmm," I said. "He didn't stop here to make a delivery, and I would bet he's not here to play checkers. Someone must've called him, told him we were asking questions. Maybe Carl." I took Smiley's hand as we crossed the street and walked down the sidewalk toward the Manor.

"Surely Jack's not …"

A dark car with tinted windows drove slowly past us, but not before I caught a glimpse of its driver through the front windshield. I stopped and turned around as the car pulled into Mike's.

"Boss has also arrived."

The slick pawnshop owner stepped out of his car, glanced over to where we were standing, and then ducked inside.

"Maybe the guy plays checkers," Smiley said. "Probably open to any man in Sweetbriar who is so inclined, don'tcha know."

"Charlie said Boss was a regular, but something doesn't set right. Seems to me we've got to keep all options open. What did you think about the other men in there?" I linked my arm through Smiley's as we continued toward the Manor.

"I don't think Walter is the killer."

"Why not?" I asked.

Smiley chuckled. "He doesn't have enough strength to kill a fruit fly."

I bit my lip as I considered his words. "What if he's faking his injury?"

"Nope. That dog won't swim," Smiley said.

My head shook before I could stop it. "You mean hunt."

"No, I—"

"Never mind. I have a bad feeling about Walter Jones. He's always been like a fox stalking a flock of chickens. Even my precious Miss Margaret steered clear of him. She can sense a person's character. That man bears watching. On the other hand, why do you think Carl left the room in such a hurry?"

Smiley made a face. "Heard him spitting up gunk in the bathroom. Terrible cold. Almost made me lose my lunch."

"Or he's guilty as sin, and the others are covering for him. If Carl killed Josiah, Walter could be charged with accessory to murder if he had information he didn't share. Right?"

We came to a stop and faced each other. "You're reaching, Sis."

I brushed a piece of lint from his shoulder. "Did you notice anything else?"

"Hmmm, nothing I can recall."

"Carl wore brown Apache boots with orange stitching."

Smiley frowned at me. "Why do his shoes matter?"

"Josiah wore that same kind of boot, same leaf design, same stitching. I remember them when he worked for us. Never saw him wear any other shoes. Whenever he'd wear a pair slap out, he'd save his money and order more. From Nashville. I'd bet the farm those are Josiah's boots."

"Didn't you say your friend was a big man?"

"Yes. Why?"

Smiley shook his head. "Carl is a skinny fellow. How could they wear the same size shoe?"

"Maybe he stuffed them with newspaper. A man who would steal a dead man's boots would not let the wrong size stop him."

Smiley raised his cap and scratched underneath. "Looks like we're getting nowhere fast. Who else is on the radar screen?"

We continued on our way as I answered. "Larry, our deputy sheriff. I don't think he murdered anyone, but somehow he's involved."

"How do you figure?"

"My daddy always said to never trust a man with shifty eyes. Don't you remember he tried some phone sex business with Shirley until she confronted the weasel?"

"Doesn't mean he—"

"The morning I found Josiah, Deputy Larry was as nervous as a hemmed-in cat. And he was sweating like he'd hiked up Jeter Mountain in July, not up to Charlie's gravesite in October. And he had a stun gun attached to his belt. Proud of it too."

"Not enough, Sis. Not even circumstantial. You just don't like the man."

He had no idea how much I didn't like the man. "There's more."

"I'm listening."

"He's good friends with Walter Jones. I suspect Walter's gamecock business has never been shut down because of their friendship. Always wondered how he could raise those birds when everyone knows they end up in cockfights."

I turned up my jacket collar and shivered. The temperature had dropped significantly. "Josiah gambled," I said. "And he was in debt to someone. When he tried to walk away, I imagine he found out he couldn't. Because he knew too much about some illegal shenanigans, someone got rid of him. We also need to consider another possibility."

Smiley stopped dead in his tracks. "Another suspect?" He turned toward me and placed his hands on my arms. "Who?"

"What if Mike demanded payment for Josiah's truck repairs? Seems to me he has some unresolved issues simmering under the surface. Righteous anger is a powerful motive."

"Seems far-fetched to me. Have to think on that one." We had reached the old stone wall surrounding Sweetbriar Manor. "I can't believe Jack has anything to do with this whole business," Smiley said as we climbed the stone steps.

"I've always felt like Jack has a good heart, but maybe he's fooled me. We can't let my soft spot blind us to the truth, wherever it takes us. Don't mention to Shirley we saw him at Mike's."

"Absolutely not, Sis. My lips are sealed as tight as a new hat."

I hoped he would keep his word. We reached the Manor's front walkway and picked up our pace.

✳ ✳ ✳

"We've got to strike while the iron's hot," I said to Smiley as he opened the front door to our home. "If this turns into a cold case, it will never be solved."

We stood in the foyer and removed our jackets and hats. I spotted Shirley coming through the kitchen door and into the dining room. She carried a tray of small vases filled with miniature mums. When she looked up, I waved. She immediately thumped the tray onto the nearest table and motioned for us. We followed her bouncing blonde pouf into the kitchen.

While all my other friends worried over the future of Sweetbriar Manor, Smiley, Shirley, and I were in a stew over the man who murdered Josiah—and how to prove it.

"Jack insists on taking me to Blind George's after supper," she said, drying her hands on her apron with so much vigor her dangling earrings jiggled. "I had planned to slip off down there by myself. How am I going to talk to any other man besides my Baby? He would have a pure hissy fit."

This was not good. "We need to throw a monkey wrench into Jack's plans."

"Not possible," Smiley said.

"Doesn't he sometimes have to work late on Saturday nights?" I asked.

"If Mr. Case has a truck coming in to be unloaded," Shirley said. "Usually happens in the summer with tomatoes or strawberries and such."

"What if you asked him to delay Jack, say an hour. Maybe Mr. Case could give him some extra chores to be done without delay. Would he do it?"

"Mr. Case has known me nearly all my life. He probably would, but he might ask why."

"Tell him the truth, only not all of it. You need to talk with another man. Right?"

Shirley nodded as her eyes widened. Then she laughed. "He'll think I'm trying to have two fellows on a string at one time, but we can count on him to keep this close to his vest pocket."

Later, Shirley served vegetable soup and cornbread for supper, along with slices of lemon pie set to the side. I told her to hurry on down to Blind George's, and I would see to cleaning up the kitchen. "It might buy you some time," I said.

"Law, honey, I can't let you do my job."

"All of our dear friends will lend a hand. Right?" I looked around our table and saw a few reluctant nods. "Come on, people, this is important." I turned to Shirley and shooed her away. "You go on. Smiley and I will be there directly."

She untied her apron and laid it on my lap. "Tomorrow, I'm making Mississippi Mud Cake for dessert. Agnes, and anyone who helps her, gets an extra big piece." She gave me a quick kiss on my cheek. "Ain't detective work the most excitin' work in the whole world?" She grabbed her Kut'N Loose bowling jacket off of the coatrack and fairly floated out of the dining room and out the front door.

"What on earth did she mean, Agnes?" Francesca asked with a sour look on her face. "What are the two of you up to?"

"If I promise to tell you later, will you organize the cleanup?"

Francesca picked up her knife and began directing. "William, get a tray out of the kitchen and two big dish tubs. Grab a soapy rag, and start loading the dirty plates and silverware. If people haven't finished eating, tell them we haven't got all night. Lollipop, you can wipe down the tables and push the chairs in, and sweep the floor and …"

Even Nellie pitched in to help. She also slipped a spoon inside her pocket, but I didn't have time to confront her.

Mr. Lively appeared like a thundercloud. "What in tarnation's going on down here?"

"I'm assigning cleanup duties," Francesca said. "Would you like to help?"

"Where is Miss Monroe?" he barked.

"On an urgent, personal errand," I said. "We'll have this place shipshape in no time."

"Humph," he said with a smirk. "I suppose this was your idea." He rocked on his heels and glared at me.

"We volunteered to help our friend, Shirley. She works hard and is not appreciated enough around here."

Mr. Lively thumbed his cloth suspenders, embroidered with Confederate soldiers, of all things. "You don't say."

"Yes, we do," William said as he stepped toward us. He swept his arms out to include the whole dining room. "Let's get to work, folks. Make Shirley proud."

Mr. Lively turned away shaking his head. He clomped up the stairs to his living quarters.

Smiley and I left. With Francesca having the time of her life, we headed to Blind George's. I was thankful it was located in the next block.

Chapter Eleven

"Looks right spooky out here," Smiley said as he grabbed the handrail on the porch to steady himself. I laced my arm through his. Maybe we could keep each other upright and out of trouble.

"Fog can make the ordinary look eerie," I said. "Watch your step. This old sidewalk has humps and bumps."

"Maybe we should've stayed home. Didn't get to finish my pie. Lemon's my favorite."

I squeezed his arm a little tighter as he swayed. "I saw some extra in the refrigerator. We'll have a piece when we get back and maybe some hot tea. We can talk in the dining room."

By the time we finished our business and returned to the Manor, the Hand-and-Foot card game—a regular event on Saturday nights after supper—would be over. I dearly loved the silly game and loved to win even more, but our detective work could not wait.

We reached the pool hall in no time and fell in step behind two couples wearing jeans, plaid shirts, cowboy boots, and hats. I hoped we could slip inside unnoticed. The air was toasty warm, and the jukebox swelled with "Ruby, Don't Take Your Love to Town." The smell of onions, chili, and popcorn floated in a haze of cigarette smoke. I spotted Shirley dancing with Deputy Larry.

Judging from the smile on her face, she was either a good actress or having a grand old time. She waved, but I looked away, not wanting to draw attention. We found two empty barstools and climbed up, which was no easy task.

Blind George stood behind the counter drying a glass with a ragged towel. He had earned his name for ignoring the sins of his customers as well as the shortcomings of his rundown poolroom. He thumped the bar with a hairy fist, and I jumped like a frog's leg on a hot griddle. He laughed and rubbed his unshaven face. "Hello there, Granny. What brings you here? You got some more questions, or are you and this fella on a hot date?"

I leaned forward. "Walter Jones here tonight?"

"Nope. Little early for him. And he don't always show up. Heard he had to hire someone to help run his farm. Knee's givin' him fits. Says he's not much good for socializin' these days."

"Told you he wasn't faking," Smiley said as he poked me with his elbow … and then slipped off his stool.

George grinned. "What can I get you folks?"

After we both straightened ourselves, I said, "Two cokes, some popcorn, and some answers to a few questions."

George dried his hands on his dirty apron. He looked at me as if analyzing what I said. After he served us, he leaned over the counter. "Ask away, Granny."

I had to raise my voice more than I wanted to in order to be heard over the music. "Does Walter ever talk about cockfights?"

"Sure. Brags about his birds comin' out the winner. Most folks think he raises those birds, and that's the end of it. But between you and me, that ain't all he does. Asked me if I wanted to know where the fights were bein' held these days. Said it was close by, and no one would ever guess the place. Told him I didn't want no part of goin' to cockfights. Got enough problems of my own."

Don't we all? "So, he sells the birds and fights them too."

"You got it, Granny, only you didn't hear it from me." George filled two frosty mugs with beer and slid them down the bar to a waitress. He wiped the cracked countertop with a wet rag.

I motioned for George to come close again. "Think Carl will show up tonight?"

"The man's been on edge lately. Even his fancy bourbon don't settle him none." Then he leaned over to me and whispered loudly in my good ear.

His words made me sit up a little straighter. *Could the bartender be right?* "Carl said that? About Josiah's bagpipes?"

George nodded.

"Ten thousand?"

"Yep. Sounded far-fetched to me too. Claims they're made from some African wood, trimmed in ivory from a woolly mammoth, as well as genuine engraved silver from Edinburgh. Who woulda thought? Every week I seen Josiah goin' through the dumpster out back. Always toted his bagpipes along, all zipped up in an old leather bag. Reckon he didn't have a safe place to leave 'em."

My thoughts were racing. "Do you think Josiah knew they were valuable? He could have sold them. For sure he could've used the money."

George shrugged his burly shoulders. "Beats me. Carl also told me they were made by some famous person years ago, like the violin. What's it called?"

"Stradivarius?"

"That's it. People can come up with all sorts of crazy notions, can't they? A homeless man riflin' through the garbage on Friday nights totin' around a priceless bagpipe. Don't make no sense."

I glanced at Smiley, who was watching the dance floor and swaying to the music. Not paying a bit of attention to what he should've been. "Pretty crazy all right," I said as I focused on more questions for George. "Did he ever search through other dumpsters? Like Begley's or the Dixie Diner's?"

George shrugged again. "Never asked. Anyway, after I seen Josiah in the alley out back, we talked and ended up makin' a deal. He came by three days a week to clean the bathrooms and sweep the place. I fed him all the hot dogs he could eat. A good trade on my part."

"Did he have any connections to Walter?"

"Frequented his cockfights and lost money gambling, but what difference does it make?" George said, scratching his chin. "Josiah's dead."

"Exactly. And someone killed him." I steadied myself on the stool. *Didn't anyone in this town care that Josiah was murdered?*

George inspected a glass and rubbed it with his towel. "Not what the paper said."

"You always believe what you read in the newspaper?"

"Good question," he said picking up another glass and holding it to the light.

"Did the two men ever come in here together?" I sipped my coke and glanced at Smiley, who still had his eyes glued to the dance floor.

"Nope," George said. "But more often than not they had their heads together in some deep discussion."

"Did they ever argue?" I had a hunch I was on the right track. Walter Jones had a strong motive if Josiah was fixing to become a whistle blower.

"Sure did. Walter has a mean streak too. I threatened to call the sheriff more than once. I might overlook a lot of things, but I can't have a fight destroy my fine establishment."

"Absolutely not," I said. Smiley reached across me for a handful of popcorn and stuffed it in his mouth. Some help he was. I turned my attention back to George. "Did you hear what they argued about?"

"Yep. Gambling. Seems Josiah was good at losing."

I tried another line of questions since it seemed we had reached a dead end. "If Josiah wouldn't sell his bagpipes, did he ever mention pawning them for extra cash?"

Our friendly bartender washed and rinsed three glasses and set them on a towel. Had he heard me? "Hmmm," he finally said. "Never did say anything to me, but come to think of it, I overheard Carl try to convince him—"

Loud voices and a scuffle on the dance floor brought an end to our discussion.

"Get your filthy hands off her!" Jack yelled. He shoved the deputy, who had a shocked look on his face.

Shirley screeched, "No, Baby! No!" She wedged herself between the two men, their fists raised.

Blind George appeared among them in a flash. "Finish this outside," he said. He pushed the men toward the door, then turned to Shirley. "Get Jack away from here before he gets arrested."

She grabbed her jacket and made a quick exit. In less than a minute, the deputy came back inside long enough to get his hat, which he slapped against his leg as he left again.

"Let's go, Sis," Smiley said. "You can talk to Blind George another time."

"But he was getting ready to tell me some valuable information."

He frowned. "Doesn't matter. We're leaving."

"Oh, all right. Go ahead and pay the bill. But I'm coming back here as soon as possible."

"I'm sure you will. And I'm coming with you, but I don't like it."

On the sidewalk underneath the streetlight, Larry threw down his cigarette and ground it underneath his boot. Instead of his deputy uniform, he looked like a regular cowboy, except for a stun gun hanging from his belt. He probably always carried it. Red neon signs flashed around us, distorted by the wispy fog.

The deputy looked up, and his left eye twitched. "You tell your friend he don't know who he's messing with. I'll be watching him. And I'll get him soon as he steps over the line. You tell him. You hear?"

"Loud and clear," I said.

I grabbed Smiley's hand, and we hightailed it back to the Manor as fast as we could manage.

We stopped short of the porch, which was bathed in a yellow light, where Shirley and Jack were in the midst of a humdinger of an argument. We froze beside a giant camellia bush—Pink Perfection and Pearl's favorite—but our two friends wouldn't have noticed if we had climbed the steps and paced right along beside them.

Shirley's high heels struck the porch beside Jack's boots as he thumped one foot and dragged his stiff leg along. They huffed and spewed angry words like a tornado. Suddenly he stopped, turned, and grabbed her arms. Her face was red from crying. His was puffed up like a blowfish.

Jack exploded. "What were you thinking? Don't you realize the power of those blue eyes of yours?"

"You've been drinking," she said. "You promised you would—"

He dropped Shirley's arms, and she reached out to him. He pushed her away.

"Baby," she said, "when you've had too much to drink, it makes you crazy, but we'll talk about it later when you ... well, when you can think straight. I can explain about tonight. You've got to trust me."

"Ha!" he said. "I seen it with my own eyes. Why him of all people?"

Shirley reached out and grabbed Jack's arm. "I had my reasons."

He jerked away and shoved his hands into his pockets. "I'm listening."

"I ... I can't tell you yet."

"So, you're saying you can't trust me." Jack took a step back and crossed his arms over his chest.

"I'm sayin' nothin' of the kind."

He jammed his cowboy hat onto his head. "I'm headed home. You let me know when you're ready to talk."

Shirley reached for him again. "Please don't do this. Stay awhile. I'll fix some coffee."

"Good-bye, Shirl." Jack clumped down the steps without a backward glance and disappeared into the fog.

Jack had shown us his jealous side—and his drinking side. His scooter sputtered like an old lawn mower but soon roared to life as he sped away. When he was gone, the street fell deathly quiet. Shirley stared into the darkness for a moment before she trudged inside, her head and shoulders drooping.

Smiley and I caught up to her in the foyer. Not only to offer comfort but to find out if she had learned anything from flirting with a sleazeball. Before I could do either, Mr. Lively appeared at the head of the stairs.

"What's all the racket down there? You must realize, Miss Monroe, entertaining men in this house, or on the front porch, is not allowed. This is not a bordello." Then he fixed his bug eyes on me. "And what might you be up to, Agnes? No good, is what. I don't want to hear another peep out of either of you ladies, or one day soon I will see you both in my office. And it won't be pretty."

Shirley and I tiptoed toward her room, minus one fellow detective. Smiley had disappeared as soon as Mr. Lively started yelling. I sat on her bed, and she pulled a straight chair over for my feet before plopping down beside me.

"Jack showed up sooner than I thought he would. And he'd been drinkin'. A lot."

I gave Shirl a hug. "I figured as much."

"We've had arguments before, but this one was a doozy. I'm afraid of what he might do to the deputy." Shirley reached for a tissue.

"Would Jack have exploded like he did tonight if he had found out about your friendship with Josiah, or Josiah's feelings for you?"

Shirley's face turned pasty white. "Don't matter anyhow. Josiah's dead, and my Baby's innocent. Those are two facts you can count on as sure as rain on a stormy day."

I patted her leg. "It's going to be alright, honey. I just know it. Tell me what you learned tonight."

"Some damagin' evidence. First of all, Larry thinks cockfights should be considered a sport and legalized. You reckon Walter has a thrivin' business sellin' his birds and runnin' some fights because of him?"

"Could be. What else?"

"There was a cockfight the night Josiah was killed. Carl was there. So was Josiah. They got into an argument. A shovin' match led to a few blows, and both men were told to leave and not come back."

My wheels were turning. "Damaging information. We need to ask someone else who witnessed this fight. Like Jack. You could convince him to come forward."

Shirley scooted off the bed and stood. She slipped out of her short skirt and shook it. "I need a long, hot bubble bath." She held her garment up to her nose and sniffed. "Merciful heavens. I've got to wash every stitch of my clothes. My hair too. I stink like a pool hall."

"What about Jack?" I asked again.

"He was there," she said sadly. "Part of the reason we argued. On the way home, I asked if he could tell me about the night Josiah died."

"What did he say?"

"Said I was askin' too many questions. I've never seen him so steamin' mad."

I gave her another hug. "Let him cool off. And sober up. We'll think of something."

When I left Shirley's room, I headed for my own bubble bath. A good place to think. I didn't like the path our investigation was taking. Jack had moved from a person of interest to a suspect, even if Shirley had been blinded by her feelings for him. Carl, who had the audacity to wear a dead man's boots, was another suspect. Had he and Josiah argued about his bagpipes? Even if they were valuable, why would Carl want them? Walter Jones was not home free either, even if he did seem injured. I needed a way to find out for sure. And what about Boss Brown? Perhaps his only crime was selling a hot set of pipes to a rich customer. Hmmm. I didn't like Boss's reaction to my questions at his pawnshop or the appearance of a woman from the women's prison. And why did he sic his goon of a bodyguard on me if he didn't have something to hide?

I turned on the hot water in my tub and immediately turned it off as my thoughts took another direction. I returned to my bedroom, grabbed my notebook and three pens, and headed back to see Shirley. She finally answered her door wrapped in a towel.

"Get something on and meet me in Smiley's room."

Chapter Twelve

S miley opened his door wide, clad in blue-striped pajamas.
"We need to talk," I said. "Shirley's on her way."
"Certainly, Sis. Come on in." He cleared a stack of old newspapers from the love seat underneath his window and plumped a pillow before dropping it behind my back. "Sorry my room is a mess," he said. "Been a little busy lately with—"

"Pearl?"

He twisted in his seat and blushed.

"I'm not here to talk to you about Pearl. This is about Josiah's killer. I don't want to accuse anyone, or even talk to the sheriff until I'm certain. I could use your input. You're good at seeing all sides of a situation. And maybe you or Shirley will see clues I've missed. Like motive."

"You got it, Sis. I've got a right smart to share with you too, don'tcha know. About us. Been wanting to talk with you, but here lately seems like …"

I leaned over and hugged him around his neck. *I dearly love you,* I said, but the words were only spoken in my heart. Maybe one day I would whisper them in his ear.

I gathered my feelings to myself while he continued to blush like a schoolboy. A barefooted Shirley joined us, tying the sash of a skimpy red and gold Japanese robe around her waist. She obviously wore nothing underneath, and I hoped that sash stayed tied. She pulled up a straight chair as I opened my notebook.

"I'm going over each name, alibi, motive, opportunity, and means." I handed my two friends a pen and a piece of notebook paper. "When I finish, we'll all write down the person we think is the killer. If we have a match, our evidence is strong. Do you both agree?"

They nodded.

"Who's first?" Smiley asked.

"Walter Jones."

We discussed and considered each suspect—except Jack of course since Shirley didn't know he had not only been a person of interest but a suspect as well. My suspicions were short-lived. Before filling my bathtub for a bubble bath, I concluded Jack's problems were personal ones, and they had nothing to do with Josiah. I couldn't prove it but went with my gut instincts. Jack might be rough around the edges—even too jealous of his Shirl—but he had a good, kind heart, and I believed he was no killer.

Smiley picked up a nearby magazine, laid his paper on it, turned his back, and began writing. "I think I know who killed Josiah," he said.

I wrote down a name. "So do I."

"Land's sake. Can't be but one," Shirley said.

We finished and held up our papers. Our names were the same. *Carl Swain.*

Maybe it was time to take our evidence to the sheriff. I wanted to talk with Betty Jo first, inform her of our conclusions, but she didn't answer the phone. I left several messages as I sat in my crooked rocker with my feet propped up on the end of my bed, phone to my ear.

The next morning after breakfast, I headed back to the kitchen and Shirley, my notebook in hand. She could help me line up our clues for the sheriff. We needed to present a logical, airtight case against Carl.

Our kitchen discussion included plans to see Sheriff Caywood come Monday morning. Everyone knew he reserved his Sunday afternoons for fishing, a tradition since his granddaddy was alive, and he wouldn't take our interruption kindly. We needed him to be in a good mood and willing to listen. He would surely agree with us, thank us profusely, and make an arrest promptly. Only one thing bothered me. Why had he not come to the same conclusions as we had?

I shook off any worries and headed for my room to choose a church outfit to wear with my black-feathered hat, as well as one to offer Pearl. She loved hats as much as I did, but she didn't own a single one.

As I passed through the foyer of the big house, the tune of "Dixie" blared forth. *Strange.* Normally, no one had a visitor on Sunday morning.

I opened the front door as Shirley joined me from the kitchen, wrapped in an aroma of dish soap, her blonde hair peeking out of her hairnet.

The sheriff stood on the porch, hat in his hands. "We need to talk," he said.

Something terrible must have happened to keep the sheriff from his fishing date. Shirley's face turned white as talcum powder. She was probably wondering if something had happened to Jack. We sat down at a dining room table near the kitchen.

The sheriff glared at me and then Shirl. "Seems we have a murder on our hands," he said as he retrieved his buckeye from a shirt pocket.

I gasped. "Another one?"

"Not my Baby," Shirley said, gripping the edge of the table.

The sheriff placed his buckeye on the table and retrieved a small notebook and pen from his jacket. "Found him late last night in the alleyway behind Begley's."

Shirley's hand flew to her mouth.

"Jack?" I asked. My mouth turned as dry as dust.

"Carl. Shot in the heart. Holding a whiskey bottle. A few gold coins were scattered across the ground, so it wasn't a robbery." The sheriff turned to a blank page in his notebook.

"Carl? Are you sure? But he . . . why are you talkin' to us?" Shirley asked. She twisted her dishtowel into a knot.

"Jack's whereabouts. When did you last see him?" Sheriff Caywood clicked his pen, wrote in his notebook, and looked up at Shirley.

Her blue eyes widened. "Jack? Last night but—"

The sheriff picked up his buckeye and studied it. "Had he been drinking?"

"Why do you ask?" Shirley and I looked at each other with an unspoken question. *Are we going to lie?*

The sheriff glared at both of us before he cleared his throat and returned his buckeye to his pocket. "I see."

What did he see? That Jack had been drinking, and we were trying to cover for him? Whatever he thought, he didn't press us, but he scribbled something else before closing his notebook.

He turned his back to me and faced Shirley. "Were he and Carl drinking buddies?"

"I ... I don't know," Shirley said in a low voice. "I don't think so."

Enough was enough. I stood and gripped the back of my chair. "Shirley doesn't have to answer any more of your questions unless you tell us where this is headed."

The sheriff pushed back his chair, but instead of standing, he placed a hand on Shirley's arm. "Jack's fingerprints were also on the whiskey bottle. He's not a suspect. Not yet. But for dang sure, I need to ask him some questions. Can you tell me where he is?"

Shirley shook her head as tears ran down her cheeks. She would never tell the sheriff where to find her Baby.

❉ ❉ ❉

By the time the sheriff left, the grandfather clock had already struck ten thirty. No time to dress and then walk to church. Nellie and Pearl appeared arm in arm and headed out the door. Their hats looked suspiciously familiar, like some stored in the back of my closet. But maybe I only imagined they did.

How could we warn Jack? Josiah's murderer had been killed, shot in the heart, and the sheriff was looking for him.

Shirley lost no time. She flew out the front door. Jack lived in a rundown part of town called The Bottom, a few blocks past my yellow rental house where Juanita and Frankie lived. I had walked there myself a couple of times, but now it was entirely too far. Besides, today I could never keep up with Shirley, a woman dead set on a mission to save her Baby. I looked out a front window. She was already out of sight.

By the time Shirley returned, she was limp as a dishrag. "I couldn't find him anywhere," she said. "Even Mr. Case hasn't seen him, and Jack promised to help him unload some pumpkins this afternoon."

❉ ❉ ❉

Days went by. Still, no one had spotted Jack, a man easy to recognize with his jerking stride and long, thick hair. Our investigation was as stale as week-old bread. Shirley had cried a bucket of tears, and my aching knee announced a change in the weather.

I was thankful for any diversion, even when Halloween ushered in a cold, blowing rain. Not long after dark, we were startled by fists pounding on the Manor's front door. We had finished our supper of chili and cornbread and lingered over our apple crisp desserts. Everyone turned toward the racket as Shirley grabbed a plastic, candy-filled pumpkin and rushed toward the door.

"Hold on! I'm coming!" she yelled.

Instead of a bunch of impatient trick-or-treaters, six dripping-wet adults entered the foyer. The men were dressed as Union soldiers and the women in fancy dresses. They looked like madams of a past era.

One soldier stepped forward and introduced himself. "Captain Wilson at your service, ma'am. We have come many miles for a chance to encounter General Sherman's ghost … or his lady friend's."

The grandfather clock bonged seven times. No one said a word, not even Shirley.

"This *is* Sweetbriar Manor, isn't it?" the captain asked.

Mr. Lively opened his office door. "What in thunder—"

Shirley found her voice. "There must be some mistake. There are no ghosts here."

"But the website said—"

"You folks come on into the dinin' room," Shirley said. "We'll make room. You're soaked to the bone and probably hungry. Miss Agnes can tell you some stories about this place when it used to be a house of ill repute, and maybe some tales 'bout Sherman himself."

Shirley dipped up bowls of chili for our guests while I filled their ears full of gossip I had heard as a child. Then Pearl walked over and stood beside me as I told them a true story about the two of us when Sweetbriar Manor had been a bordello. I explained how, curious about a fancy woman named Dakota, one night we hid next to the porch in the hydrangea bushes, hoping to catch a glimpse of her. When the front door finally opened, my daddy stepped outside with a woman wearing a sparkling red dress. We were old enough to understand what he was doing there, and the most beautiful woman we had ever seen had to be Dakota. Pearl listened with wide eyes and clapped at the end. Maybe she remembered a time when we did such foolish antics.

Before the ghost-seekers moved on, they shook every resident's hand, thanked Shirley for her hospitality, and left money on the tables. Mr. Lively said it would help pay for the food, but we overruled him. We told him we were adding it to the Juanita and Frankie fund. He left us in a huff, as usual.

As soon as he was gone, I hurried over to William and Francesca who were in a heated argument. "He's bound to find out you're behind this nonsense," she yelled.

William stuffed his cigar into a shirt pocket. "He will if you don't pipe down. Right, Red?"

"Mark my words, your computer games will be a catastrophe," Francesca said as she wheeled away from us.

"Don't go," I said. "Let's think this through."

"Come on, sweetie," William said.

Francesca stopped, then turned her wheelchair around and whizzed past us toward the dining room.

We gathered at a nearby table, empty of dishes and food. The clanging of pots being scrubbed and bluegrass music drifted from the kitchen.

Francesca pressed her lips together and frowned. She had not gotten over her hissy fit.

I ignored her snit and turned to my burly friend. "William, your website has reached people far and wide, even out of state. What if we zero in on the locals?" I asked. "I need both of you to help. Can we work together?"

Francesca nodded. Barely.

William looked at his lady and then at me. "You got it, Red."

"Good. We'll use the list of signatures you've gathered. William, you will convince a few people to write letters about the Manor possibly being haunted. Give them some background information about Sherman not torching Sweetbriar, and suggest why he changed his plans. Shouldn't take many facts to get some juicy rumors started."

He retrieved his cigar from his pocket and stuck it in his mouth. "Okay, but what do I do with these letters?"

"Nothing. The people who write them will send them to the *Timely News*, editorial page."

Francesca leaned forward, a slight smile on her face. "What can I do?"

I knew she would come around. "You have the list of repairs needed on the Manor, right?"

"Of course," she said, waving her diamond-covered hands.

"Contact the Historical Society of Sweetbriar. They'll be distraught when they learn this place is nearly in shambles. It isn't that bad, of course, but you might stretch the truth just a tad. Encourage those folks to also start a letter-writing campaign to the *Timely News*."

Francesca laughed and slapped the table. "I like it."

We said our good nights, and my two friends headed to William's room chatting about their assignments. Between social media and our local paper, perhaps something would help to stop the sale of our home. We had to be willing to try anything.

The next morning as Shirley cleared the dining room tables, she hugged a stack of plates and bowls to her chest. Without warning, the stack tipped forward. She steered the dishes to the table with a thud, followed by an avalanche of flatware.

In the deafening silence that followed, she sank into a nearby chair. Her pale lips quivered. "My Baby's not ever comin' back," she announced. "He's gone for good."

Chapter Thirteen

"You must be mistaken," I said. "Maybe Jack went somewhere to sort things out in his mind. He'll come back. You'll see." *Did I really believe that?* Someone besides Shirley could have warned him that the sheriff was looking for him, maybe for good reasons.

She shook her head of teased fluff. "I haven't seen or heard from him since … since we had that awful argument. And I couldn't find him after the sheriff questioned us that Sunday morning. I thought at the time he was only avoidin' me, but somethin' awful has happened to him. I can feel it clear down to my fingernails. This is my fault for flirtin' with a low-life deputy, besides askin' my Jack too many questions, and naggin' him about his drinkin'."

I patted her shoulder but didn't say what I was thinking. Jack was acting guilty of something. But what? Jealousy and drinking too much were his only crimes as far as I could decipher. Was there more? Had I missed something?

Shirley blew her nose. "I stopped by his place to see if he would talk to me since I haven't heard one peep from him in days. His landlady told me he's gone. Paid his rent and left. Headed south. All I could find out."

"Ha!" Francesca said. "Running from the law. There's a crook if there ever was one. He's probably connected to the string of robberies I've been reading about in the newspaper. The sheriff ought to be notified."

"Who's a crook, pretty lady?" William said. He had come to push his wheelchair-bound friend to the sitting room's piano, where he was content to listen as long as she was willing to play her favorite Bach or

Beethoven.

On her way out of the dining room, Francesca turned to us. "A handsome young man who seems nice to old people has his own agenda. Mark my words," she said as she flounced back around. "Let's go, Willy."

I scooted my chair close to Shirley's. "Jack must have had his reasons for leaving town. He's a thinker, and he'll explain as soon as he gets his mind straight. Don't give up on him." Jack was angry with Shirley. Did he think she had fallen for the deputy? Were we wrong about Carl killing Josiah? Would Jack kill someone in a jealous rage after hitting the booze? Or was he running from the law because he was a thief like Francesca suspected?

I found a clean hanky in my purse and held it out. After honking into it like a goose, Shirley said, "I know Jack loves me. I do. I only wish he would share his life with me, the good and the bad."

"Give him some time. Ask the Lord to send His angel army to protect Jack."

She looked at me like a lost little girl. "Really?"

"Certainly. One time my Charlie delivered a load of tobacco to the auction warehouses over fifty miles away, and it came a freak ice storm before he got back home."

"What happened?" Shirley blew again and blinked back tears.

"I paced the floor and prayed. Soon as Charlie walked in our front door, he grabbed me and twirled me around. He had come within a hair of being creamed by a tractor-trailer. Jackknifed right in front of him. Turned out it happened the same time I started praying."

Shirley took my hands in hers. "Let's pray," she said.

And so we did.

As we both said *amen*, Mr. Lively passed through the dining room. "Ladies," he said to Shirley and me, "we need to talk."

❉ ❉ ❉

The three of us squeezed into Mr. Lively's tiny office. It smelled like it needed a good dose of sunshine. He paced back and forth in the small space with his hands behind his back. He finally stopped and faced us like a drill sergeant.

"Miss Monroe," he said with a scowl, "if you weren't such an excellent cook, I'd fire you. Might do it anyway. I haven't forgotten …" He tapped his clipboard with a pen. "It's all right here. You have left your duties to the residents three times at least, and maybe more if the truth be known. You have invited people in off the street as if we were a tourist attraction. And you even fed people after a funeral service without my permission. Improper behavior and some of it probably illegal."

Then he glared at me. "Agnes, I can't fire you, but I can call your daughter and tell her to come get you. Somehow, you have managed to be connected to every disruption that has happened since you moved here, and it has to stop. Or else."

I managed to swallow before I said, "All because some of us gave Shirley a little assistance? Or we welcomed a few people to come inside out of the rain? Or we served some food to the Salvation Army? Ridiculous. We have not committed any crime. One more threat, and you'll hear from my lawyer."

"Rubbish. You don't even have one."

"Have you heard of Mr. Thompson? Meanest lawyer in the whole county."

The administrator's face turned fiery red. "Country lawyers don't scare me. What I have to say to you ladies is more important than your disrespectful behavior. I've been itching to lay some facts on the table for some time, and I've made a decision."

Shirley and I looked at each other. What on earth was he talking about?

He puffed out his chest and thumbed his suspenders. "Your protest march will never take place on my watch, your petition will never see the light of day, and your list of *urgent repairs* will never stop the sale of this place. And I suspect you're behind those pesky letters that keep popping up in the newspaper. Be assured, I will find out. Your *detective work* has to cease immediately. I've talked to the sheriff. He not only agrees, he's going to sit on the drugstore shooting as long as possible, keep it away from reporters until he knows more facts."

Unfortunately, Mr. Lively was not finished. "The rumors and gossip you're spreading could potentially ruin Sweetbriar's stellar reputation, the town's as well as the Manor's. I can't have any more disruptions interfere with my work schedule. Go on, get out of here," he sputtered. He waved his arms and shooed us away.

We passed back through the dining room and into the kitchen. "How dare he threaten us," Shirley said as she plopped skillets into a sink full of soapy water. "Who put a burr under his saddle?"

I climbed up on a stool, glad Lollipop was sweeping the dining room. "He's full of hot air," I said as Shirley attacked the skillets with a scrub pad.

Then she loaded plates into the dishwasher. "Do you really have a lawyer?"

"I know Mr. Benley who specializes in real estate. He's the best."

"But you said—"

"I asked Mr. Lively if he *knew* Mr. Thompson. And I believe he does." Shirley chuckled. "Mercy in abundance."

✻ ✻ ✻

When Jack vanished, our meals turned into disasters. Breakfast, more often than not, consisted of burnt toast, dry scrambled eggs, and undercooked bacon. Shirley mourned her Baby. Her blonde hair stayed a tangled mess, and her eyes were as puffy as biscuit dough.

I rummaged around in my purse, found my phone, and called Betty Jo. "We're marching in three days, permit or not." As soon as I hung up, I banged on Francesca's door and gave her the same message. "And bring your posters if you have any decent ones." Then I told Smiley to bring his.

✻ ✻ ✻

Our detective work had come to a screeching halt. Would I ever discover the truth about Josiah's murder when our prime suspect had also been murdered? Now what? What men were left on my list? And did the killer do away with both men, or were the two deaths unrelated?

I headed down to Begley's Drugstore. Perhaps I could talk to Carl's boss. I had known Mr. Watson all my life. Surely, he could shine some light on a stalled investigation.

When I entered the store, he was decorating a Christmas tree, even though Thanksgiving had not yet arrived. It was aglow with tiny white lights, doves, and red balls. "Almost puts me in the mood to shop," I said.

"Too much trouble if you ask me. Have to take it all down in a few weeks. Then it'll be valentines, leprechauns, the Easter bunny, and—"

"Can I ask you some questions about Carl?"

"Suppose so. Young man sure had me fooled," he said, pulling more decorations out of a box.

"How so?"

"Sheriff said he was passing stolen merchandise out the back door. Not anything from the store, mind you, but the alleyway must have been a pickup point."

I moved closer to the tree and touched one of the red balls. "He told me one time about working until nearly midnight."

"He was working all right. Say, what would look best as a tree topper?" He held up a big red ribbon in one hand and an angel in the other.

"The angel for sure." I straightened one of the doves. "Why do you think he was killed? Ever have any drugs missing?"

Mr. Watson reached up and placed the angel on the tree. "Those are locked up tight, and we're strict on the records we keep. I don't see how anything could be missing without our knowledge."

"Well, that certainly is a relief, isn't it?" I stood back and admired the finished tree.

"Yep. He might have had a lot of faults, but I don't think drugs was one of them. Say, why are you asking such questions anyway?"

"Curious is all," I said as I settled my purse onto my shoulder. "The sheriff said some gold coins were scattered around his body. Do you know if they were regular ones or rare?"

Mr. Watson stacked the empty boxes and pushed them aside. "Deputy showed me some. They were unusual all right and not actually coins, but metals from the Scottish games. Up at Highlands."

"My oh my." I was getting far more information than I had anticipated. "Had they been stolen?"

"Yep."

A clerk called for Mr. Watson's assistance, so I made my exit. As I slowly walked back to the Manor, leaning heavily on my cane, I pondered my findings.

If Carl had not handed drugs to the large man in the ally the night Jack had seen him, what had been in the package? More stolen items? For whom? Did Jack know more about the exchange than he had shared? Maybe there was no other man in the alley that night. Jack could have received the package, then he and Carl could have killed Josiah because he was a witness. But a witness to what?

Back to square one—bankrupt and no get-out-of-jail-free card.

❋ ❋ ❋

The pot of clues, suspects, and speculation—along with skimpy evidence—continued to simmer on low. We needed to turn up the fire. But how? Shirley, Smiley, and I had discussed the case every way from

Sunday.

When the day of Sweetbriar Manor's protest march arrived, I welcomed the diversion. At least we were taking action on the home front.

As I passed through the sitting room, Ida Mae, Miss Johnson's mother, rocked in a corner with Juanita by her side. The old woman needed to be in a nursing home, but her daughter had convinced the owners of the Manor she could take care of her here. Now with Miss Johnson serving time, I wondered what was going to happen to her mother.

Ida Mae turned her white frizzled head toward me, clapped her hands, and laughed. She might not understand what was happening, but as sure as rain, the old woman was happy. At least she rarely traipsed around stark naked anymore like she did when her daughter had been in charge, but she continued her love affair with her pink toy phone. She held out the receiver. "Mama's fixing biscuits and gravy. You coming?"

I leaned down and spoke into her phone. "Sounds delicious. I'll be there."

The old lady grinned up at me.

Juanita hugged her charge and patted her back. Their faces shone bright with a genuine love for each other, and Juanita's freckles seemed to dance. Not only was the young woman the perfect caregiver, she earned more money now than she had working at Case's Produce Stand. Even so, her paycheck would not cover all her living expenses, which included my rental payments. *Gee whiskers. How did my life get so complicated?*

Juanita secured Ida Mae's lap blanket around her legs. Who would have thought a young slip of a girl could take on such a big responsibility and do so with such ease? My admiration for her raised ten notches.

"Have you ever considered becoming a nurse?" I asked.

Juanita looked at me, blinked fast a few times, and turned away. "Used to. Maybe someday."

I gave her shoulder a quick squeeze. "Don't give up on your dreams. Never, never, never give up. Winston Churchill."

"Who?" The girl scrunched her face.

"He encouraged the Brits during WWII."

She stared at me with furrows across her brow.

"I often forget how young you are," I said. "Never give up. Agnes Hopper."

She laughed as she brushed Ida Mae's long, wispy hair.

Had I given Juanita false hope? How could she go back to school when she had a toddler and not even two nickels to rub together?

I said my good-byes and started toward the front door as Mr. Lively swooped into the room and stopped in front of the two women. He puffed out his chest and thumbed red suspenders holding up his rumpled pants. "We have finalized relocation arrangements for Miss Ida Mae."

I turned and went back to stand beside Juanita. "What? How can you do such a thing?" I asked.

"This is none of your business, but for your information, her daughter designated me as her guardian, so it's all legal."

Juanita froze with the hairbrush in midair. Her mouth hung open, and her freckles darkened against her pale skin. I put a protective hand on her shoulder.

"Agape Center has agreed to take her," he added. "We are fortunate indeed."

"When?" I asked. My hackles were going into overdrive.

"Ten days. Time to get her packed up, the proper papers signed, and her medications transferred. And we'll need to contact a transport service. Can you take care of all the details with securing Angel's Wings, Miss Juanita?"

"Yes, sir. Cer ... certainly."

"This has been a most productive day." He turned on his heels and left us.

"Miss Agnes, what am I going to do?" Juanita said with a shaky voice.

"You will visit Ida Mae as often as you can, and you will find another job. You knew one day she would need more care than you could give her."

Juanita began brushing Ida Mae's hair again, but the brush fell from her hands and bounced onto the floor.

"I'll ask Henry if he's heard of any place hiring," I said as I picked up the brush.

What was going to happen if Juanita came up empty-handed? She would no longer be able to make rental payments of any size.

We could both be in a worse fix.

Chapter Fourteen

The residents gathered on the Manor's front porch, squeezed between Betty Jo and her garden club. They were assembling, but not to join our protest. Armed with stepladders, pine garland, and a wreath—along with magnolia leaves and fruit—they had their own agenda. The decorations released an intoxicating fragrance.

"Do you have our permit?" I asked Betty Jo.

She tossed me a sideways glance. "Would I let you march without one?"

"When will these people be out of our way? We're behind schedule," a sour-looking woman said, clipboard in hand.

"Cool your heels," ordered a young woman with blue-streaked hair. "Where's your Christmas spirit?"

The garden club women shifted to give us more room, but an undercurrent of grumbling continued.

We needed to get cracking, but first I had to convince Lollipop he couldn't go with us. I had promised his brother, who insisted he not participate. Lollipop edged closer to me as he slurped on a sucker, tugged on my sleeve, and waited. He looked like a child Santa had forgotten.

I looked into his sad face. "What if your brother calls, like he does every day before lunchtime, and you're not here? He would be sick with worry. You wouldn't want to upset him, would you? He loves you dearly."

His lower lip quivered, and his eyes filled with tears. I took him by the hand and led him back inside. "Besides," I added, "Shirley needs your help with lunch. She's fixing your favorite dessert, brownies with chocolate chips and walnuts. She's probably wondering right this very minute how she's going to chop all those nuts."

He stared at me for a moment. Then he straightened to his full height. "Shirley needs me?"

When I nodded, he hurried toward the kitchen. I didn't have time to let Shirley know he was coming, but she would look after this gentle soul until we returned. Our chief cook had also planned to join our march, but Mr. Lively told her if she did she could kiss her job goodbye.

"Land's sakes, honey," she told me while refilling my coffee cup at breakfast, "he's got me over a barrel with my shoes off."

The fruit-and-pine-scented air had turned cooler than a few minutes before. I pulled out my gloves and red knit cap from my coat pockets. My purse was too heavy to carry on our walk to town, so I had asked Shirley if I could leave it in a big drawer of pots—since it probably wouldn't be safe in my room.

"Certainly, honey, but my kitchen don't have a lock on it."

Was I becoming too paranoid? I didn't trust Nellie and her sticky fingers. She might be Minnie Pearl's cousin twice removed as she claimed, but what if she had acquired the skill of opening locked doors? Like mine. Did her reason for staying behind include stealing?

Excited chatter filled the air as I slipped my cane, along with an umbrella's loop, over my arm. Nellie had insisted I carry hers because Francesca predicted rain was coming. The leopard print fabric looked brand new. I spotted a price tag and wondered if she had stolen it from some store, but I had more urgent things on my mind.

Mr. Lively—looking like a plump Ebenezer Scrooge—suddenly stood among us. Silence dropped like a cloak. "I hope you folks realize this whole affair could backfire. The community of Sweetbriar will see the economic, social, and political benefits the new owners will inspire. Change is in the air, and you cannot stop it."

Betty Jo stepped away from her quiet-as-a-tomb garden club ladies and handed him an envelope. "The residents of Sweetbriar Manor can at the very least let their situation be known. They have rights. You will see we took care of the legalities in this matter. We have covered all our bases thanks to our competent lawyer."

Mr. Lively crammed his hands in his pockets. "You don't say."

Betty Jo continued. "When their march is finished, they expect no harassment to come from you or from anyone else, from here to the head office in Tennessee. Consider yourself forewarned. And please tell Shirley they will be returning in time for lunch."

"I don't take kindly to threats." He glared at our group, his bug eyes as narrow as they would go, but he didn't say more. He spun around, grumbled to himself, and marched back inside, slapping the envelope across his open palm.

As soon as the front door slammed, excited chatter started up at a low pitch, but it could build into a frenzy of voiced fears. Some might get cold feet, afraid of repercussions.

I walked over to the old farm bell hanging on a post. Miss Johnson had rung it six times to announce the supper hour and her blessing of it. Today, one clang was all it took. "Get this show on the road," I said. "William, you and Francesca take the lead."

"You got it, Red," he said with a wink and a salute.

"Good luck!" yelled the young woman with blue-streaked hair.

I gave her a thumbs-up as we followed behind Francesca. Red and green helium-filled balloons had been tied to her wheelchair and floated above her. They added bright colors to a gray morning. I breathed a sigh of relief but soon had other worries.

Smiley, who had been too quiet at breakfast, lagged behind near the end of our line. He wore a charcoal gray overcoat with a red-plaid scarf tied around his neck, but without his usual baseball cap. His white hair, fluttering in the breeze, looked like feathery angel wings. He took out a handkerchief and coughed into it.

I dropped back to talk with him. "At least you didn't wear those sandals of yours today, the ones you're fond of wearing with your black dress socks. Where are your hat and gloves, by the way? And did you forget your Old Spice? Not like you at all."

He coughed again.

I didn't like the sound of it.

He gave a weak smile but said nothing.

"Shouldn't you go back home?" I added. "You're too sick to be outside in the damp air."

He shook his head. "Got a little cold, Sis, don'tcha know. I wouldn't miss this for the world."

"I would give you my knit hat if you would wear it."

He looked at my head and grinned. "Not on your life."

"Well, at least stick your hands inside your pockets."

He nodded and followed my instructions.

"Promise me you'll rest on a bench if you get tired," I said.

"Stop worrying so much, Sis. I'll be fine."

I wasn't convinced but made my way toward the front of our procession with the red and green balloons waving overhead.

We soon reached Blind George's Pool Hall and stopped to let the stragglers catch up. When I turned to look behind us, Smiley dropped onto a bench. I was thankful to see him there … until Pearl joined him. I could not tear my eyes away as she took the scarf from around his neck and tied it over his head and ears. Then she turned up his coat collar and gave him a kiss on his cheek. *A kiss.* And I could tell my silly friend loved her fussing over him. *Drat. And double drat.*

"Let's go, Red!" William yelled. "We don't have all day!"

Blind George and his cleaning lady stood on the sidewalk. He dried his big hands on a dirty apron, and she leaned on her mop. They watched us in silence as we moved by.

I waved to George.

He yelled, "Way to go, Granny! You show 'em!"

The old woman got into the spirit of our march. She whooped and danced a jig with her string mop.

I yelled to George, "Aren't you coming?"

"Thought you'd never ask," he said as he jumped into the middle of our group.

"I asked you a week ago. Did you forget?" But I don't think he heard me over the noise and commotion. Hard of hearing and forgetful. Two changes in myself I didn't want to claim, but then we were all getting older—like it or not. Even George. Even Pearl and Smiley, my two best friends, sitting on a bench together. *Drat.*

"You all stop in on your way back!" the old woman hollered to the residents of Sweetbriar Manor. "Hot coffee and doughnuts. On the house."

George looked her way and frowned, but then he smiled. "Yes, yes. Coffee and doughnuts," as if it had been his idea.

Our group shouted as one loud voice, "Yay!" We clapped our hands. Nothing like free food to get seniors excited.

Our protest march had turned into a celebration. As we approached the center of town, I was thankful I had remembered to bring my cane. I couldn't have managed without it.

The sounds and scents of Christmas in the air added to the festive feeling. I was glad the town of Sweetbriar had decided to get into the spirit early this year. Maybe Nellie should have come after all. Then I wondered who was left behind to keep an eye on her. Gee whiz, she could be shuffling through some private items in my chest of drawers, even messing with my tabloids. Maybe that's why she had been nice to me lately … so I might let my guard down around her.

"Rudolph the Red-Nosed Reindeer" swelled through large speakers from the courthouse square. The song reminded me of my past and a simpler time. As a child, my family and I would return home after shopping in town, cut a tree from our farm, and decorate it with fat, colored bubble lights, candy canes, and aluminum icicles tossed by the handfuls.

Lost in my thoughts as we crossed the street, I nearly bumped into the side of a mule, outfitted with a rank-smelling canvas pouch tied so it hung suspended behind his rear. The muscular animal clomped along pulling a carriage filled with people talking and laughing. The special transport, provided by Sweetbriar's Chamber of Commerce—and driven by a man decked in tails and a top hat—was trimmed with greenery, red ribbons, and jingling bells.

"Merry Christmas!" I yelled. Everyone returned my greeting and waved as they moved on down the street.

Our permit allowed us one trip down the middle of Main Street, starting at the courthouse square and ending at the corner of Main and Washington, the location of Begley's Drug Store. After our march, we would walk back to Blind George's for warmth and refreshments and afterward continue the short distance back to the Manor.

The sheriff assured us he would block the street for the time we would require. I'll have to say Hershel Caywood was as good as his word. He stood beside his cruiser parked sideways across Main at the other end of town. His vehicle was positioned so no one could squeeze past him—if someone decided to be foolish enough to try.

He wore white gloves and directed traffic away from Main, down First Avenue where people would have no choice but to turn onto King Street. His deputy performed the same sort of maneuver at the other end. We had no cars on the street, only seven residents from the Manor, George, and the mule-drawn carriage—the only vehicle allowed to continue its regular back-and-forth trek. A scattering of people gathered along the sidewalks.

We held Smiley's signs up high. He had worked hard getting them ready since Francesca had apparently never completed hers. Where were Smiley and Pearl anyway? I squinted and looked all around. There they were on another bench. She handed him a bottle of water Santa's elves were busy passing out to the crowd. I forced myself to keep my attention on the task at hand.

Smiley's posters were colorful and perfect in design. They were also discreet and polite because I had promised Betty Jo to follow her plan. "Subtle wording will win the people over," she said. "Honey is better than vinegar, after all."

"Honey attracts flies," I said.

She had only rolled her eyes … as usual.

I looked over our posters held overhead. *Sweetbriar Manor Is Our Home. A Retirement Home is an Asset to Sweetbriar. Your Senior Citizens of Sweetbriar Manor Help Support the Local Economy.*

Then I spotted one that spelled trouble. Naturally, it was held by Francesca. Then duplicate ones began popping up from underneath her lap blanket. It was no wonder she had kept them a secret.

In bold black letters, each one said: *Seniors or Criminals as Your Neighbors? Your Choice!*

I maneuvered my way over to her. "What are you trying to do? Get us arrested?"

Her chin jutted forward as she raised the sign higher. "No need to pussyfoot around. The citizens of this town need to learn the truth."

I grabbed for her sign, but she jerked it out of reach.

"Hold on, Red," William said. "I think she's right about this."

"Of course you do," I blurted. "Love is blind."

"I'm disappointed in you, Agnes," Francesca said as she waved her sign. "Your wimpy posters will accomplish nothing."

"Maybe. Maybe not. But yours will stir up trouble. We've got to be smart about this, work every angle like a politician. I don't want those women living in our home, but we've got to use the legal channels. We're marching to make the people aware of what's going on. Remember, we need their signatures on our petition. Getting folks agitated won't help our cause one bit."

The woman pulled another sign from underneath her blanket and handed it to William. "You've been listening to your daughter too much is all I have to say."

I tried once more to grab her sign. "And I listen to Henry. We have, by the way, found another possible location for the women's halfway house."

She huffed. "I don't believe it."

I envied Francesca for taking a stand. Our posters were meant to protest the possible influx of women criminals into our community, but I had agreed to try to work through the system.

"Let's go, Red," William said as he pushed Francesca past me. "We're falling behind."

Our group picked up the pace, and we were spared any further discussion for the moment. Smiley's posters were either being tromped upon by dirty shoes or sticking out of trashcans. Francesca's kept multiplying. *How many did she make anyway?*

Lucy, a waitress from the Dixie Diner, stood along the curb among a group of men and women. Then I spotted Boss, of all people. Why wasn't he working at his pawn shop? He leaned against a lamppost, one foot raised behind him, with his arms folded. I looked back as our group passed by. He caught my eye and tipped his hat, a smirk on his face. Almost like he was taunting me. Then he turned his attention to a large woman with spiked hair who appeared beside him—the same woman who had come to Sweetbriar Manor from the prison system, and the same one I had later seen at the pawnshop. They fell into a deep discussion. *What on earth could those two have in common?*

Then Lucy the waitress began chanting, "Seniors, yes! Criminals, no!" Others joined her, and their voices swelled until they swept over us like a tsunami. I smiled and waved to the growing crowd, praying Francesca's posters were exactly what our cause needed. Otherwise, we could lose our home in the flood and even drown ourselves. And what would such a disaster accomplish?

Out of nowhere, it seemed, a red scooter sputtered alongside me. "Mind if I join you?" a man in a dirty jumpsuit hollered over his noisy contraption. It was Mike from the garage.

"Mike?" I yelled. "What are you doing riding Jack's bike?"

He shook his head, unable to hear over the racket. Not only was he breaking the law, he was riding Jack's beloved scooter. How did he acquire it, and why did he think he could crash our protest march? He puttered on ahead and waved his hand in the air. We had promised no motorized vehicles. I hoped our law enforcement didn't have the manpower to shut us down.

Chapter Fifteen

I spotted Betty Jo on the sidewalk in front of Henry's Hardware. She must've left the Christmas decorating to her garden club friends. She glanced my way and winked, even smiling ever so slightly. Surrounded by other spectators, she attempted to appear neutral to our cause, but I made a mental note to thank her again for working behind the scenes to obtain our permit, even if it was at the last possible minute.

A muscular, bald-headed man walked up and stood close behind her. Boss' bodyguard and nephew looked even more menacing in his leather jacket. He leaned forward and said something to Betty Jo. She stared straight ahead, her eyes growing wide. Then he vanished. *Why would he be talking to my daughter? What could he possibly be up to?* I moved toward her until she spotted me, waved me on, and gave a thumbs-up. I rejoined the march. Talking to her would have to wait.

Henry and Miss Margaret, who was thankfully on a leash, stepped off the sidewalk and joined the Manor's residents. Blind George had taken it upon himself to carry one of Francesca's signs. He held it up high, swung it back and forth slowly, and turned it in all directions. The chanting swelled and followed us down the street. When I glanced back where I had seen Betty Jo, she was gone.

Well, sir, maybe it was the excitement of the moment, but it was like we had given the spectators a signal. All sorts of people—children, women with packages, teenagers with cell phones and earplugs, and finally a staggering, drunk man—joined our march. People were laughing and talking and even singing, "We Shall Overcome." I'd never seen a more uplifting demonstration in all my days on this earth. My heart swelled with pride, and I even forgave Francesca. Well, maybe not totally.

The *Timely News* van pulled up, and a young man jumped out and took pictures. Lots of people used their phones to capture the moment. I wanted to do the same but couldn't manage anything beyond limping along with my confounded cane. A sharp pain made me wince. Whoever said getting old was not for wimps knew what she was talking about.

George returned Francesca's sign to her with a bow, and she looked as proud as a queen at her coronation. Our crowd swelled in size, and some of the teenage boys elbowed their way through us. They were having a good time, but they could also knock someone down who could get trampled. I could have set into worrying good, but we had other concerns.

The scooter backfired. Three times. It sounded like gunfire. Before I could blink twice, a deputy from the town of White Pine appeared among us. Our sheriff had apparently hired outside help. He ran over to Mike and pulled him off the bike. Then he frisked him from head to toe, handcuffed him, and sat him on the sidewalk, all in a flash.

Mike jumped up and yelled, "You ain't got no right! This is harassment!"

The deputy pushed him back down. The growing crowd booed. It was a good thing Shirley had not come, for she would have recognized Jack's scooter and wondered why her Baby was not driving it.

I marched over to Mike and turned to the White Pine officer of the law. "Aren't you overreacting? Let him park the bike so he can join our peaceful march."

The deputy's hands fisted at his sides. "He broke the law with his contraption."

"Maybe. But handcuffs? Is that really necessary?"

Voices rose in agreement, especially from the Manor's residents who had circled around us.

The out-of-town deputy scowled at me. "I can shut this whole thing down. Call for backup and arrest the lot of you for causing a disturbance."

I crossed my fists on top of my cane and steadied myself. "Go ahead. Arrest me."

"Now, Miss Agnes, be reasonable," said our own deputy who suddenly appeared by my side.

"Arrest me too!" yelled Francesca as she held her fists in the air.

One after another, the residents of Sweetbriar Manor and a few townspeople followed our lead.

A WLEX newsman with a movie camera on his shoulder filmed the crowds, as well as Mike, who stood on the sidewalk in his greasy, garage jumpsuit, grinning from ear to ear.

Then Francesca shouted, "Criminals or seniors?" The chanting began again. She held her sign up high as the camera turned her way.

"Looks like we'll make the news," I said, mostly to myself as I gazed up at the dark cloud that had suddenly appeared above us.

Raindrops splattered onto the pavement, and a cold rain began to fall in earnest. Wind whipped the rain around until it seemed to come from all directions. I managed to open Nellie's umbrella, but a gust of wind flipped it inside out. The crowd quickly dispersed. Out of the corner of my eye, I saw Betty Jo, the sheriff, and Mike huddled underneath the awning of Dot's Antique Shop. Was I the only one who recognized the scooter as Jack's? I had plenty of questions bubbling, but they would have to wait.

I managed to locate Smiley, who looked worse than a shipwreck survivor. Henry, holding Miss Margaret in his arms, ran on ahead of us. I grabbed Smiley's arm—with Pearl latched onto his other one—put my cane to good use, and we headed toward the pool hall. For good or bad, our protest march was over.

Smiley sank into the nearest chair, and Henry brought him a glass of water. Pearl and I sat nearby and sipped on cups of hot chocolate. As soon as everyone dried off a bit with some of Blind George's bar towels, we would head to the Manor.

Then, out of nowhere, a man wearing a grungy Army jacket and sporting a full beard leaned down close to my ear. "Something you ought to know."

He smelled like a sour goat and looked even worse. He led me away from the noise into a darkened corner. My heart fell into my stomach, but I squared my shoulders and looked him in the eye. "What is your name, and what do you want?"

"Name's not important, but I've got information you might find interesting."

I squinted at him in the dim light. "Why would you tell me anything?"

"Because Josiah was my friend."

"Land sakes! Please go on." Was he a homeless man? I tried not to cringe or stare at his long, dirty fingernails when he reached out and touched my arm.

"I overheard Josiah talking to the sheriff one night," he said.

Could I trust this stranger? "You sure? Where? When?"

"Underneath the bridge, where we sleep sometimes. Sheriff come poking around, looking for him. About two weeks before Josiah was killed."

"Go on."

The man leaned a little closer. "They argued. The sheriff was as mad as all get out."

I looked around to make sure no one was listening. "Are you going to tell me what they said?"

"Keep your britches on, little lady. I'm getting there. The sheriff said, 'You need to back out. Now. Ain't worth dying for.' Then Josiah says, 'We made a deal. I'm getting close, and I'm sticking with it.'"

"Don't suppose you overheard exactly what they were arguing about."

"They seen me looking and listening, then the sheriff stormed off."

I tore a napkin in half, wrote down my phone number, and handed it to him. "Thank you for the information. Call me if you think of anything else."

"You can count on it," he said as he stuffed the piece of paper into his pocket.

✳ ✳ ✳

Smiley said he didn't want any lunch, so I laid out some dry clothes for him and went to my room where I changed into a pair of soft, old jeans, a flannel shirt, and my fuzzy, kitten slippers. Then I wrote down the new information in my notebook.

When I checked on Smiley later, he was sound asleep. I went into the kitchen and told Shirley we would both be missing her lunch of ham and cheese quiche with a Greek salad on the side. My dear friend needed to rest, and I had work to do.

I sneaked past Francesca while she had her head turned toward William and returned to my room. Notebook in hand—and my purse I had retrieved from the drawer of pots—I went to the beauty shop where I shut and locked the door. No one would think of looking for me in here, especially Nellie, who seemed to pop up out of nowhere.

Here I could study my detective work, and if I needed to use my phone, this location had the best signal. I tried to consider all the evidence with fresh eyes. One thing for sure, I had a bone to pick with our good sheriff. Obviously, something had gone on between him and Josiah, and it smelled worse than the homeless man at Blind George's.

My phone rang, interrupting my thoughts. It was Betty Jo, breathless with worry.

"Yes," I said. "I know Boss' nephew. What did he say to you?" I walked over to the beauty shop windows and gazed outside at the fountain. "Slow down. I can't make out what you're saying."

Pearl moved across my line of vision carrying a tray of pansies. I moved away from the windows before she could see me. She would want to know what was wrong.

"He said what? Yes, I'll be here. No, don't come. Henry either. You might scare him away. No, I'm not afraid."

We ended the call. I had lied. I was definitely afraid of being in the same room with Billy. He was coming to see me tonight after supper.

The aroma of Shirley's ham and cheese quiche drifted into the beauty shop, making my stomach roll.

The residents of Sweetbriar Manor made the local news, which we gathered around to watch before dinner on the sitting room's television. The commentator's report painted us as old fuddy-duddies who refused to adapt to change—seniors who had hardened our hearts toward young women seeking another chance at life.

Smiley seemed to perk up a little, but at supper he hardly touched his spaghetti with meatballs, even though he had not eaten lunch. I picked at my supper also, but for a different reason.

Maybe Billy wouldn't show up. I told Shirley to let me know if he did, but I didn't tell her why. After all, I didn't know myself. Pacing the floor in my room—then the sitting room and the dining room—did not produce one ounce of peace. Finally, about nine o'clock, I was headed back to my room when the doorbell rang. Thankful Mr. Lively had gone out for the evening, I opened the door, and "Dixie" rang out.

Billy, dressed in full motorcycle gear, held his helmet in front of him. "Miss Agnes, can I come in? I ain't got long."

The sitting room was empty, but we went to a far corner beyond the piano in case anyone should wander in. My heartbeat sounded like a bass drum in my ears. When we sat down, I held my hands together to keep them from shaking.

Billy didn't waste any time or mince any words. "I seen what happened to Josiah."

Fifteen minutes later, Billy was gone. Was he a reliable witness or someone with a score to settle? My mind was in a whirl.

The next morning during breakfast, everyone pored over the *Timely News* Saturday edition, which featured pictures—in color no less—of a crowd of people led by a woman in a wheelchair with red and green balloons. The headlines read: *Seniors' Protest Runs Amok. Scooter Driver, Mike (of Mike's Garage), and protest leader, Agnes Hopper, Fined.*

Fined? Protest leader? "Francesca was the one in charge, not me." I didn't know how much I had been fined, but I didn't have any money for such nonsense, nor the time to even think about the news report after last night's visit.

My intentions were to ask Smiley if the newspaper could be wrong about this, but another matter took first priority. He had not eaten a bite of his scrambled eggs, cheese grits, or bacon. He picked up his napkin and coughed.

"I knew you had no business getting out in the cold air yesterday," I said. "And then getting soaked clear to the bone didn't help."

"Ah, Sis." He coughed again. It sounded like a rattlesnake in his chest.

I laid my hand on his forehead. "Just as I thought. You have a fever. Have you taken any medicine?"

He shook his head and wiped his face with a napkin.

I stood and helped him up from his chair. He shook worse than a broken-down ladder as he tried to protest my help.

"Listen here, Sam Abenda, if you refuse to take care of yourself, somebody's got to do it for you. Like me."

He attempted to wave me off but didn't have the strength of a flea. I caught Shirley's eye and motioned to her.

She rushed over and put one arm around Smiley's waist. "Honey, lean against me. We're gonna get you to your bed where Miss Agnes can look after you while I call the doctor. And don't you go to shakin' your head. That's exactly what we're gonna do whether you like it or not."

I hurried ahead of them to Smiley's room to turn down his bed and get him some Tylenol, a glass of water, a thermometer, and an ice pack. Before I could get my mission accomplished, there was a loud thud, and the floor trembled behind me.

Shirley yelled, "Oh, merciful heavens!"

I pulled out my cell phone and called 911.

✱ ✱ ✱

The kind EMS woman said, "Don't worry, ma'am. We'll take good care of him."

Then they whisked him away. My dear friend looked tiny and fragile and as pale as wallpaper paste—a mere shadow of himself with a ragged breath. A sob caught in my throat. "Don't you dare go and die on me," I muttered.

Mr. Lively appeared beside me. "Did you call your daughter? Maybe she can carry you to the hospital."

I nodded and blinked back the tears. "Three times. Doesn't answer."

"Don't worry. I'll get my car. Meet me down front."

My eyes went wide. *Maybe the man does have a heart underneath those suspenders.*

I had never seen his car before, didn't even realize he had one. I expected to see a ragged, old-model Ford or Dodge to match his personal appearance. Instead, a spiffy red sports car pulled up to the curb. I opened the door and plopped inside, but the seat was much lower than I expected.

"Haven't had this baby out of the garage since I arrived in Sweetbriar," he said. "I've missed her. Named her Bonus Baby. Soon as I close the deal, I'll pay her off. Yes indeed." He patted the dash as we sped away.

I didn't feel like asking questions or making any small talk, but I was certainly grateful for a ride. "Thank you for taking me."

"Doing this for your friend. He seems to dote on you for some reason, though for the life of me I can't fathom why."

Smiley dotes on me? I was at a loss for words.

"Mr. Abenda has a stronger constitution than you might think," he added. "Reminds me of my granddaddy. Ninety-eight before he passed."

My insides quivered so hard I trembled all over. Was Mr. Lively trying to reassure me? I silently cried out to the Lord. *Please don't let him die.*

When we pulled up to the emergency room entrance, I managed to push myself upright with my cane and shut the car door. Mr. Lively sped away as I hobbled inside.

A woman with rouged cheeks and black curls piled on top of her head spoke from a desk behind a glass enclosure. "Who are you here for?" she asked, checking her records.

"Sam. Sam Abenda."

"Family?"

"Sister. Can I go back?"

She shook her curls. "They'll tell us when. Might be awhile. You can wait over there." She pointed to a row of green, plastic chairs.

"Say," said another woman with *Doris* pinned to her chest, "haven't I seen you somewhere before?"

I shook my head. "I don't think so."

She slapped her desktop. "Yes. You had a run in with the law. Started a riot on Main Street."

"That's not what hap—"

"Old people or criminals? I'm not sure which is worse." Doris's nose twitched as if some stench had offended her. "If you ask me, Sweetbriar Manor ought to be turned into a classy B & B and featured in *Southern Living* instead of plastered across the newspaper like we're all a bunch of rednecks. Disgraceful is what it is. Disgraceful. And another thing … what's all this blarney about the place being haunted?"

"You don't understand …"

The double doors swung open, and an ER attendant stood in the opening. "Anyone here named Sis?" she asked.

I moved forward, one painful step at a time. My knee had chosen a bad time to act up.

* * *

I lifted Smiley's hand and held it in both of mine. His dark brown eyes fluttered open. He managed a weak smile, and I let loose a great sigh of relief.

"Don't try to speak," I said. "Save your strength. Nurse says you have a bad case of bronchitis. On the verge of pneumonia, I might add. You are one stubborn man."

"You worry too … too much …" he sputtered, which sent him into a coughing fit. Then he collapsed against his pillow.

"Don't you say another word. The nurse says they'll decide in a couple of hours if you should be admitted or discharged. Either way, it's complete bed rest after we get you back home. They've started you on a round of antibiotics, and they want you to get checked again in about ten days or sooner if you spike a fever again. I promised them you would follow their instructions, and I would see to it you did. No sweet-talking me or wiggling out of anything. You gave us a scare."

He sighed but had no energy left to resist. Like it or not, Mr. Sam Abenda was going to behave. He wouldn't be able to talk much for a while, but when he was on his way to recovery, he could listen. And I had plenty to tell him.

With the help of cough syrup with codeine and oxygen fed through a tube in his nose, Smiley settled down and slept, but each breath rattled in his chest. I scooted a chair close to his bed, lifted one of his hands, and held it in both of mine. His skin was clammy, even though his temperature reading on the monitor had returned to normal. Pneumonia was nothing to be trifled with, and I hoped the doctors knew what they were doing.

As Smiley slept, I remembered Mr. Lively's words as he drove me to the hospital. I knew why he was totally obsessed with a timely sale of Sweetbriar Manor. When he closed the door on our home for the last time, he would be paid enough money for a brand new red sports car.

Chapter Sixteen

Three hours later, with Smiley breathing on his own and his oxygen level staying at ninety-eight percent, he was discharged to go home. Betty Jo rushed in and left again to bring her car around to the entrance since Mr. Lively had returned to the Manor.

I insisted on wheeling him toward the ER's exit under a nurse's distinctly chilled supervision.

"I'm not an invalid, don'tcha know," Smiley said as he looked up to me with a weak smile.

"No, but I'm the one in charge here," I said. "Sit back and enjoy the ride."

Sheriff Caywood was talking to Doris, the admittance person. She batted her long eyelashes at him as she gathered her long, smooth hair into a ponytail, but he didn't seem to notice. Two orderlies were on their hands and knees scrubbing the floor.

I stopped Smiley's wheelchair beside the sheriff and leaned on the handles. "I've been wanting to talk with you since Carl was shot. Do you know who killed him? I would bet my last penny it wasn't Jack."

"Can't answer. Ongoing investigation."

Can't or won't? "Seems to me there's a bunch of questions with no answers. What *can* you tell me?"

The sheriff crossed his arms over his large belly. "Happened in the alley behind the drugstore. A clerk emptying the trash found him."

"I learned those details earlier. Sounds like we have a crime wave in Sweetbriar."

"We have nothing of the kind, but I reckon I can share this with you since it has your name on it. Picked it up from the crime lab this morning."

My eyes narrowed. "You make a habit of carrying evidence around with you?"

"Do you ever stop asking questions?" The sheriff groaned and rubbed the back of his neck. "For your information, I intend to get the opinion of a buddy of mine."

"Well, I'm glad you're not letting every crime fall by the wayside. Now, what did you want to show me?"

He held up a dirty, bloodstained piece of notebook paper encased inside a gallon zip bag. "Found it stuffed inside Carl's jacket. Understand, you can't take it out, but maybe you ought to read it."

Agnes was written across the top in large, printed letters. *Senile old woman, stop poking your nose where it don't belong or you will be snuffed out when you least expect it and planted beside your no-count husband.*

What on earth did the words mean? *Snuffed out? Me planted beside Charlie?* I trembled until the bag left my hands and fluttered onto the wheelchair and Smiley's lap.

The sheriff picked it up. "Looks like you and me have some things to discuss. I'll be in touch, Miss Agnes. Soon. Don't be doing nothing foolish. Matter of fact, don't be doing nothing at all. My deputy will be close by, your invisible shadow until this is resolved."

The sheriff turned away to talk with a man in a white lab coat who held the plastic bag up to the light as he read the note. They lowered their voices, but not before I heard the man ask about Josiah's autopsy report. I couldn't make out anything else before they whirled around and walked away.

Smiley lifted his hand. "Sis?"

I leaned down with my good ear close to his mouth.

"Listen to the sheriff. Please."

The nurse—who had been amazingly patient and quiet—loudly cleared her throat. The three of us moved through the automatic doors and loaded Smiley into Betty Jo's car.

Early the next morning, Sheriff Caywood stood in the foyer of Sweetbriar Manor, hat in hand. He bent over and looked me dead in the eye. "You've stirred up a bushel of trouble. Didn't I tell you to leave matters to the law?"

"Yes, but—"

"No buts. These boys play for keeps."

Francesca wheeled past us but stopped at the dining room door. She turned her wheelchair around and headed back to where we stood. *Just what I need.*

Thankfully, William came to our rescue. "Where have you been, sweetie?" He winked at me and whisked her to the dining room under sputtering protests.

"Let's find a place to talk," I said, leading the sheriff to two wingback chairs in the far corner of the sitting room, the same spot where I had listened to Boss' nephew. I was not ready to share what he told me. The aroma of bacon and coffee drifted in, as well as the hum of residents gathering for breakfast.

The sheriff dug his buckeye out of a shirt pocket and set about rubbing it. "I would advise you to tell me everything you've come by, as well as your sources."

Everything? Not hardly. "Well, for starters, since my number one suspect is dead, I'm stumped. I figured since Josiah had big gambling debts, someone hired Carl—since he had karate skills—to rough him up, but his blow to his neck landed harder than he intended. Maybe he then decided to finish the job with a scarf, which was found underneath Josiah's body, probably left behind by mistake. Plus, whoever hired Carl helped him place Josiah on a bench in Beulah Cemetery."

"Interesting theory."

"Some things I know for certain about Josiah. He didn't drink, he cared about people, and he worked for the Salvation Army."

The sheriff rubbed his buckeye a few times and then looked up. "Yes, he did. I'm going to share some information about him, but you have to swear you'll keep it to yourself. This is for your ears only, *and* for your protection."

I nodded. "You have my word."

"He also worked for me. But not officially, you understand."

"He did? Forever more. The two of you … First Pres … on Wednesday mornings. Why didn't you tell me about him working undercover?"

"Didn't think there was a need. How did you find out about us anyway? Oh, never mind, I don't need to know. Maybe you'll understand how serious this whole situation is. He was not on the payroll, but he was the best informant I've ever had. He stopped in one day, told me all about his gambling on cockfights and how he was trying to leave it behind. Said he had some information I might find useful. Then I asked him if he was willing to work with me, let people think he was a bum hooked on gambling, so we might catch some of the big-time criminals."

"Oh, my. I knew he was a good man, but I had no idea about—"

"He was close to meeting a crime boss when he was killed. When Carl Swain was gunned down, I thought the two deaths were connected, but now I'm not so sure."

"So, you knew Josiah was murdered. But how could you—"

"Release a false report?"

"Exactly." This new information was buzzing around in my head like a swarm of yellow jackets.

The buckeye disappeared into his shirt pocket. "Had to give the killer enough rope to hang himself. Only I didn't count on Carl getting in the way."

"So … you know who murdered both men?" I asked, hopeful he would be honest with me.

"Still mulling over the evidence. All circumstantial. Has to be airtight or it won't hold up in court. Besides, the coroner, who is a good man, has to report his findings in five more days. That's the deadline, and if he doesn't comply, he could lose his license. He can't help me cover up Josiah's cause of death any longer."

I closed my eyes to think about what he'd said and to shut out the chatter coming from the dining room. "Merciful heavens. Five days?"

The sheriff stood and paced the floor. "I've asked you to back off. Now I'm telling you. We'll find out who killed both of these men. But we'll do it our own way in our own time, with or without help from the coroner. And with no help from you. This is dangerous business. Promise me you'll stop asking so many questions."

I stood and squared off with him. "Hershel Caywood, it's a pure shame you didn't take after your granddaddy. He knew how to ask for assistance when he needed it. How did you get to be so stubborn? I knew Josiah didn't die from exposure, but as far as who killed him … well, since you won't share the name of your prime suspect, I'm back to square one, thanks to you. I must have overlooked something."

The good sheriff gave me his best no-nonsense look. "Miss Agnes, if you're looking to be a hero, you could end up a dead one. You think about that."

I walked him to the front door—since he declined to join us for breakfast—and promised I would. Think about it that is. Who had possibly killed two men? And how could I possibly not stay involved?

I could see my casket lowered into the ground beside Charlie's grave.

✳ ✳ ✳

Few words had passed between Smiley and me since he had returned from the hospital, so we lingered over our after-breakfast coffee in the dining room. We were alone except for Lollipop using a carpet sweeper underneath the tables.

I turned to face Smiley. "Did I tell you the sheriff mentioned organized crime?"

He took a sip of his coffee. "Didn't figure you were going to stop turning over rocks. What if a snake happens to crawl out?"

I slapped the table with my palm. "We've got to be ready to chop off its head with a garden hoe."

Smiley shook his head, rose from his chair, and coughed. It sounded ragged and rough. When he recovered, he stood up straighter, looked at me, and said, "Morning paper's calling."

I bit my tongue, but that didn't stop me. "Well, for goodness sake, spread a blanket or your afghan over your lap first. You don't need to take a chill and have a setback."

"Ah, Sis, no need to fuss over me, don'tcha know."

"You might be napping before you finish the front page, but I'll peek inside your room in a bit to check on you."

I kissed him on the cheek and left him standing in the dining room.

During lunch, I hardly listened to any of the conversations around our table. The sheriff's words kept nagging me until I could think of little else. *Dead hero. You will be a dead hero. Leave the investigation to the professionals.* Was I truly in over my head? Would I swim … or sink?

If Carl had not killed Josiah, then who? Should I depend on the testimony of a man who not only looked like a thug but probably was one? I needed a place to think, to sort through the suspects who were still on my list.

I called my daughter. "I know you've heard about Carl Swain. You can't deny he was murdered. And so was Josiah. The sheriff so much as said so. No, I can't tell you exactly what he said. Not yet. Yes, Billy scared the living daylights out of me, but I'm not ready to tell you what he said either. No, I didn't call only to deliver upsetting news. I need you to carry me out to the farm. I have my reasons, and they're important enough to interrupt your day. Yes, now. Don't start giving me excuses why you can't. Since Henry closes the store early on Wednesdays, tell him he can come too. For sure, bring Miss Margaret. She could use an outing."

Betty Jo groaned and told me to stop yelling.

"What? I'm not yelling." I lowered my voice anyway. "If it weren't important, I wouldn't ask you. No, I can't tell you why I need to go. Not yet."

She let out one of her martyred sighs.

"I'll wait for you on the sidewalk. Beside the *No Parking* sign."

When my daughter pulled up to the curb, I heard another car's engine start up. I glanced down the street as Deputy Larry's cruiser edged forward—the sheriff's idea of protection, even though his deputy and I were always at odds with one another. I climbed into the Buick's back seat with Miss Margaret who greeted me with happy little grunts. I hugged her and rubbed her behind her ears. I didn't mention to Betty Jo we had an unwelcome bodyguard following us. I slipped an apple out of my coat pocket and dropped it onto the floorboard.

"I don't allow food in my car," Betty Jo said.

"She'll swallow every smidgen, and you won't be able to even imagine she rode in your pristine car. She's cleaner than any persnickety fussbudget, of whom you take the prize."

"I declare, Mother, you have a blind spot when it comes to your stupid pig."

Miss Margaret rooted underneath her blanket. She had gobbled up the apple, but the scent of it lingered.

"Henry busy?" I asked.

"Straightening his stock room. I expect he'll finish in no time. Won't have to stop to play with your silly pig."

Before I could reply to her continuing insults, she said, "How about some music?"

She had not mentioned Carl or Josiah and neither would I. Maybe when the case was solved, we could put some of our own issues to rest. If she didn't talk about what had happened to her all those years ago, she would never have any peace.

She pushed a CD into the slot and turned up the volume on Carolina Girls. "When Henry retires, we're moving to Myrtle Beach," she announced.

"Whatever for? Does he know this?"

"Not yet, but he will when the time is right." She tapped her brightly polished nails, bluer than the ocean, on the steering wheel and sang—off tune I might add.

"And when do you think this might occur?" I practically shouted. "If you think running away will solve anything, you're mistaken. Sweetbriar isn't the only town with crime. It's everywhere."

She turned the volume down a bit. "Not sure when I can convince Henry to retire, but I'm taking shag lessons, six weeks beginning this Saturday."

"My, my," I said as I set aside the retirement news, not to mention moving. *Maybe I should at least try being more pleasant with my difficult daughter.* "Sounds like fun. When you learn the steps, you can teach us at the Manor. Or maybe teach us how to line dance. No one has to have a partner, and for sure we don't have enough men to go around."

"I'll think about it. If you're still living there."

"The dining room would be the perfect place, hardwood floors and all. I'm sure Henry could help push the tables out of the way. I'll bet Shirley and her Baby can cut a rug, like in the movie *Dirty Dancing*. Can't you just see it? Her wearing those spike heels she's fond of. And him? He would wear his black cowboy boots with the silver toes, like always. He must only have one pair of shoes to his name."

"Most likely."

The tune changed to James Taylor's "How Sweet It Is."

How could I think of Jack dancing with Shirley? He was no longer around and, according to Mike, he left his scooter behind because the old bike wouldn't make it as far as he needed to go. Jack had taken a bus. Mike wouldn't tell me where he had gone, and neither would Mr. Case, Jack's former employer at the produce stand. Even if Jack had killed Josiah, he wouldn't have sneaked back in town to do away with Carl. Maybe the two murders were unrelated.

"I'll need to start looking for some shoes," I said to give my brain a rest from trying to figure out the puzzle. "No ordinary ones will do. Dancing shoes. I used to tap dance, you know." I thought back to the shopping program that had featured fancy shoes—those sparkling red flats with tiny straps I saw on the same day I learned of my financial woes. But shoes cost money I didn't have. Maybe they were on sale. Wouldn't hurt to check it out. No harm in looking.

"Hmmm, I never knew you tap danced."

"Could be a lot of things you don't know about your mother," I said under my breath. I hurried on, raising my voice. "William and

Francesca boogie to his old Elvis records. Her being in a wheelchair doesn't stop those two."

My daughter hummed to the music and didn't respond.

"Before she died, Alice told me one of her regrets was not dancing more when she had the chance. Did I tell you already?"

"Several times. I suppose I do have most of the tunes we would need."

"Absolutely."

Music continued to fill the car. Would my daughter really teach us how to dance? Maybe. Unless she became obsessed with her ridiculous notion of moving to Myrtle Beach. If she did, why, a runaway freight train couldn't stop her. Grieved my heart to think she might not always be around. I would even miss our spats.

Dark thoughts. My daughter gone. And what if the sale of my farm never materialized? Who would want it? No one bought small farms these days. Too much work and too little profit. I had made some inquiries but had not placed it on the market yet. I had been procrastinating, but it was not an easy decision.

I could see a bill collector chasing me down the road. Papers fell from a hefty woman's clenched fists and, of course, she wore red shoes, reminding me of the ones I coveted. In an instant, she advanced close enough to pounce on me. I sucked in my breath. My worst nightmare swallowed any happiness of imagining I could ever dance to the sounds of beach music. I gazed out the side window, and then looked behind us.

Yep. Larry was still there, along with my wacky thoughts.

Chapter Seventeen

Betty Jo turned onto the farm's dirt lane, overgrown with tall weeds swaying in the breeze. Honeysuckle vines had swallowed a wooden enclosure near the main road. Charlie had built it to keep our garbage cans out of sight and away from prying raccoons. Miss Margaret started squealing and hopping around.

"What in tarnation is wrong with her?" Betty Jo yelled.

"She can smell the farm," I said. "Drive down the lane a little further. Park near the house, and I'll let her out."

As soon as we stopped, I opened the backdoor. My sweet pig raced toward the pond between the house and the barn. Her favorite place. I looked around for the deputy's car but didn't spot it anywhere. Maybe he figured this was a safe place. Besides, I certainly didn't need anyone guarding me.

More than a year had passed since the fire, yet gazing into the charred remains of my farmhouse was much harder than I expected. The burnt-wood stench rose into the air. I could still picture orange flames licking their way up my kitchen curtains and a fireman carrying me outside to stand underneath our big oak tree.

Our front porch had collapsed, swallowing the strings of morning glories in an instant. And the swing Charlie had built when we were hardly more than newlyweds stood on end. It remained where it had fallen.

My chest tightened. It was an effort to breathe. Finally, I said, "I'm going to walk down the lane a short way or maybe past the barn. I've got my cane, so I'll be moving slow. No need for you to come with me." I needed some time to clear my head in order to solve a crime, and alone would be best.

I stood on a slight rise beyond the barn where Josiah had practiced his bagpipes. From here, the view had once been fields of golden burley tobacco and meadows sprinkled with grazing Holsteins. Beyond them were rolling hills as far as the eye could see. The abandoned fields and meadows had sprouted goldenrods, butterfly weeds, and clumps of a dusty-blue flower. I didn't like the change, even though the overgrowth had its own kind of beauty. Here was a place where I hoped to sort through the evidence and determine who killed Josiah—and Carl— beyond any doubt. It was time, past time, to close the investigation.

I sensed Betty Jo's presence beside me. She rummaged in her pockets, found a tissue, and blew her nose. "Why did we have to come out here?"

"We had some good years on this place," I said. "You don't have to stay. Didn't you say you needed to go to the Winn Dixie?"

"I can't leave you here alone. What if you should fall?"

"Nonsense. Miss Margaret and I lived on this land, just the two of us, after your daddy died and before the house burned. Besides, you wouldn't be gone more than an hour or so at the most."

She reluctantly agreed. "Okay. Check your phone. Do you have a signal?"

I slipped it out of my pocket. "Three bars. I've got some thinking to do. Yes, I'll be careful."

I turned back toward the barn, watching my feet with every step until distressed animal noises caught my attention. Miss Margaret—in a streak of pink—chased a flock of squawking geese out of her pond territory.

"You go, girl!" I yelled. In a tiny snapshot, my precious had lifted my spirits. She gave me hope. I could, no I *would* come to grips with Sweetbriar's terrible, baffling crimes and understand how to solve them while I stood on this land of Charlie's and mine.

A hawk circled overhead against a clear, blue sky. It glided downward and disappeared on the other side of the barn. In the next moment, I turned to look behind me as a faint rumble, a motor of some kind, grew louder. Soon, an old pickup truck topped the ridge and barreled down the lane toward me. I froze in place. When it didn't slow down, I managed to step aside but nearly lost my footing as the truck skidded around me in a cloud of dust and rocks. The driver sped up and kept going. I watched the churning trail of dust leave my property and continue onto Walter's. He must have cut an opening in our fence. I had seen his face when he flew past.

What in thunder was he doing here?

Suddenly—as if by divine intervention—I knew. I moved toward the barn, my detective antennas on alert. I stopped short in front of the double doors and turned around to look at the flat swatch of land around me. As if plowed by a drunk, tire tracks and ruts crisscrossed each other in all directions. Obviously, many vehicles had come and gone here, some fairly recently.

I managed to push open the big doors with rusty hinges.

Light fell into the barn. Particles of sawdust danced in sunbeams, spotlighting a circular, roped ring. Edging closer, I stepped on a chicken's foot and then spotted some feathers. A sour stench filled the heavy air. It was obvious what had taken place here, probably orchestrated by Walter. This had to be the new location of the cockfights Walter had wanted to share with Blind George.

I backed out of the barn until a cool breeze touched my neck. I took a deep breath and made my way around the barn where I had seen the hawk swoop down and disappear. I hadn't gone far when another vehicle approached. I turned, leaned on my cane, and watched as Deputy Larry drove down the lane toward me. He pulled his squad car close to the barn, killed the engine, and got out.

"Some help you are," I said. "Walter could've run me over, and I could be dead or dying."

"I saw him," Larry said. "Maybe he was taking a shortcut to his place. And maybe you ought to put up some *No Trespassing* signs."

"In spite of your incompetence, I've stumbled upon something you and the sheriff will be interested in."

Larry scratched the inside of his ear with one finger. "You don't say."

"The barn doors are open. Look for yourself."

He disappeared inside, and I waited for him, expecting him to thank me and then immediately radio his boss.

"Well?" I asked when he returned and stood in front of me with his fingers on his stun gun.

"You may have something. I'll talk to the sheriff when I get back to town."

"*May* have something? *Talk* to the sheriff? Is that all you have to say?" Once again, my hackles went into overdrive.

"Miss Agnes, suffice it to say we're keeping an eye on the situation.

Why did you come out here anyway?"

Like I owed him an explanation. "Needed a place to think. I've certainly not committed any crime."

"I'm parking up near the highway until your daughter comes back for you. Sheriff says you need protecting. Reckon I've got to do my duty."

"Some protection you are," I grumbled to his back as he left me there.

I moved around to the back of the barn. As I suspected, dead gamecocks had been thrown into a pile and preying animals, probably coyotes, had claimed most of their parts. I gagged at the smell of blood and decay. Deputy Larry—and most likely the sheriff—knew what had taken place here. But why were they protecting Walter?

Now I understood why, soon after Charlie's death, my neighbor had made an offer to purchase our farm at a ridiculously low price. He would not get away with any of his shenanigans. He knew how Charlie and I hated the so-called sport of cockfighting. And to hold them in our barn, on the sly ... some nerve he had. A man this sneaky, this low-down would think nothing of murder if someone got in his way. Josiah or myself, and maybe Carl.

The evidence against my neighbor as a killer was compelling, yet another suspect had to be considered. *Boss Brown.* At least if I believed his nephew as a reliable witness. Greed ruled in the lives of both men, but I needed evidence as reliable as the good book.

As I watched my precious splashing in the pond, I pondered how to solve this case. Then I remembered the words Charlie had said to me one day after he returned from his weekly checker game. Instantly, one person stood out from the others, but was it possible to use this piece of information? Could it be considered evidence?

I hollered for Miss Margaret, who was busy rooting around the pond's edge for heaven only knew what. She ignored me. But when I promised her a Granny Smith, her ears perked up. She left her search for treasures and ran lickety-split to where I stood in the lane. I pulled the apple from my coat pocket and heard the sounds of yet another vehicle approaching. Was the deputy returning? No, this one putt-putted along, and no sign of a deputy followed behind it. Larry had probably answered another call, more urgent than babysitting an old woman.

I held onto Miss Margaret's collar in case this driver also proved reckless, but there was no need. An old Ford Fairlane crept into view.

Someone sightseeing or lost was my guess. The car pulled off the lane and parked beside our burn barrels. A young woman with a mop of curly brown hair jumped out and waved.

"Yoo hoo! You the owner of this place? If you are, we need to talk." She ran toward me waving her arms like she was flagging down a bus.

I hoped she didn't break her high heels on the rocky ground or stumble in her short, tight skirt. We waited for her to reach us, Miss Margaret sniffing my pockets for another apple.

The young woman arrived huffing and puffing, but she didn't slow down. "Please tell me you're Agnes Hopper," she said in high-pitched excitement.

"I am."

"Fabulous! I've been trying to reach you. Did you receive my letter?"

I frowned at her and shook my head.

"No? Are you sure? I drove all the way here from Atlanta. Decided to look you up and knock on your door but swung in here on the way. Good thing, huh? Sweetbriar Manor is where I was headed. That's where you live these days. Right?"

I nodded again, completely baffled about this peculiar state of affairs. Miss Margaret pranced around me until I retrieved the last apple from my pocket and tossed it underneath a hemlock.

"I'm forgetting my manners," the woman said, reaching out to shake my hand. "I'm JoAnn Dixon with Countryside Realty. Have you considered selling this place? I have a client ready to make you an offer."

Oh, my. Merciful heavens.

I rummaged in my purse for a peppermint to calm myself, as well as to stall. *Have I considered selling?* It was important not to act too anxious. *Shoot.* More than anxious, I was desperate. After finding a mint, unwrapping it, and popping it into my mouth, I strolled down the lane toward the house, leaning on my cane as if totally disinterested—when my purpose was to prevent her from getting a whiff of the carnage that had taken place in the barn and behind it. The young woman followed alongside me, studying my face as we walked.

I stopped near the potting shed where Charlie had placed two stumps underneath an apple tree, a favorite spot to rest before we washed up for supper. As soon as I sat down, Miss Margaret stretched out by my feet, licking her lips and obviously satisfied for the moment.

JoAnn planted herself in front of me with her arms folded. "Well, have you?"

I looked up and squinted at her as she stood against the bright sky, trying to contain my excitement. "The idea has crossed my mind a time or two. This place, on this very ground, is where my dear Charlie and I shared many good years. Why, it would be like … like selling out my Charlie. I don't know—"

"Think about it." JoAnn held out her business card. "I'll get back in touch with you. And soon. If you're willing to let this place go, I'll share everything with you then. I think you'll be pleased with our offer. Just promise me one thing."

What was this woman up to? "If I can."

"Don't commit to anyone else until we have a chance to talk."

That I could do. "You have my word."

Think about it? That's all I'd been doing since Mr. Lively handed me his office phone, and my banker informed me my checking account was overdrawn, even though I couldn't bring myself to put the farm on the market yet. This young woman had a client ready to buy. Had Mary Lou, the clerk at the register of deeds, shared the information that I hoped to sell my farm someday? I had confided in no one else. Maybe gossip was a good thing after all.

JoAnn's dusty car sputtered and coughed as she drove away from the potting shed and continued on down the lane toward Highway 421. I hoped she made it to wherever she was staying.

I waited for Betty Jo on the stump where I could see her Buick approach the house. A glance at my watch told me that in about fifteen more minutes she would arrive, and she would be in a hurry to get back home. My purpose in coming to the farm was to clear my thinking about Josiah and Carl. I prayed for guidance to finally settle the case, put it to rest so to speak.

The farm could be as good as sold if I agreed on the offer. Charged with excitement over the possibilities of this new turn of events, I would have to contain myself until, or if, I signed papers and closed the deal.

My thoughts turned to other pressing matters. Walter Jones had not only been trespassing, he had been using my barn for his cockfights. He had some nerve, but did his lack of scruples make him a killer? I reached down and rubbed Miss Margaret behind her ears. She sighed with contentment. My eyes closed as I visualized the note Sheriff Caywood had found stuffed inside Carl's jacket while trying to remember the exact wording. Something about it didn't set right.

Senile old woman, stop poking your nose where it don't belong or you'll be snuffed out when you least expect it and planted beside your no-count husband!

Which of the suspects talked like that? And which one thought Charlie was no good? I brought up each one up in my mind and tried to remember the times we had spoken. Words, attitudes ... I jabbed the ground with my cane. *Yes!* Now I was certain. A piece of the puzzle had fallen into place, and I thanked my dear husband for one additional clue that had finally made my suspicions crystal clear. But how could I best use it? It would come to me in due time if I could contain myself and not get all in a dither.

Chapter Eighteen

Miss Margaret settled herself on the back floorboard of Betty Jo's car. Before we reached the end of the lane, she was sound asleep and snoring. Our visit to the farm had done us both a world of good.

"I know you're in a hurry," I said to Betty Jo, "but stop at Sheriff Caywood's. I won't be long."

She nodded and didn't argue. Her face looked as drawn as a wrinkled bedsheet. I had told her about Walter nearly running me down with his truck and about finding cockfighting evidence in the barn. That was enough. I hadn't shared anything about talking with a Realtor or my conclusions about Josiah's killer.

When I reported Walter's shenanigans to our good sheriff, he said he would "look into it" and perhaps I needed to get some of those *No Trespassing* signs and install a bar across the lane. Almost exactly what his deputy had said. *Pete and Repeat.*

"I'm sure you agree," he added, "our first priority is to solve a murder. Everything else has to take a back burner."

He sounded worse than his deputy, but I kept my thoughts to myself. "I understand. How about solving two murders?"

"Speculation and circumstantial is all I've heard from you, and neither cuts it with the law," he said with a sigh.

"I'll have proof soon. Concrete proof. And before we have another murder on our hands." *Which could be mine.*

"This case is complicated, and you've gotten in over your head. I'm telling you to leave it alone. Do you hear what I'm saying, Miss Agnes?"

"What if I can line up all the evidence like checkers before a game?"

He laughed. "You think you can deliver? Alright. It's against my better judgment, but you've got my attention. You're on. Since you won't listen to reason, if you can present rock-solid evidence—without getting yourself killed in the process—I'll eat my hat."

Things were finally looking up. "I'll use the element of surprise. It won't hurt to have several witnesses, so bring your deputy along."

He appeared to size me up before he answered. "Where and when?"

"Clear your Saturday afternoon schedule, and meet me at Mike's Garage," I said. "Yes, I'll have the evidence. I'm fairly certain the killer's going to be there. Be prepared to make an arrest." I could hardly wait to get back home and share my good news with Smiley and Shirley.

When the sheriff stood, his buckeye fell onto the floor and rolled under his desk.

I opened his office door, turned, and looked back at him. "By the way, would you like your hat soft or hard boiled?"

Back at the Manor, I headed to the kitchen to find Shirley and to share my conclusions about a murderer among us. Then I would have to find Smiley. As soon as the sheriff arrested a killer, we could celebrate … maybe with our friend's fried chicken, rice, and gravy.

Lost in thought, I nearly fell over Nellie in the dining room on her hands and knees among a scattering of letters and bills and such. I reached for the back of a chair to steady myself. "What on earth?"

"Flew out of my hands," she said. "Are you going to help me or stand there like a numskull?"

I joined her on the floor as something snapped in my good knee. What if I couldn't get back up? I tried to concentrate, to make sense of what was strewn before us.

"Looks like you've got tons of mail here, but none of it's opened." I picked up one envelope. It was addressed to Mr. William Statton. "This isn't yours," I said, even though that fact was obvious.

Nellie snatched the letter out of my hand. "I found it."

"What else have you *found*?" I asked, picking up other pieces of mail as a shiny black feather floated from the pile in my hands.

"Give me those. They're mine," she said, reaching for the ones I held.

"Where did you find this feather?" I picked it up and suddenly knew. "You stole it from my jacket. After you took my candy, you came back, didn't you?"

Nellie looked at me with wide, watery eyes. Her chin quivered. "I came back to tell you I was sorry. For taking your candy. I found the feather on the floor beside your bed. I thought you would be sure to pick it up and throw it away, so I took it. And that's the truth."

I dropped the feather into my purse and snapped it shut. "Look, if you'll help me deliver all of this to the right people, I won't call the sheriff and tell him what you've done. And I'm so glad to have this feather returned, I might forgive you for taking it. *Might.*"

Nellie helped me stand, and we made stacks on a nearby table. At least half of our residents had two or three pieces of mail. Though some looked like junk mail, others appeared important. One was addressed to me from Countryside Realty. Maybe it would have some valuable information about the offer to buy my farm. I could hardly contain myself. I stuck the envelope in my purse, tucked the rest of the mail underneath one arm, and grabbed my cane with my free hand.

After we delivered the last piece, I brought Nellie along with me. As we entered the kitchen, Shirley whisked a pan out of the oven. Roasted butternut squash, lavished with cinnamon and sugar, filled the room with a heavenly aroma.

"Nellie has volunteered to scrub your pots and pans three times a day for six weeks," I announced.

Shirley fanned herself with her apron. "Land's sake! Best news I've had in a coon's age. Lollipop's plum tired of kitchen duty these days."

"I'll be in the sitting room reading my mail. Then I'll be talking to Mr. Lively for a while if you should need me before I come back to bring you up to date." I glared at Nellie.

She scowled back. "You're mean."

"Yep. Mean and madder than a wet hen. And don't you forget it."

Shirley's eyebrows rose up underneath her blonde bangs, but she got Nellie busy scrubbing. I hoped Mr. Lively would try to get some help for this woman. Her latest episode was far more serious than stealing candy bars or a coaster lying around, or even a valuable feather.

In the sitting room, Smiley had nodded off with his newspaper collapsed in his lap. William sat on the other end of the sofa with Francesca parked close to him in her wheelchair. They only had eyes for each other these days. I hurried to an overstuffed chair in a far corner. Finally, I could open my mail. I looked at the date stamped on the envelope. Almost three weeks old. *Merciful heavens.*

I read the letter twice because I had trouble taking it all in. JoAnn represented an Atlanta developer in the process of designing a subdivision, and they had their eye on our farmland as the perfect site. No mention of the amount of their offer, but they wanted to close in thirty days, less since my mail had been stolen and their letter delayed. I promised Charlie to make certain I received a fair price.

With the farm sold, it would be easy to move forward and resolve my money issues. Or not. It would take more than closing a real estate deal. It would be necessary to make some wise investments, or I'd eventually fall into the same old sinkhole. I needed enough income to live comfortably for years to come. That would mean not succumbing to those confounded shopping channels again. I was addicted as sure as Nellie was hooked on taking what didn't belong to her.

I stopped at a side table in the dining room where Shirley was preparing a large coffee pot for our evening meal.

"Mercy in abundance," she said after I explained my conclusions about Josiah's killer. "I dearly wish my Baby was here. I knew he was innocent all along."

Shirley had prepared one of my favorite suppers—pinto beans, corn bread, fried potatoes with onions, and butternut squash, but my mind was in such a whirl I hardly tasted anything.

"We'll talk soon," I said to Smiley before heading for my room. I had shared my findings with him earlier, and even though I was certain of Josiah and Carl's killer, I wanted to be prepared. There could be no surprises.

"No problem, Sis," Smiley said. "Got some urgent business of my own."

He didn't say so, but I knew. His business was with Pearl.

✳ ✳ ✳

During lunch the next day, I turned to Smiley and whispered in his ear, "Will you go with me to Mike's Garage on Saturday?"

"Why?" He looked into my eyes. "Oh, jumping Jehoshaphat. I know why."

The front doorbell rang, but before anyone could think about answering it, the door flew open and banged against the wall as "Dixie" filled the air.

"I thought we voted to disconnect that thing," I said.

"Mr. Lively says he likes it," Lollipop piped in.

All heads turned toward the entryway.

"I do declare. Speak of the devil," Francesca said, wrinkling her nose as if Jack's appearance offended her.

Jack Lovingood stepped into the dining room, dragging his bad leg along like always. He looked around the room, removed his cowboy hat, and held it in front of his chest as if ready to make a speech. Instead, he stood at attention and grinned. Jack looked different somehow, even though he had only been gone a couple of weeks. His long curls were pulled into a neat ponytail. He was clean-shaven and … his clothes. Jack sported a pink collared shirt underneath a leather jacket, a pair of new jeans, and his black cowboy boots with the silver toes had been cleaned and polished. He had always been able to sweep any woman off her feet no matter what he wore or what he might have done, but this transformation made him even more of a dreamboat.

Francesca wouldn't admit she had swooned over his presence since the first day he appeared on our porch with a basket of strawberries. Why couldn't some women say they enjoyed looking at a handsome man?

"We aren't above being human, after all," I said.

Smiley questioned me with his eyes.

Francesca ordered William, "Call 911. This instant."

William mumbled something in reply, but he didn't jump up to do her bidding.

"Where's Shirl?" Jack asked, his grin still in place.

We all pointed toward the kitchen where a radio boomed with a rousing old-time gospel song, "Send the Light."

Jack moved through the swinging door. Each resident seemed to be holding his or her breath. A couple of seconds passed, though it seemed like forever. A large pot clanged onto the floor. Shirley screamed. Then complete silence followed. A men's quartet belted out another hymn on the radio, "When We All Get to Heaven."

At last, the kitchen door opened. Shirley and Jack stood among us, grinning like lovesick Cheshire cats, their arms entwined around each other's waist. We could all breathe again. We clapped and cheered, even Pearl who didn't have a clue what was happening. Except for Francesca. Her face looked like a thundercloud, and her long string of pearls was in its usual knot. She thrived on the misfortunes of others. She would be delighted if Jack turned out to be a killer or at least a robber. A happy ending gave her no fodder to chew.

I bit my tongue because I still had some misgivings about Jack. Was he mixed up in some of the good-old-boy gambling and illegal mischief? I suspected he was. Along with our sheriff and his deputy who chose to ignore the cockfights being held in my barn.

After the excitement died down, I told Francesca to organize another cleanup. She refused, but William winked at me and rose to the occasion.

I told Shirley and Jack to go someplace where they could talk. I hoped they didn't go to her room because the way those two were looking at each other, they might never come out.

"We're headed to Case's Produce," Jack said. "Picked up my scooter from Mike's. Purrs like a kitten. Got my old job back, and I need to check in."

Smiley and I went as far as the porch. I yelled to Shirley, "Don't hurry back."

She turned long enough to wave her hand in the air.

We watched as they climbed onto the seat of his red motor scooter and putt-putted down the street with Shirley's blond fluff rising above them. They were headed toward The Bottom, the poorest part of town where they both used to live. I prayed Shirley would remember to return to us. I truly didn't know what we would do without her, and I didn't want to find out.

Smiley reached for my hand. "Let's you and me find a place to talk. My room or yours?"

✳ ✳ ✳

"You will go with me to Mike's Garage on Saturday afternoon, won't you?" I asked Smiley as I made myself comfortable on his loveseat.

"Wouldn't miss it for the world. Mighty fine detective work you've accomplished, I'll say. And the sheriff would say so too if he wasn't too stubborn to admit it."

"Probably not going to happen, but the important thing is I kept my promise to Charlie and to Betty Jo."

"Exactly. Say, how about a cup of hot tea? Dining room ought to be cleared out, and I'd like to talk to you about me and Pearl."

I wanted to hear what he had to say, yet at the same time … I didn't. What if he said he could only be true to one woman, and that one woman was not me? Could I still be his friend without pining for more than his friendship? I didn't think so.

The dining room had a few stragglers, but the kitchen was empty, so we sat on stools pulled up to the antique workbench—one of my favorite spots in the Manor. I took a deep breath and braced myself, but as Smiley talked on and on, I never could have guessed what he had to say. I listened and gradually relaxed. I nodded and a few times said, "You don't say" or "I do declare."

Smiley's excitement about learning how to express himself on canvas filled my heart with pride, even though I was more than a mite jealous.

"Mostly, I watched Pearl while she worked," Smiley said, "with my canvas set up beside hers. I tried to repeat everything she did. She never laughed at my first attempts though even I could see they looked like a first grader's."

"But you didn't give up." I hoped he could see the pride in my eyes.

"Nope. Since Pearl's not too good at explaining what comes natural to her, I signed up for an online art course, thanks to William. He's a computer whiz, don'tcha know."

"Did you swear him to secrecy too?"

"Now, Sis, don't be too hard on him or Pearl. I wanted to surprise you, and they agreed to help me."

Who would've thought? He continued talking about mixing colors, the importance of light and shadows, and depth perception. Amazing for a man who hadn't seemed to have any spark of creativity in his bones until a short time ago. It was as if he'd been asleep and had suddenly woke up, raring to go to make up for lost time.

"What are you going to do with your paintings?" I asked. "They might fetch a good price, and Henry would let you hang some in his hardware store like he does with Pearl's."

Smiley stopped with a spoonful of honey halfway to his tea. His look told me I might as well have said he should start a bonfire with them.

"How could I sell them? They're … they're like my children. You want me to sell my children?"

"But they'll soon multiply like guppies. Your room won't hold them all."

He methodically stirred the honey into his tea. "I'll have to think about it. It would break my heart to put a price on them."

I tried to lighten the mood. "How many do you have?"

"Two. Working on a third."

"I have an idea," I said, getting excited about the possibility. "What if you put them on display, like a one-man show, here at the Manor? The entry hall would be greatly improved, and so would our dining room. As a matter of fact, you and Pearl should both hang up some of your artwork."

"Might be a solution," he said, sipping his tea. "But would Mr. Lively agree? Our home being for sale and all."

"Maybe I can convince him. Improve the looks of this place for sure."

Smiley's grin spread across his face. "Absolutely." Then he surprised me. "When I finish the third one, I want you to choose one for yourself. As a gift."

"You bet." I hugged him tight, nearly knocking him off his stool.

On the way to my room, I knocked on Mr. Lively's office door. It was quiet as a tomb, so I knocked again. Surely, he was not taking an afternoon nap in his tiny office.

"Mr. Lively? I wanted to let you know I'm going to call the main office in Tennessee. We need someone around here who's available— more than a suggestion box—to talk to."

There was a slight shuffling inside the office. I waited and thumped my fist on the door. Finally, the lock turned. The administrator looked more rumpled than usual. His hair stuck up in all directions, and his bulging eyes were bloodshot.

"What do you want?" he growled.

His breath nearly knocked me over. He was not taking care of his hygiene. He was obviously an unhappy man, and maybe even depressed to be working in a job he was ill-suited for. But I would not excuse him.

He took off his glasses and rubbed his eyes. "Where's Miss Monroe? Have you seen her?"

"Uh, she had an urgent errand and ought to be back shortly."

"Well, when you see her, tell her she can't run off whenever she pleases and not tend to her duties. This kind of thing is getting to be a habit, and she will find herself looking for another job." He started to close the door.

"Wait," I said.

"Also, tell Miss Monroe pork chops, rice, and gravy sounds good for supper. You might also inform her I'd like her fried chicken dinner in a week or so. I'll let her know exactly when, and to prepare for at least five extra people. We'll be closing a deal on this place. By the way, Shady

Acres has some openings. Exactly the sort of place where most of you people belong anyway is my way of thinking."

"What about due-diligence on Sweetbriar? I haven't seen any inspectors around here. Assisted-living? None of us will be going there. We might be old, but we're not feeble."

"No skin off my nose where you people go, but you'd best be making plans. The clock is ticking, and we'll all soon be outta here. My boss promised me a big bonus once this place is shut down. I'm close enough to smell it." He slammed his office door and turned the lock with a loud click.

"Not the only thing that smells around here," I said, thumping my cane on the floor. I had forgotten to ask about displaying Pearl's and Smiley's creations. What difference did it make anyway? Our home was as good as sold. Francesca and William had their names on a list. Smiley had talked about doing the same. I had thought we could never lose our home. I even said I would not let it happen no matter what. Had I only been fooling myself? Was Sweetbriar Manor done for? Maybe our time was running out.

At least I knew why my two friends were spending so much time together. *A common interest is a good reason, right?* Then doubt started creeping in.

Were they really as innocent as two newborns, or were they using their art as an excuse?

Maybe they were both as guilty as sin.

Chapter Nineteen

Shirley and Jack floated inside the foyer like two lovebirds as the grandfather clock struck once. Three-thirty.

Jack kissed his Shirl on the cheek and said, "I've got to go. Mr. Case got in a load of Christmas trees, and the truck needs to head back. Save me some supper. I'll be starving after my meeting. What's on the menu?"

I waited for "Dixie" to play out before speaking, but they were so lost in each other, I don't think they knew I stood nearby. "Pork chops, rice, and gravy. Mr. Lively's request."

Shirley looked at me and then the clock with a startled expression. "Goodness gracious, I'd better get moving." She gave her Baby a hug and rushed off toward the kitchen.

Jack turned to go.

"Wait a minute," I said.

He stopped with his hand on the doorknob. "I know what you've been up to, Miss Hops." He grinned, showing his dimples.

"You do?" *How would he know unless Shirley told him?*

He squared his hat onto his head and saluted. "Yep. And I've got some information for you."

I leaned on my cane, wishing I had a place to sit. "About the deputy? Why he threatened you?"

Jack frowned. "He's got a big bark with no bite. Besides, he's not why I left."

"He's not?" *Someone must've warned him about the sheriff asking questions.*

"Nope," he said as he straightened up and puffed out his chest. "Took the bus to Fair Hope up near Pineville and admitted myself."

I couldn't believe what I was hearing. Jack was confessing. "You're an alcoholic?"

"Yep. Say, got to run. Got to get to work and then to my AA meeting on time. Convinced my counselors I was ready to leave Fair Hope in only half the time. Them meetings was part of the deal."

I raised my hand. "Wait. Can't we talk first?"

He hurried out the door with a wave. "Nope."

I caught up to Shirley in the kitchen, who was already busy flouring and browning pork chops. "I talked with Jack. Briefly."

She faced me holding a floured chop in the air. A grin spread all over her face. "Ain't it wonderful?"

My hands flew to my hips. "Because he's an *alcoholic*?"

"Because he went and got help. On his own. He's the finest man ever." Shirley dropped the chop in a bowl and picked up another.

I reached up and brushed some flour from her cheek. "He knows we've been investigating Josiah's death. But I'm not surprised you told him."

"Law, honey, we had a bunch of air to clear. We promised to never keep secrets from each other again." She cut her eyes toward me. "Are you mad?"

I shook my head. "Already got over it. I may have to ask for your forgiveness one day."

"Whew! Thank you, Lord."

"Jack says he's got some information about our good deputy. Did he mention it to you?" I hoped Jack wasn't throwing a monkey wrench into what I thought was an airtight case.

"We were too busy to talk about a sleazeball." Her face turned a rosy red.

"I can only imagine," I said, patting her on the back. "When he comes by to eat supper, would you come get me?"

"Yes ma'am," she said. She flipped a few chops in one skillet, lifted some from another, and added more to brown.

The aroma was heavenly, and I could almost taste the gravy over mashed potatoes. "Can I start peeling?" I asked.

"Thanks. Sure would help a bunch."

I sat at the island to rest my knee and got to work. When all of this was over, maybe I'd ask Doc Evans to recommend an orthopedic doctor. Maybe. While potato peelings flew, I said, "Mr. Lively told me our home is as good as sold. And he says the whole bunch of us belong in nursing homes. And he has ordered mashed potatoes and gravy and fried chicken for the new owners, whenever they come to sign papers. A celebration meal. Do you think Francesca's prediction is coming true?"

Shirley stopped, walked over to me, and laid her arms on top of my shoulders with her floured hands in the air. "Remember what you said when I first realized Jack had left town, and I didn't know if I'd ever lay eyes on him again?"

"Sometimes prayer is the only answer," I said.

"Seems to me we need to be asking for the good Lord's help again." And so we did.

✳ ✳ ✳

I couldn't get Jack off my mind. Could I trust his information, or was he trying to make the deputy look guilty of a murder he didn't commit? Did jealousy continue to fester in his heart as he saw a way to get revenge?

When I called Betty Jo, she assured me the sale of Sweetbriar Manor was not as close as Mr. Lively had indicated. "Or it could be closer than we think. Either way, he's trying to scare you."

"Well, he's doing a dang good job. And he plans on celebrating with Shirley's fried chicken." That man was much too busy keeping my panties in a wad.

Betty Jo's voice turned serious. "Have you been taking your blood pressure medicine?"

"Certainly. I think so." *Had I? I would have to be more careful.*

I said good-bye and turned off my phone before she could call me back.

At nine thirty-five, Shirley knocked on my door and stuck her head inside. "He's here."

We slipped through the foyer as quiet as two ghosts. A thin strip of light shone underneath Mr. Lively's door.

Jack sat on a kitchen stool hunched over his plate. He looked up long enough to give me a nod and Shirley a grin. "Best food I've had in two weeks," he said as he sopped up the last of his gravy with part of a roll.

"You must be starving," Shirley said as she whisked his plate to the stove and piled on more food.

I pulled up a stool to the old workbench across from him and climbed up. "What do you have to tell me about the deputy?"

"The deputy? Nothing except he better stay away from my woman."

"But you said—"

"No, you did. This is not about him." He cut into his second pork chop and stuffed his mouth full of meat, potatoes, green beans, and corn. He finally swallowed and drained a glass of iced tea. Then he picked up a knife to start the procedure all over again.

I laid my hand on his arm. "Tell me. Please."

"I understand you visited Boss' Pawn Shop."

The very thought gave me the shivers. "He gave me the runaround."

"Figures. I was in there the day after Josiah was killed."

I leaned in and almost fell off my stool. "You were? Did you see his bagpipes?"

"Nope." Jack drained another glass of tea.

"Did you see or hear anything?"

"Yep."

"Are you going to tell me?"

Jack finally turned to face me. "Boss was on the phone telling some dude to knock on the back door after ten o'clock and he'd take a look at what he had to sell. Then he added, 'No fake stuff, neither. I know my Celtic jewelry.' When he hung up, a woman comes walking in. A heavy-set woman, and not much of a looker, but she and Boss start kissing and hugging each other like they were long lost sweethearts or something. Paid me no mind whatsoever. In case they did, I moved over to a motorcycle on display and pretended an interest."

"Oh, my," I said, my mind in a whirl.

"You ain't the only one who can do detective work," Jack said.

He was right. At this point, I would take all the help I could get. "Go on."

"Boss says to his lady friend, 'I told you it would work. This town won't know what hit 'em, and if they ever do figure it out, we'll be rolling in dough and living in Switzerland, or on some tropical island. You stick with me.'"

I tapped my fingers on the workbench. "Then what?"

"Then she says, 'Are you certain the closing will …'"

I waited as Jack grabbed a napkin and wiped his mouth.

"Boss said, 'I won't be there, you understand, but you will. Everything's set to run smooth as silk.' Then they look at each other all lovey-dovey, and I figured it was a good chance for me to slip out of there."

"That's all you heard?"

"Ain't it enough? Those two are up to no good."

"I know who that woman is," I said as I eased off my stool.

Shirley nearly overfilled Jack's tea glass but caught herself in the nick of time. "Land's sake. Who is she?"

"Don't know her name, but I first saw her and Boss when I was downtown visiting my bank, and again when they were watching our protest parade. Then she was in the pawnshop working at a desk when I stopped by."

"Can you tell us what she looked like, Miss Hops?" Jack said with a grin.

"She had spiked hair, a rose tattoo on her neck, and instead of her prison-gray suit, white blouse, and laced up shoes, I would bet when you saw her she was stylishly dressed."

Jack laughed. "You got it."

Shirley looked from me to Jack, her face a question mark.

"One of the women from the prison system," I said.

"But what on earth do those two—"

"Beats me," Jack said. He got up, kissed Shirley on the neck, and carried his plate to the sink. "You and Miss Hops are the official detectives, but I'll keep my eyes and ears open. By the way, her first name's Irene."

❋ ❋ ❋

Back in my room, I recorded Jack's information in my notebook. Boss and his lady friend, Irene, had a scheme going, but I couldn't figure what it was. Why would Boss care if the women's prison system owned Sweetbriar Manor? And what, if anything, did the sale of our home have to do with the murder of Josiah? Or Carl? If there was no connection, did Walter Jones remain my number one suspect? Maybe I would have to ignore what my Charlie had told me.

Chapter Twenty

Betty Jo called to say she was doing her best to legally stop our home from being turned into a halfway house, but she also said her pastor told her we needed to love all people—especially women who had lost their way. Henry had contacted the Chicago firm who represented the women's prison system about taking a look at Sweetbriar's old elementary school under renovations, soon ready for apartments. They said their goal was to purchase a place, not rent.

Then Betty Jo said, "I've been thinking about what you said about helping you with your detective business, driving you to no telling where—where you have no business going. I've decided I simply cannot go against Sheriff Caywood, who says no crime was committed in Beulah Cemetery."

I didn't tell my daughter I no longer needed her services. Fairly certain I had enough evidence to close this case—if my conclusions were correct—I had only two more days before the sheriff said the coroner would have to release his report. According to the good sheriff, his disclosure would make Josiah's killer go into hiding or leave the country, never to be seen again.

Was he right? Did he have a suspect I knew nothing about?

❋ ❋ ❋

Before supper, Smiley and I gathered in the Manor's foyer with Francesca and William, like some of us often did before a meal. We discussed any options we might have at this late date to stop the sale of our home.

"What if we contacted the prison system and talked to them directly?" I said. "Fill them in on the shortcomings of Sweetbriar Manor. And we could hint our mayor is not happy with a halfway house locating in our town. We've got to play every card we can think of."

Francesca smoothed her pearls and said, "I declare, Agnes, you can attract more trouble than a prostitute standing on a street corner. I don't know how you manage to do it. You've got to face the inevitable and find another place to live, like the rest of us."

"I say go for it, Red," William said with a wink and wiggly eyebrows. "What could it hurt? One thing's for certain. We haven't had a dull minute around here since you came. If you hadn't taken on Miss Johnson and convinced us we needed to do the same, we would've stunk worse than a barrel of sauerkraut left out in the sun too long."

Francesca flounced in her wheelchair. "That's enough. Let's go to dinner, Willy. This discussion is going nowhere. Agnes is one hardheaded woman who doesn't know when to give up."

"I'm hardheaded? You're the one who will never admit to being wrong about someone." *Like you've always been suspicious about Jack,* I almost spit out. "You're as stiff-necked as the Israelites who wandered in the desert for forty years."

Mr. Lively opened his door, and we froze in place.

"How about holding it down out here. I can't think with all this yelling going on. I've got work to do, and some of it is urgent. Have some respect."

The grandfather clock bonged, like the lowest piano note, six times. The sound vibrated in my ears as he turned and slammed the door. The bulldog statue, always parked near his door, teetered and shook before standing guard once again. My friends and I walked into the dining room.

Shirley passed us carrying a tray with Mr. Lively's dinner. The aroma of fried chicken floated behind her.

"He must be practicing his celebration meal," I muttered.

"Do you have a good lawyer?" Francesca asked from her end of the dining table. Apparently, she didn't hold a grudge against me for calling her stiff-necked, and I had already forgiven her for calling me hardheaded. Because, after all, that described me pretty well. I was not about to give up.

"I know one who specializes in real estate," I said. "Why?"

She narrowed her eyes. "I'm surprised your daughter didn't advise you better. You can bet our Tennessee owners have a slew of them. How do you plan on defending yourself if they say you need to move to one of those places for old people with mental issues? Or what if they declare you're incompetent, and Betty Jo agrees and signs the papers to put you away? We may all have to get a lawyer before our claims are settled."

I slumped in my chair. "Do you think it could come to such drastic measures? Wouldn't they have to have proof and not someone's opinion?"

Francesca pointed her knife at me, her diamond rings flashing. "Get your head out of the sand, Agnes. They can *prove* whatever they like."

A burning sensation flew up my neck like a hot flash of years ago. I didn't like the way this conversation had turned. Francesca sure had a way of imagining the worst.

"Mr. Benley is the best lawyer I know," I said. "He's good and kind and honest."

"He won't do. You need the meanest one available. The same one I got for my son, Edward." She asked William for a pad and pen—which he magically produced for his lady—and she jotted down the information she said I needed. The meanest defense lawyer in three counties.

I took the slip of paper, dropped it in my purse, and promised her I would think about it.

✻ ✻ ✻

At breakfast the next morning, Mr Lively appeared in the dining room as we were finishing our biscuits, sausage, and gravy. He looked like he had been up all night. Even though his clothes were more mussed than usual, his face unshaven, and his bug-eyes had bags underneath, a half-smile played around his mouth. He could not hide his happiness behind his shoddy appearance. I held my breath for the bad news bound to come.

"The present owners of Sweetbriar Manor and representatives from the prison system are coming into town for final negotiations," he announced. "One week from now, after our dinner, we'll close the deal. I expect every last one of you ..." he stopped to glare at me ... "to be on your best behavior. And by the way, I might not know who he or she is, but your computer guru has been stopped cold. The haunted house nonsense and the so-called candlelight ghost tours have been deleted from cyberspace."

For a moment, no one spoke. We sat perfectly still, stunned by his announcement. No one dared look at William, but I could see him out of the corner of my eye. He appeared to be choking on something, but then his shoulders began shaking. He was apparently trying to contain the laughter ready to bubble over. Thankfully, Mr. Lively didn't notice and left us promptly.

"Whew," William said as he wiped his eyes with his napkin. "Not to worry. My grandson can bring old Sherman's ghost back. And his lady friend's."

I refilled my coffee cup. "We can't depend on imagined spirits to save us."

"And what would you suggest we do?" Francesca asked.

"I have a plan." I stirred my coffee and took a sip.

Francesca clattered her silverware onto her plate. "Well, are you going to share it with us?"

"Can't. Not yet."

Grumbling set in, but I left before anyone could mutiny.

It was sunny and crisp on Saturday afternoon when Smiley and I entered Mike's Garage, once again ignoring the *Closed* sign on the door. The dirt and grease smells greeted us. A wood fire sizzled in a potbelly stove, and coffee perked in an aluminum pot sitting on top.

We stood quietly for a moment to adjust to the dim light. Anticipating what I was about to do set my nerves on edge and sent a shiver up my spine. Mike and Jack, facing each other on the edges of metal folding chairs, were hunched over a checkerboard. Boss Brown watched the game from the seat of a metal step stool. Walter Jones read a newspaper as he slouched in the dirty wingback chair, with his feet propped on an upturned box of motor oil. His crutches leaned against a nearby pole. In unison, the four men raised their heads and stared at us.

It was Jack who broke the silence. "What brings you down here, Miss Hops? Women bring bad luck to a betting game. It's like jinxing a coal mine." He spoke in a gruff voice, but then halfway grinned. "When Mike loses, he's gonna blame you. Won't be pretty. Maybe you and Smiley best head back to the Manor."

Had he figured out why we had come? Did Shirley tell him of my plans to expose the killer today? Maybe he was trying to protect me.

"Don't let us interrupt," I said as I removed my gloves. "We were out for a walk and thought we might warm up a bit before heading back home." I moved over to the stove, held out my hands, and Smiley followed suit.

I couldn't imagine what had possessed me to set foot in this place without giving Sheriff Caywood time to arrive first. What if he didn't come? I couldn't accomplish anything without him here. Smiley and I could be like fish tossed onto a riverbank to flop about until we sucked in our last breath. How deep would the men's loyalties to each other go? Jack might back us up, but would anyone else?

I whispered to Smiley, "Think of something. Stall."

He immediately did. "Since we're here, any ideas for last-minute shoppers? Like for stocking stuffers? Could be most any small item. Candy, beef jerky, a ballpoint pen, even a bandana. Christmas is almost here, don'tcha know."

I took his lead. "Point us to where we might find such items, and you boys can get back to your game before you forget whose turn it is." I removed my hat and jammed it into a coat pocket already bulging with a scarf and gloves.

Mike pushed back his chair and stood. "Beats all I've ever heard, but I reckon I've got a few things." He brushed past us and headed toward the back of his store. "I've got some suckers and cinnamon balls along the side wall over there, but there's air fresheners, small thermometers, suet for birds, or those bandanas you mentioned down this way. You'll have to scrounge around, but you might get lucky."

"Mercy in abundance," I said as I leaned on my cane. "Your place is full of treasures."

"Let me know when you're ready. I'm officially closed, but I reckon I have time to take your money." Mike hurried back to his game and apologized to Jack for the interruption.

I gave Smiley a quick hug. "My stars, you were quick on your feet. Did you bring any cash?"

"A little. Maybe the good sheriff will show up directly."

Time dragged by, it seemed, but when I glanced at the RC Cola clock on the wall, only ten minutes had passed. Smiley made a pile of stocking stuffers near the cash register while I was certain we had reached the bottom of Mike's gems.

"Let's go check out the candy," I said, trying to buy more time. "I think I saw some Lollipop might like."

The men looked up, but only briefly, before Jack, the winner of the current game, challenged Walter, who reached for his crutches and maneuvered over to Mike's seat. Bets were placed, a serious exchange. Boss wrote in a small notebook, collected the money, and dropped the bills into an old cigar box. When the pawnshop owner shed his jacket and draped it over the back of a kitchen stool, I couldn't help but stare at a bulge. Did he have a gun inside his coat's breast pocket? What had I gotten myself into?

Smiley and I edged toward the suckers. After studying the collection, we selected an array of Tootsie Pop flavors. "I'm sure he'll love these," I said. "A ribbon tied around them will look festive."

Mike's door opened, which ushered in a rush of cold air, as well as the sheriff and his deputy. The two men were in a heated argument.

"You can't drag me down here on my day off!" Larry shouted.

"You're always on call if you want to work for me," Sheriff Caywood answered.

Boss clenched his jaw and glared at the officers.

The deputy's fingers drummed the head of his stun gun. Was he thinking he might need it?

"We're here, Miss Agnes," the sheriff said.

"I see you are," I said, much relieved and partly amused he had brought his unwilling deputy along as I had requested.

Walter Jones stood. He grabbed his crutches and tucked them under his arms. "I need a smoke," he said.

Before he took a step, a short, white-haired man burst inside. "My car's on fire! Help! You gotta help!"

Mike and Jack grabbed fire extinguishers and ran to the man's aid. The garage emptied out behind them. Flames shot from underneath the hood of a red SUV. Black smoke billowed upward.

The sheriff called the fire department, but by the time the fire engine pulled underneath the Stagecoach Express sign, the danger was over. The car's engine, hood, and front windshield had been covered with white foam.

Mike and the car's owner—whose name turned out to be Joe—began discussing damages, repairs, insurance, and such.

"No sense trying to play checkers around here," Walter said. "I'm headed home."

"Not yet," Jack said. "I've got money riding on this game. You're obligated."

Walter's face turned a blotchy red. "You can't tell me what to do."

"No," the sheriff said. "However, Miss Agnes requested this meeting, and nobody's leaving until I say so."

The sheriff had actually listened to me?

A vein bulged in Walter's neck. "Let's get this over with. What about him?" He pointed a crutch toward Mike, who was engrossed with Joe's problems.

The sheriff opened the door. "Him too."

The fire truck pulled away. The SUV was ruined, and Joe—who had no means of transportation—joined our group. He pulled a phone out of his pants pocket. "My wife will have to pick me up, and it'll take her an hour or so to get here. What's the name of this town anyway? Are all the folks around here as crazy as you people?"

Jack put his arm around the man's shoulder. "You've asked a good question," he said with a grin. "You can use your phone back here. Better signal." He led him to the back of Mike's and returned in short order, but the men didn't resume their checker game. Walter stood and leaned on his crutches bunched together in front of him, a scowl on his face.

The sheriff walked over and stood beside me. "Let's hear what you have to say, Miss Agnes. You've got our attention."

Chapter Twenty-One

I straightened my shoulders, shot a glance at Smiley, and mustered all the courage I could. "First of all, contrary to what some of you believe, Josiah Goforth was murdered and transported to a bench in Beulah Cemetery. His death was staged to look accidental."

Murmurs bounced around the small room.

"She doesn't know what she's talking about," the deputy said as his left eye twitched.

"Let her finish," the sheriff said.

"At first, I was puzzled about some evidence I found near the body." I pulled out the gamecock feather.

Walter laughed and pointed toward the feather. "What does that prove?"

"Nothing," Larry said. He looked as nervous as a hemmed-in cat.

I examined the object in my hand as if looking for clues, then held it up. "The killer planted this feather on Josiah to ensure we linked him not only to someone who raises gamecocks, but to the same someone who held his gambling addiction over his head. Josiah couldn't shake his habit, even though he lost more often than not."

Jack looked amused. "That all you got?" he asked.

"Circumstantial," Walter said.

"No, gentlemen, I have this." I held up a small plastic sandwich bag.

The sheriff took it from me and studied it. "What have we got here?"

Smiley stepped forward. "No ordinary pocket knife. I can tell the sheep from the goats, don'tcha know."

"What on earth is he talking about?" Walter said.

"Smiley is an expert," I said. "He was a Fuller Brush salesman and used his Case knife to rap on doors back in the day."

"Geez, Louise, can we get this over with? My knee's killing me," Walter said. He sank into a greasy, overstuffed chair.

Boss Brown, who had not uttered a word, sat with his arms tightly crossed.

"Get on with it, Miss Agnes," the sheriff said. "What about this?" He held up a chicken's foot he pulled from the bag.

"I found it in my barn. Look familiar, Walter?"

Walter shrugged. "They all look alike. What's your point?"

"You thought you found the perfect place to hold your cockfights. Even the sheriff and Deputy Larry looked the other way because they were hoping to snag a bigger criminal than you. Josiah was working undercover when he was killed. Only his death was not the result of a gambling operation." I held my breath as the tension in the room mounted.

Walter pointed one of his crutches at me. "I had nothing to do with any of this. I'm totally innocent."

"Not hardly," I said. "But let's get to what matters most. I would venture to guess Boss lost his knife when he and Carl pushed Josiah up the hill in a wheelbarrow."

Jack and Mike cut their eyes at each other, then back at me. Neither moved or said a word.

Boss jumped up, knocking the metal stool to the floor. "Don't try to involve me in your nonsense. You're senile and delusional."

I sidled a little closer to the sheriff before speaking again. "Boss Miller Brown, your initials look mighty fine and fancy on your knife. For a while, I thought Carl had killed Josiah with a karate blow to his neck and then called on you to help him dispose of the body. Seemed to make sense at the time since Carl had threatened Josiah—who had witnessed an exchange behind Begley's. I thought Carl was selling drugs out of the back of the drugstore, but it was something else."

"You got no proof," Boss said. "Carl was a dangerous man, and he had access to all sorts of drugs. Got me some painkillers and charged me three times what they were worth. Threatened me if I told anyone. He had a black belt, you realize."

"Ah," I said, "yes he did, but after I talked with Billy—your nephew and also your bodyguard—he was most cooperative because he liked Josiah. Seems Carl stole small items for you, for your Celtic Room, and that night in the alley he gave Billy a package of gold Scottish crosses, antique and rare. You didn't display them or any of your other stolen items but sold them on the sly."

Boss glared at me but didn't move or speak.

"When I finally remembered something my Charlie told me, it cinched the case against you. He once heard you call your own grandmother *old and senile and no-count*. The same words written on the note to me you stuffed inside the pocket of Carl's pharmacy jacket. Charlie also said you would get rid of your own grandmother if she stood in your way. Seems Carl was in your way, wasn't he? Was he going to confess and turn you in?"

Boss balled his fists and stepped toward me.

"Stop right there," the sheriff said. "Don't make another move. Let her finish."

I swallowed my fear and kept going. "When Carl found out he couldn't live with his guilty conscience, he talked to Blind George. From him, I found out Carl had provided the wheelbarrow, the pickup truck, and what was thought to be the perfect place to dump a body."

"You don't know what you're talking about, you crazy old woman," Boss said. His nostrils flared, and his eyes darted nervously around the room.

The sheriff finally drew his gun and pointed it at Boss. "Stay where you are."

Smiley cleared his throat. I hadn't realized until then that he stood so close to me. He squeezed my shoulder. "You can do this, Sis."

I took a deep breath. "Walter told Carl to 'rough up Josiah,' not only because he hadn't paid his gambling debts, but because he had been asking too many questions. You see, Josiah was on the verge of exposing a gambling operation. At first, I thought Walter hired Carl to kill him, to keep him quiet—which was a strong motive, and it threw me off course. Until Carl was murdered."

I looked at the sheriff, and he nodded for me to continue.

"Josiah's death had nothing to do with gambling. Boss killed Josiah out of pure greed. He wanted his bagpipes, a valuable instrument, for a special Highland Games customer with deep pockets. Josiah had sold some of his small Celtic items to Boss in the past but would never consider giving up his bagpipes. The owner of Last Chance Pawn Shop doesn't like to be turned down."

"Ridiculous! Sheriff, you don't believe any of this, do you?"

The sheriff kept his gun pointed at Boss. "Go on, Miss Agnes."

"Seems Boss strangled Josiah with one of his silk scarves. Snuck up behind him when he came in his shop after hours to sell a gold medallion. Unknown to Boss, Billy was in a back room at the time. Didn't realize what had happened until it was too late, so he hid behind a door. He stayed there. Didn't move for nearly thirty minutes. When Carl came into the pawnshop, Billy peeked through a crack and saw Carl helping Boss carry Josiah's body out of the shop—until they stopped long enough for Carl to remove Josiah's boots. At the time, Boss didn't realize a surly man with a black belt would develop a conscience. When Boss found out Carl was ready to confess his part in the murder—which was to help dispose of the body—he shot him."

"Outlandish!" Boss shouted. "An old woman's speculation." He looked around at the other men. "Somebody back me up here."

"There's more," I said. "Something else Charlie told me about Boss. Said he always carried a silk scarf tucked in one of his pockets. Ordered a dozen at a time from Atlanta. Kind of like carrying a rabbit's foot for good luck. I wonder if he's replaced the one he used as a murder weapon?"

"We'll see," the sheriff said. He motioned to his deputy. "Frisk him."

With his gun still trained on Boss, the sheriff glared at the man. "Don't be so foolish as to try anything."

The deputy moved forward, patted the pawnshop owner down, and found nothing but a billfold and some change.

"His jacket," I said, moving closer to the kitchen stool.

Larry picked up the jacket, reached inside the vest pocket, and pulled out a silk scarf. Red paisley, similar to the one left at the cemetery. It slipped out of his hand and fluttered to the floor. When Larry bent down to retrieve it, he received a kick in the face. He collapsed onto the floor and groaned. "Ohhhh! My jaw's broke."

In an instant, Boss snatched the deputy's pistol from his holster and lunged for me. When he twisted my arm behind my back, my cane fell to the floor. "You're going with me," he said between clenched teeth. He nodded to the sheriff. "Drop your gun."

Sheriff Caywood slowly laid his gun on the floor, never taking his eyes off me.

I stole a glance at Smiley, who looked like he might pass out. "You're making matters worse," I squeaked.

"Shut up, you old windbag!" Boss growled. "You're my ticket out of here."

My heart thumped in my ears. We edged past the sheriff who

whispered, "He's not going to let you live."

Suddenly, Joe—whom I had forgotten about—ran from the back of Mike's. "Help! Toilet's overflowed!"

Everyone looked his way, including Boss.

Out of the corner of my eye, I saw a crutch swing toward me. It knocked against Boss' hand. The gun fell and slid across the concrete. In a flash, the sheriff retrieved it and jumped between us.

"On the floor. Face down. Now! Hands behind your back," the sheriff growled in Boss' face. In no time, Boss had handcuffs clamped around his wrists.

Smiley retrieved my cane, handed it to me, then grabbed me in a fierce hug. "Are you all right, Sis?"

"Absolutely. I … I think so." A weak feeling came over me as the room spun. "I've got to … to sit down."

Smiley led me to an overstuffed chair beside the pot-bellied stove, and I sank into it. "You had me worried," he said, leaning over me. "Don't know what I would do if …"

I reached up and touched his smooth cheek. "I love you too."

He grinned. "Ah, Sis." As he hugged me around my neck and patted my back, I caught a whiff of his Old Spice. A familiar comfort.

After I caught my breath and the room stopped spinning, I walked toward Boss, who was now sitting on the floor with his hands cuffed behind his back. His plaid bow tie was cockeyed, his white dress shirt dirty and torn. I knew not to get too close. He looked up at me and sneered.

"There's one thing I haven't quite figured out," I said in a low voice.

"So? Why would I tell you anything?"

"If you don't, most likely I can get in touch with Irene. I'm sure Sheriff Caywood would like to hear what she has to say. The two of you had a scheme going, didn't you?"

"You don't know when to quit, do you?"

"Do you think she'll visit you in prison? Maybe she's wised up and understands you were using her. Do you want to tell me why or do I talk to the sheriff?"

Boss fidgeted around on the concrete floor and cursed.

"Settle down over there," the sheriff hollered, looking up from his paperwork.

"I'm listening," I said as Smiley walked up beside me and slipped his arm around my waist. I was grateful to lean on him a little.

"Irene planned on running the halfway house."

"Sounds innocent enough, but there's more isn't there? Tell me everything or—"

"She was going to help me in my business."

"How exactly."

"Uh … well … she would get the women living at the halfway house to bring me things to sell."

"How would they? Why would they? Oh, I see. Irene would know enough dirt on these women to blackmail them into stealing valuables for your backdoor business. Am I right?"

Boss looked down at the floor and nodded.

"I need a strong cup of coffee," I said. Smiley and I made our way over to two greasy chairs. I sank into one while Smiley hurried to the stove and poured steaming coffee into two mugs.

I would soon tell the sheriff everything I had learned. If Irene and Boss had been successful, our town would have been infested with crime. Our investigation into Josiah's death had accomplished more than I ever thought possible. I shut my eyes a moment and gave thanks.

By the time Joe's wife walked into Mike's to pick up her husband, she found an angry man handcuffed to a metal pole, a deputy with an ice pack on his face, a sheriff writing a report while he sipped on a fresh cup of coffee, and Jack working on a toilet.

And my former neighbor—the apple farmer who probably saved my life—was also handcuffed. He sat in the back seat of the patrol car while the sheriff waited for backup. Charges of holding illegal cockfights were forthcoming, the sheriff assured me, as well as trespassing. Not enough evidence to arrest the big-time gambling operators they were hoping for, but who knew? Maybe Walter would make a deal for a lighter sentence.

Before the sheriff drove him away, I leaned inside the car's back window and asked Walter, "Why did you back me up in there? Could have turned out differently if you hadn't."

"You and Charlie were always good to my Helen before she died. Flashed in my mind. Might have to answer to her one day."

"My goodness. I always liked Helen, but now even more so."

Mike bagged our purchases and handed us the stocking stuffers. "Merry

Christmas," he said. "On the house."

Smiley and I were glad to be leaving, but as we opened the door, the sheriff was returning inside. "Forgot my buckeye," he said. Then he stopped. "Miss Agnes? Don't you be leaving town, you hear? I'll need your testimony, along with that of Boss' nephew. Besides, I have some questions for you."

"Oh, I'm not planning on going anywhere. You can find me at Sweetbriar Manor any time you need my services." At least I hoped so. An issue not yet resolved.

By the time Smiley and I made it back to the Manor, he looked as limp as overcooked spaghetti. Together, we managed to climb the handicap ramp.

"I think all of the excitement took the starch out of us," I said. "Are you sure you're alright?"

He nodded. "Boss could've killed you, don'tcha know. Without thinking twice."

As we stood facing each other on the porch, he looked like a little orphan boy. My heart melted into a puddle of love. I threw my arms around him and pulled him close. "I don't know what I'd do without you either," I whispered in his ear.

"Ah, Sis, you and me understand each other pretty good." He smiled like his old self, and I smiled back.

I kissed him on the cheek before we went inside. We stood in the foyer and removed our jackets, hats, and gloves. "Boss will be locked up for a long time to come, maybe forever," I said. "Walter won't be holding any more cockfights. Ever. Josiah helped put an end to pitting those beautiful birds against each other, even though the sheriff didn't catch the big-time operator."

Smiley took a deep breath. "Think I'll lie down before dinner and rest my feet."

I watched him as he headed toward his room. Right there on the spot, I made a decision. I would do everything in my power to become Mrs. Sam Abenda in the near future. Life was short, and we needed to be together while we still had some time to enjoy each other's company.

Chapter Twenty-Two

I sat on a stool in the kitchen and told Shirley every detail that had taken place in Mike's Garage. When I finished, my dear friend hooped and hollered and danced a jig around the kitchen island. Then she turned around and realized she had an audience. Lollipop, Francesca, and William had moved into the kitchen. They looked at Shirley as if she had lost her sanity.

"Well, are you going to tell us what happened?" Francesca asked.

I told the story once again—a rather condensed version—while Shirley put on a kettle for tea.

Everyone had questions for me. *What clues led me to identify the right suspect? When did I know? Was I ever afraid?*

I glanced at my watch. It was nearly five o'clock. "Oh, my goodness," I said. "I have an appointment, and I don't want to be late."

"What are you up to this time?" Francesca asked.

"Some personal business of mine and Charlie's. Maybe you folks can talk with Shirley."

Shirley's face lit up. "Only if I can get some help with dinner."

Since it was past time for me to be on my way, I pushed on the swinging door and nearly knocked Pearl down in the process.

"What's happening?" she said. "Is there something I need to know?"

With no time to reassure Pearl, I left Shirley to deal with my overly anxious friend.

I opened the front door for the Realtor, JoAnn, which I had recently learned how to do without setting off the tune of "Dixie." I truly wanted my private business to stay as my own until the deal was done, assuming we could come to an agreement. As we chatted in the foyer, I spotted

Henry coming up the walkway. I held my breath and inched the door open for him to join us. Mr. Lively never appeared. *Perfect.*

The three of us stepped inside the dining room. After introductions, I led them through the kitchen and toward the entrance to the beauty shop. Everyone stopped their chatter and watched us in total silence until Francesca said, "What on earth?"

I had no doubt Shirley could handle the situation without spilling the beans. Henry would be my witness, and he would know if the land developer's offer was a fair one or not.

A card table and folding chairs Shirley had set up for us, served as a place to work. JoAnn pulled out a stack of papers from her briefcase, and we settled down to business. The aroma of beef tips and onions drifted onto the small, enclosed back porch where Shirley still gave manicures once a week.

Turned out the offer for our farm was more than I had expected, and certainly more than Walter Jones had once offered. After papers of intent were signed, and I had agreed to the amount of their earnest money they would deposit in my account Monday morning, we stood and shook hands.

"We have a name for Sweetbriar's new housing development," JoAnn said. "Charlie's Acres. What do you think?"

"It's perfect," I said, at a loss for more words. I reached out for Henry, who steadied me by slipping his arm around my shoulder.

Charlie would have been so proud.

After JoAnn left, I talked with Henry about some of my future plans, and he gave me his wholehearted support. "Let me know the outcome on the farm," he said. "I predict the sale will be finalized without a hitch, but I'll hold off telling your daughter until it's a done deal."

My son-in-law was a true gem, and I told him so. "Selling the home place wasn't easy, but it had to be done. I know Betty Jo. She'll come around. By the way, ask her why she cared so much. About Josiah, that is. She needs to talk with you about something that happened years ago. Maybe she can finally put it to rest."

We said our good-byes. Henry was in a rush to pick up Miss Margaret from his store, drop her off at Ben's farm, and scoot home. Betty Jo didn't like for him to be late, but she would be much relieved Josiah's case was solved, his killer arrested.

❋ ❋ ❋

On the following Tuesday night, Mr. Lively—in a green and yellow plaid sports jacket and his usual rumpled khaki pants—presided over the extra table Shirley had arranged in a far corner of the dining room. He uncorked a large bottle of white wine and poured glasses all around to the gathering of two men, the present owners of Sweetbriar Manor, as well as two women, probably the potential owners from the women's prison.

I wondered what had happened to the stocky woman with spiked hair and a rose tattoo on her neck. Her partner in crime was in jail. Had she been allowed to talk to Boss? She should know by now he had murdered two men. Maybe she had crawled back to whatever rock she had come from.

The boisterous group laughed and talked and toasted as they enjoyed their chicken dinner, while most of the Manor's residents picked at their food and spoke in whispers.

"Looks like we're done for," Smiley said to everyone sitting at our table. He turned to me and lowered his voice. "Where will you go? How long do you think it will be before we'll have to move? We should have gotten our names on a list somewhere. Anywhere. We'll probably have to go to some sad, dirty, awful place. This is worse than a dozen cats thrown in a sack and dumped in the river."

I placed my hand on top of his. "Reach down inside yourself and grab ahold of a piece of optimism like you are known to do. And don't let go. Remember when you said we would survive no matter what? *We.* You and me."

Smiley slipped his hand from mine and added more sugar to his coffee. "I remember, but it seems like ... like Sweetbriar Manor's finished and so are all of us."

"Show's not over yet," I said. "Remember Winston Churchill. Never, never, never give up."

Gradually, the dining room emptied of most of the residents. Shirley poured more coffee for those sitting around Mr. Lively's table and for the few people who lingered over their apple cake, like Smiley and me.

Shirley stopped at our table and leaned in close. Her white-knuckled hands gripped the coffee thermos, but she couldn't keep it from trembling. "Mr. Lively says they're holding their meeting here in the dining room after supper, and they want everyone else out. Their words, not mine. I feel just awful how things have turned out. Makes me sick to my stomach. I've got to get busy and clear their table. Bring your cups to the kitchen, and I'll put on a fresh pot. We've got to figure out where we're going and what we're going to do. All I know is, I'm turning in my apron as soon as you good folks are gone."

I leaned toward Smiley. "You go ahead with Shirley. I may be awhile. If you've gone to your room, I'll knock on your door."

"You're up to something," he said. "I can see that gleam in your eyes."

I reached for my cane. "Say a prayer. And keep on praying. I'll need every single one."

❋ ❋ ❋

I walked over and stood beside Mr. Lively as conversations around the table lessened and then ceased altogether.

"This is a private meeting," Mr. Lively said as he scowled at me.

"Understood, but I have a question." I tapped my cane on the floor.

"Agnes Hopper, you have no business—"

"Let her speak," one man said.

I glanced his way. He looked familiar. Then I recognized him. He was one of the owners of Sweetbriar Manor, along with five other retirement homes across the southeast.

"What purchase amount is on the table?" I asked.

"The nerve of some people. You can't …" Mr. Lively sputtered.

"We're satisfied it's a fair price," the man said.

I tapped my cane again. "What if you received a better offer," I said. "Can we talk about it?"

The two ladies representing the prison system immediately stood. "This is outrageous!" one shouted. "We had a verbal agreement, an understanding, and we're holding the present owners to it. The amount we offered was at the top of our budget. We can do no more. We refuse to discuss the matter any further."

I moved my cane in front of me and leaned on it since no one had offered me a seat. "My son-in-law has been doing some research for me. What if I told you of a perfect location for your halfway house for less money? Would you be interested?"

"We're listening," one woman said as the two sat back down.

❋ ❋ ❋

An hour later, we had made a deal. Contingent upon the sale of my farm, I could become the new owner of Sweetbriar Manor. Breathless by the turn of events, I also welcomed into my heart a measure of peace and happiness.

Even the women from the prison system were excited. Tomorrow, a Realtor was coming to show them the Last Chance Pawn Shop. Boss didn't own the two-story brick house, so his upcoming trial and prison sentence couldn't hold up a sale. The owner, Mr. Green, had been anxious to find a buyer for some time. Between Henry's real estate connections and William checking online, we had discovered all the details we needed.

The former funeral home had been kept in good repair. The upstairs would easily convert into a half-dozen bedrooms. The structure offered a large, old-fashioned kitchen downstairs and other spacious rooms for dining and socializing. Not only was the asking price lower than they had offered for the Manor, the location was closer to Main Street and the center of town.

I knocked on Smiley's door. He pulled me into his room and placed his hands on my shoulders as he looked intently into my eyes. "Sis, I hung back in the kitchen with Shirley. We heard everything. I think you made a wise business decision, and Charlie would think so too."

"Really? Sometimes I'm not so good with money matters."

"Nonsense. You can see clear pond water when others only see the mud at the bottom, and they won't jump in."

"It warms my heart you think so highly of me, but I'm afraid I could slip back into some old habits and get into some big trouble."

"Whatever is worrying you, you can tell me, don'tcha know."

We walked over to his loveseat. He removed a stack of newspapers, and we made ourselves comfortable.

I studied his face for a moment before speaking. "Yes, I know I can tell you anything. You see, I'm struggling with an addiction and ... and I'm ashamed to admit it, but it's true."

Smiley's eyes widened. "You mean with alcohol, like Jack?"

"You had him figured out too?"

"Yep. Told me he had to reach the bottom and look death in the eye before he realized what he had to live for. Takes courage to admit our shortcomings, don'tcha know. Since he returned from that drying-out place, he goes to his AA meetings without fail. Haven't you noticed he talks more these days, and he doesn't have a short fuse ready to blow?"

I had definitely noticed the difference. "For sure he's changed, and Shirley is beside herself with happiness. How come you know so much anyway?"

Smiley's grin was sheepish. "One night I couldn't sleep, and I couldn't find you wandering around not sleeping, so I headed for the front porch. Figured a little rocking wouldn't hurt. Well, sir, the front door was open, which was unusual for the middle of the night. Then I heard Shirley crying. She and Jack were sitting on the front steps. I started to turn back, but their conversation drew me in, so I stood there and listened to two dear people trying to get their lives straightened out. And they will. They even prayed to the good Lord, so He's watching over them."

"Do you think they'll get married?" I sure hoped they would.

Smiley looked confident. "Yep."

I narrowed my eyes at him. "And how do you know?"

"Ah, another story for another time. We got sidetracked. Finish telling me how you became an alcoholic. Never would've guessed it."

"No, no. Let me tell you about my addiction. I thought I had it licked until Nellie turned on the television set in the sitting room. And there they were. Red dancing shoes brought back the same old urges."

I shared the whole shopping channel addiction mess, as well as my other spending habits without holding anything back.

Smiley was right. A shared burden didn't feel nearly so heavy. I reached for his hand. He gave mine a squeeze and leaned closer as I turned toward him. His kiss, aimed for my cheek, landed smack dab on my lips. He jerked away as if he'd landed on a red-hot skillet. He looked at me with eyes as big as a starry sky.

Laughter bubbled up inside me until it spilled out.

"Sis, I … I …" he sputtered before finally giving in to laughter himself.

We laughed so hard tears slid down our cheeks. I dug in my purse and found two clean handkerchiefs. Finally, we settled down enough to talk.

"You know I love you," I said. "Since my first day at the Manor when you called me Sis and told me to call you Smiley. Do you remember?"

"Certainly do. You looked lost and scared and more than a little angry. I knew you needed a friend."

He slipped his arm around me, and I laid my head on his shoulder. We didn't talk for a while but sat there in a peaceful silence as clear and sweet as a mountain spring. Didn't matter he hadn't declared his love for me. In time, I knew he would.

❄ ❄ ❄

The next day, I called Fruitland Bible College and signed up for their recovery counseling sessions, both Nellie and me. I was sure Betty Jo would agree to carry us there—if she didn't get snippy after I confessed about my shopping addictions. She had already discovered the pending sale of the farm. If all went as planned, Henry would inherit Sweetbriar Manor one day. Hardly two words had passed between my daughter and me since she found out.

✳ ✳ ✳

Late one night when we couldn't sleep, Smiley and I strolled around the foyer and then the dining room and gazed at the paintings hung on the walls. They were mostly Pearl's, but two now belonged to Smiley. I had chosen one of his for my own, a tobacco barn bulging with golden burley. It was my favorite.

We stopped in front of Pearl's watercolor of a hydrangea bush wet with rain and turned toward each other, my heart nearly bursting with pure joy.

Before I could tell him so, he hugged me tight and whispered, "Don't know what I'd do in this old world without you. My life would be as dull as an old, rusty pocketknife, don'tcha know."

I laid my head against his chest and lifted my hand to his face. "What are you saying?" I held my breath and waited.

"Well … uh … what I'm saying is … wanna be my girlfriend?"

I pushed away from him and stepped back. "Sam Abenda, you are as dense as a fence post if you have to ask me that question."

He nodded and studied his bedroom slippers. "Are you saying yes?"

I threw my arms around his neck and squeezed him tight. "Absolutely, you old goofus." I kissed him on the cheek and reached for his hand. "I'll be your girlfriend. Today and forever. And I won't let you forget you asked me."

Would Charlie approve of our declared friendship, even if I had hopes for more? Which I did. Absolutely.

Since neither of us wanted to turn in for the night, we went into the kitchen where I fixed us some hot tea—orange spice, our favorite. We sat at the old workbench adding lots of honey to our cups.

"So, you don't think my buying the Manor at my age is totally crazy and irresponsible?" I asked.

He stared into his teacup as if searching for an answer.

"Henry's name is also on the deed, so when something happens to me, Sweetbriar will be his to do with as he wishes," I said. "Betty Jo somehow discovered our arrangement, and she's madder than a wet hen. If it will be enough to keep her from moving to Myrtle Beach, outlasting her hissy fit will be worth it. Time will tell. Henry loves this town. Always has."

"Nobody knows what tomorrow might bring, Sis, but you're in good health, your mind is sharp, and I think if it's managed right, this will be an excellent investment. I would bet you have some ideas for improvements too."

"Exactly. Are you ready to hear some of them?"

"We've got all night, Sis, and I'm all ears."

Epilogue

The song "How Sweet It Is" ended. Smiley, dressed in thrift-store jeans and plaid shirt, asked me to sit out the next number with a cup of Shirley's pineapple-and-lime-sherbet punch. We had shagged nonstop for more than an hour. Amazing what a shot in the old knee will do. Doc Evans said it was a temporary solution, but I was thankful all the same. Even my garage sale flats, made of Italian red leather, cushioned my old feet like comfy bedroom slippers.

"You look right spiffy tonight," I said to Smiley as I gazed into his brown eyes.

"Like my new duds?" He puffed out his chest like a peacock. "Would ya like to give Blind George's a whirl Saturday night?"

"Absolutely," I said, jumping up and nearly spilling my punch. Maybe we could even find him a pair of cowboy boots instead of sandals with dress socks.

As Smiley stood, Francesca and William joined us. I caught a whiff of a recently lit cigar. "Have you been smoking that thing?" I asked.

"Relax, Red," William said. "I walked clear down to that bench underneath the magnolia tree before I did. No harm done."

"I told him you wouldn't like it," Francesca said. She twisted around in her wheelchair and shook her finger at him. "That cigar is going to get you in a heap of trouble one day. Mark my word." She turned back and faced me. "He's already burned a hole in a shirt pocket, and I saw one in his sheet just last …"

A scarlet flush moved up Francesca's neck clear to her pure black hair. She looked like she might be on fire, but not from shame. She stroked her pearls and glared at me. "We don't have to answer to you. What we do in our rooms is our business."

"Now, sweetie," William said as he patted her shoulder. "Calm down. I'll get us some punch."

As he left us, I touched Francesca's arm and looked her in the eye. "You and William should be together. That's not the issue here." Then I excused myself and followed after my burly friend. We had to address the Manor's *No Smoking* rule and nip his careless habits in the bud.

Shirley and her Baby swept past me leaving perfumed air behind them, which was welcomed.

By the time William and Francesca sipped on their punch, he had sworn to only light his cigar after his feet reached Main Street and to leave any partially smoked cigar in a potted plant by the back door. I prayed he would keep his word.

Henry, bless him, asked Pearl to dance, and she didn't protest when he reached for her hand.

"Line dancing's next," Betty Jo announced. "Come on and strut your stuff. Show us what you've learned." She turned up the volume on "Carolina Girls."

I looked at Smiley and grinned. "One more?" When he nodded, I grabbed his hand, and we joined our friends.

A minute or so later, I caught a glimpse of Sheriff Caywood standing in the arched doorway between the foyer and the dining room. With a frown on his face, he leaned against the doorframe and fished his buckeye out of his shirt pocket—a sure sign he had a lot on his mind.

Smiley said, "Go on, Sis. Looks like he's wanting to talk to you." He reached for another chicken salad sandwich. I left him, content in his munching, and walked over to the sheriff.

"Don't suppose you came to dance," I said.

"I'd like to ask you a question." He dropped his buckeye into a shirt pocket and gave it a pat.

"I'm surprised you waited this long. How about some punch?"

He nodded.

I filled our cups and walked back over to him.

"Did you talk to everybody in Sweetbriar?" he asked.

"Pretty near." I took a sip of punch.

"I guess this case is about wrapped up. At first, I suspected Carl as the murderer, like you did, but then after he was killed, I started looking closer at Boss. I questioned Billy several times, but he never had much to offer. How did you get him to put the finger on his closest relative? Family ties are strong around these parts."

"As it turned out, Billy and Josiah were good friends. Boss was family, but he was a harsh taskmaster, besides selling stolen merchandise—a crime Billy found deplorable. He was anxious to help solve the case."

"Don't that beat all," the sheriff said as he handed me his empty cup.

"What about Josiah's undercover work?" I asked. "Did it lead to any arrests?"

He smiled with a twinkle in his eyes. "Ongoing investigation, Miss Agnes."

"I can keep secrets," I said.

"I reckon you can. With what we learned from Josiah and Walter spilling his guts for a lighter sentence, we're close to arresting a big-time gambling crook."

"Josiah would be proud."

"Yes, ma'am. I reckon he would."

"What will happen to Boss?"

"Could get life or the death penalty. Looks like greed did him in. Walter too."

I walked the sheriff to the door where we said our good-byes. As I returned to the dance floor, I wondered if Francesca's son, Edward, was one of the big boys he mentioned.

❊ ❊ ❊

In the weeks that followed our dancing to beach music, I made two changes, no three, to Sweetbriar Manor.

The first was to have Henry disconnect the front door tune of "Dixie." Permanently.

The second was a sign, written in a spiffy calligraphy, that would hang proudly above the front door. *There are no strangers here, only friends you haven't yet met. W.B. Yeats*

Finally, I asked Mr. Lively if he would consider staying on as our administrator. He would have to answer to me, of course, as well as to our residents' newly formed five-member board, with Francesca as chairwoman.

"Are you out of your mind?" Francesca asked as she twisted her pearls into two knots. "Our board should have something to say about this."

"They can voice their opinions, but the hiring and firing is my decision, and mine alone."

"Mark my words," she said. "If he stays, trouble will march in right beside him."

She pulled out her tarot cards, and I hurried away to check on dinner. Shirley was trying out a new recipe for spaghetti and meatballs.

As it turned out, Mr. Lively had been ordered to close down Sweetbriar Manor. If he refused, his boss had vowed to fire him. No wonder he had been on edge when the other residents and I tried to stop a sure sale. He should have received his bonus since I paid a slightly higher price for the Manor than the prison system had offered. He polished up his red sports car and was now driving it nearly every afternoon. I figured he needed a second chance if he wanted one. *And if he stayed without changing some of his disgusting hygiene habits? Well, I'd have to figure out a way to address that issue later.*

I was actually working on a fourth change—allowing pets into our home. At least on designated days as visitors. One morning, I asked Smiley what he thought.

He stirred more sugar and cream into his coffee. "I miss my old hound dog, Daisy, almost more than I miss my Lucinda, don'tcha know."

I thought of my sweet little pig. "Yes, I do know." I set my red purse on the table between us and rummaged through it. No cell phone. "Where on earth did I leave it?" I muttered to myself. "Must be in my room. Don't go anywhere. I'll be back in a jiff." *Maybe Henry could stop by this afternoon after work—with my precious Miss Margaret, of course.*

Yes, life was good, and I could certainly get used to being in charge.

Rushing through the foyer, I nearly ran over Nellie, who quickly slipped something into her skirt pocket. That something began playing guitar music. The same tune as my phone.

"Hand it over," I said, standing my ground in front of her with my hand out.

"I found it," she said as she fished it out of her pocket and handed it over. Her eyes filled with tears.

"Just where did you *find* my phone?" I asked, more than a little irritated. "Have you been in my room again? I could've sworn I locked my door." This nonsense of Nellie picking up whatever she pleased had to stop.

She began crying in earnest, but I would not excuse her behavior. "What else do you have in those pockets of yours?" I pulled her over to the round table in the center of the foyer. "I want to see everything. Put it here." I slapped the table.

Nellie looked at me like I was ready to throw her in jail, which is how I felt. Slowly, she laid out a box of matches and two cigars.

"These look like William's brand. Have you been in his room too?

Anything else?" I asked.

She shook her head and looked down at the floor. "I was going to give everything back," she mumbled.

"When is your next counseling session?" We had to, somehow, get to the bottom of her obsession with stealing or she couldn't continue living here.

Nellie sniffed and wiped her nose on her sleeve.

"I'll find out, and whenever it is, I'm going with you."

I took her into the dining room, told her to sit beside Smiley and not to move. Then I hurried to my room to splash cold water on my face. Maybe that would help calm me.

But my room was locked, which could only happen with a key. So, Nellie hadn't been snooping around inside. Then where had she found my phone? Or the matches and the cigar?

The moment of loving *being in charge* had vanished. I had to have some answers.

I turned around and headed back to confront Nellie, but another urgent matter stopped me dead in my tracks. Mr. Lively stood next to the bulldog statue that always guarded his office door. A look of defeat was in his eyes, and a threadbare suitcase sat by his feet. As sure as my name's Agnes, he was leaving Sweetbriar Manor.

"Where do you think you're going?" I asked as I steadied myself with my cane.

"It's best this way. I don't think we can ever get past our differences." He bent down and picked up his suitcase.

"How will we know unless we try?" I stepped closer and reached out my hand.

He looked down at the floor and shook his head. Then he moved toward the front door, opened it, and was gone.

Could I, or should I, convince him to stay? How would I know unless I tried? I was certain that's what my dear Charlie would've advised.

I hurried as fast as possible to catch up with Mr. Lively.

53556490R00124

Made in the USA
Columbia, SC
17 March 2019